A DEADLY SECRET

Nina Slocum should have been the happiest woman in the world. Her books were on the bestseller lists. The man she lived with was her heart's desire. Her lovely grown-up daughter was working out splendidly as her assistant. And now, incredibly, wonderfully, she was going to have another child.

Then her daughter made the one discovery that she should not have made, a discovery that threatened Nina's career. . . . And took as her lover the one man in the world Nina did not want her to have.

Now the floodgates of mother-daughter rivalry were wide open—and Nina Slocum's perfectly arranged world was about to be shattered into jagged pieces. . . .

A DANGEROUS GIFT

Claudia Crawford

A DANGEROUS GIFT

A SIGNET BOOK

SIGNET
Published by the Penguin Group
Penguin Books USA Inc., 375 Hudson Street,
New York, New York 10014, U.S.A.
Penguin Books Ltd, 27 Wrights Lane,
London W8 5TZ, England
Penguin Books Australia Ltd, Ringwood,
Victoria, Australia
Penguin Books Canada Ltd, 10 Alcorn Avenue,
Toronto, Ontario, Canada M4V 3B2
Penguin Books (N.Z.) Ltd, 182–190 Wairau Road,
Auckland 10, New Zealand

Penguin Books Ltd, Registered Offices:
Harmondsworth, Middlesex, England

First published by Signet, an imprint of Dutton Signet,
a division of Penguin Books USA Inc.

First Printing, May, 1996
10 9 8 7 6 5 4 3 2 1

To my sisters Miriam and Phyllis,
with loving gratitude for their
sweetness and encouragement

Chapter One

Michael was wide awake and still reading when Nina drifted quietly off to sleep. After a light supper on trays, they had made love for dessert. Despite what sexologists said about postcoital gender behavior, Nina was the partner who instantly rolled over in gratified exhaustion while Michael was energized by their pleasure and took up his nightly editing chores with renewed purpose.

Now as the salt breeze off the Hudson River sweetened the early morning Greenwich Village streets, Nina awoke in the drowsy contentment of a good night's rest to find Michael fast asleep with his bed light shining in his face, his glasses on and the new Americana manuscript on his chest.

Oh, Michael . . . ! She plucked off his glasses with pickpocket skill, removed the manuscript, and turned off the light. *What am I going to do with you?*

"You could marry me."

Had she spoken aloud? Or were they so attuned

that he could hear her thoughts? "Oh, *Michael*! I thought you were asleep!" She skimmed a playful pillow at his head. He swatted it aside and wrestled her into his arms with her full cooperation.

"I'm serious, Nina. I found a gray hair last night. I've given you the best years of my life. It's time you made an honest man of me. Besides that, I love you with all my heart and soul."

Michael Ludovic had indeed devoted his life to her. She returned his love with all her heart and soul. She owed everything she was and had to him. By publishing her college thesis, *The Role of the Libido in 3,000 Years of History*, he had launched her career as America's youngest and most controversial historian. The combination of her youth, beauty, and indisputable academic brilliance had jump-started *Libido and History* onto the best-seller list and made her a star of the lecture circuit.

Michael had been shrewd enough to see that without realizing it, Nina Slocum had staked out her own patch of literary territory with her sex-and-history approach. What some called her sassy interpretations of people and events might invite debate and sometimes anger, yet her scholarship was impeccable, her research scrupulous. Noted historians might be stingy with praise. They might sneer at her jazzy style. They could not fault her on facts.

Under Michael's guidance, her sexual comparisons of historic enemies had become her trade-mark. Comparing Elizabeth I and Mary of Scotland, Nina concluded that Mary had let men use her and paid for it with her head while Elizabeth encouraged men to *think* they were using her. When they went too far, they were the ones who paid with their heads.

Her current biography compared Napoleon Bonaparte with Admiral Horatio Nelson, contrasting their respective lives in the context of the women they loved. To Michael's delight, the book was creating an uproar in both Britain and France because Nina's opening paragraph called the reader's attention to "the sexually revealing contrast between the phallic simplicity of Nelson's column penetrating the sky above Trafalgar Square and the vulvic opulence of Napoleon's Arc de Triomphe straddling the Champs Élysées."

If not for Michael, Nina would doubtless be teaching history somewhere, worrying about tenure and trying to be both mother and father to J.J. Her daughter adored Michael, the only father figure she'd ever known. The three of them lived harmoniously in the nineteenth-century town house she and Michael had bought and restored. So why did she hesitate to make their arrangement legal? It wasn't that old bugaboo about fearing to make a commitment. She had passionately committed herself to Michael Ludovic in every aspect of her life. Her love and devotion. Her work. Her daughter's happiness and well-being. Her tender desire to spend the rest of her life with him.

Perhaps it was a superstitious fear of hubris, of defying the gods by wanting everything. Right now she had everything except marriage. She was haunted by the conviction that life was a house of cards, ever vulnerable to collapse. If she played the marriage card, the gods might decide she was too greedy and blow her card house down.

"Well—?" From behind the open pages of the *Wall Street Journal,* Michael peered at her across the breakfast table. He had proposed marriage many times before and had philosophically accepted her excuses:

She was older than he. Six years older. When she was a wrinkled old crone of seventy, he would be a dynamic sixty-four.

He passionately wanted them to have a child and fretted about her biological clock. She had given birth to one child and regarded that as sufficient. J.J. adored Michael. Their father-daughter relationship was better than most based on biology.

Nina smiled at him and blew him a kiss, pretending to misunderstand. "What did you say? More jam? Forgive me, darling. I was daydreaming."

Pretending to believe her, he quietly pressed his point. "I thought we might wander down to City Hall this afternoon and pick up a marriage license."

"But, darling—we can't. Not this afternoon, anyway. Have you forgotten? The Prunella Dove interview! The whole damn crew—cameras, lights, producers—everybody will be arriving here this afternoon to set things up before the great Prunella herself sweeps in. Don't you remember?"

He lowered his newspaper. "I remember discussing it, but I didn't think you'd agreed to do it. You know her reputation. 'Swoop like a vulture; coo like a dove!' "

Nina was defensive. "The *Dove Report* sells books."

He reached across the table and took her hand. "Listen to me, Nina. Remember what that TV critic said? How Prunella makes chopped liver out of her guests and makes them think it's pâté until they see the hatchet job she does in the editing process? We don't need this media exposure. Not now. All of your books are still selling. *Napoleon and Nelson* is still a best-seller in paperback. You're just starting *Hamilton and Burr*, and that won't be out for at least a year. I thought we'd agreed you'd give Prunella a pass. Why'd you change your mind?"

"I thought I *told* you—"

He groaned. They both knew she hadn't told him.

"Tell me again." He was more hurt than angry. Candor and honesty were central to their relationship. Why had she tried to do something behind his back?

She found it hard to explain even to herself. "I was going to tell you after it was over. When you got home from the Backgammon Club. I know it's a sneaky thing to do, and you and I don't do sneaky things, do we?"

"We do not do sneaky things."

It was time to explain. "This isn't an ordinary interview. It's part of a special Mother-and-Daughter series. They're doing Vanessa Redgrave and Natasha Richardson. Debbie Reynolds and Carrie Fisher. Janet Leigh and Jamie Lee Curtis. And—ta-da!—bringing up the rear yours truly Nina Slocum, controversial historian, and her brilliant and lovely daughter, Jennifer Joy Drake, otherwise known as J.J. Vera Boyle thought it was wonderful—"

"And who is Vera Boyle?"

"Prunella Dove's producer. Everybody knows that."

"I didn't know that."

An unaccustomed guilt washed over her. She could not for the life of her figure out why she had tried to deceive him.

"Oh, Michael, I don't know what got into me. There was Vera telling me about all the other mothers and daughters and dammit, I wanted J.J. and me to be included. I'm so proud of her wanting to follow in the old lady's footsteps, and now that I've hired her as my official research assistant, I want to show her off to the entire world! Is that so awful?"

A paternal grin warmed Michael's face. "The mother hen wanting to show off her baby chick. The most basic instinct in nature. Face it, Nina. You're a mother and you're reacting like a mother. I knew there had to be more to it than plugging your books."

There was more to it. Vera Boyle couldn't be absolutely sure, but it looked like Lady Antonia Fraser and her mother, Lady Longford, would also be part of the series. To Nina, Antonia Fraser was the twentieth-century's greatest biographer. Not only was the aristocratic English beauty acclaimed for her exquisite style and vivid reconstruction of historical events, but she was also married to playwright Harold Pinter and moved in British intellectual circles that had no counterpart in the United States.

When a New York book critic called Nina "the American Antonia Fraser," she had been thrilled at first and then embarrassed. In twenty years perhaps but not now. To her chagrin, the tag line stuck and followed her to Britain, where the press, sensing controversy, had hailed her as such. As a result the Pinters had snubbed the reception given by Nina's publisher, and Antonia had sent back the review copy of the Napoleon-Nelson book without comment.

Michael had assured her it didn't matter. The book continued to sell well in Britain and the Continent. But it did matter. Through no fault of her own, Nina had dared to be what the English called presumptuous, presuming to include herself in the rarefied world of Antonia Fraser.

Nina had resigned herself to the "America's Antonia Fraser" tag. Reviewers automatically used it, as did the lecture-circuit brochures. She hated it, but she was stuck with it. Common sense dictated that she view it in public at least as a compliment.

That was why it was so important to her to be part of the series that included the two English-women. From what Vera Boyle had said, there was a good chance Prunella would schedule Nina and J.J.'s tape on the same night as Longford and Fraser. The connecting theme? Daughters following in their mother's footsteps.

Relieved at having cleared the air, Nina rose from her place, circled the table, and pulled out Michael's chair so she could sit on his lap. "Forgive me?"

"Only if you agree to marry me."

"Let's talk about it tomorrow."

He raised her to her feet and pressed his face to her breasts for a brief moment. "Just be careful. The woman's truly a vulture. Remember. Just because she asks a question doesn't mean you have to answer it. And tell that to J.J. You can always say, 'What an interesting question!' or 'I don't think I can answer that!' "

In keeping with their morning routine, he snapped on his bicycle clip and led the way down the inside stairwell to where his twelve-speed Schwinn leaned against the wall. She no longer teased him about being New York's only publishing tycoon who rode a bicycle to work wearing a Brooks Brothers suit and cordovans. She watched him strap last night's homework into his basket before giving his hair a schoolboy pat and straightening his tie.

"Nice tie, darling."

"Some sexy dame bought it for me. Refuses to sleep with me unless I wear it."

Another part of their ritual, a jocular reminder that he allowed Nina to pick his ties but remained adamant about the conservative wardrobe he had worn since adolescence. No arguments. No Armani. No jeans, even on weekends. And yet, as Nina reminded herself, he was not a total stiff. Shortly after they met she had laughingly accused him of having been born wearing a three-piece suit. "I bet you keep it on even when you take a shower." That night she had fallen in love with him when he did just that.

The hand brake released, one foot pressed to the pavement in start position, he embraced her as if he were off to war. "Why don't I skip backgammon? I think I should be here when the vulture swoops."

"Not on your life. You'll only make J.J. and me nervous."

"I worry about J.J., Nina. Is she getting enough sleep? I heard her working late last night, and when I knocked on her door this morning she was already gone!"

Nina crossed her arms with tender exasperation. "Quit stalling, Mr. Ludovic. You know very well she has her aerobics class at eight."

He could not tear himself away. "I don't think she had breakfast." He also knew very well that J.J. liked to make herself a peanut butter and bagel to eat on the way.

"*Michael*! Get going! Everything will be fine."

"You've got my number at the club?"

"I've got your number, period. Move it." She smacked his back fender as if it were a horse and sent him on his way.

Although she could hear the phone from the sidewalk as Michael disappeared around the far corner, she took her time returning to the house. Let it ring. Whoever it was could leave a message on the machine or send a fax. She wanted to spend a few moments gazing at the building's façade and remind herself that this was almost how it had looked when it was built by John Jacob Astor in the 1820s. The elegant Federal architecture of the new republic had replaced the heavier

Georgian look of the colonial period. The original Flemish bond brickwork had stood up well. On either side of the low stoop, the wrought iron handrails were turn-of-the-century copies of the originals. The leaded glass in the front door had come from another house and had been certified authentic.

She stopped to polish the brass door knocker with her shirttail, straightened the raincoats and hats on the hall rack, and entered the kitchen just in time to hear her daughter's voice on the answering machine: ". . . so, I hope it's okay . . . I knew you'd understand . . . love you . . . see you later, Mom."

Understand? Understand what? Last night J.J. had told Nina she didn't want to be on television. She had begged Nina to do the interview without her. "Say I've got hives. And laryngitis!"

Nina had brushed her daughter's hair as she always did in times of stress, and soon the truth emerged. J.J. had seen Prunella Dove in action. She was terrified the vulture would swoop down on her with questions about her real father, maybe ask if J.J. was illegitimate, maybe ask how she felt about her mother living in sin and maybe what it was like to have a mother who was not only famous but more beautiful than she could ever be.

"Who's been talking to you?"

J.J. had dissolved in tears. "The girls at the gym.

Sally Morse said anyone who goes on the *Dove Report* is asking to be crucified. And she said—"

"That little bitch! You don't have to tell me what she said. I remember what happened with those pictures of you when you got the history prize. She said you looked like the gargoyles on Notre Dame cathedral, right? Like this maybe?"

Nina twisted her face into a hideous distortion, bugging out her eyes and drooling saliva until her daughter choked with laughter and begged her to stop.

"Oh, Mom! I want to grow up and be like you."

Nina held her close. "No, you don't. You want to grow up and be yourself, your own woman. And that means protecting yourself from spoilers like Sally Morse. The best way to judge people is ask yourself: are they for you or against you? And if they're not for you, avoid them like the plague. Okay, my pretty? And remember you are pretty, you're articulate, and you're going to knock Prunella's socks off."

Reassured by her mother, J.J. said her morning classes ended at one and she would come straight home from school. Nina held her breath as she rewound the message tape. Had Sally Morse once more gotten to her daughter? If only Nina hadn't dawdled on the sidewalk. The sin of pride over her beautiful house! If only she'd been in the kitchen to answer the phone. She pressed Play.

"Hi, Mom. I just remembered something. You

know that box of clippings I was telling you about? In the Rare Book Room? Well, I just remembered the librarian said she'd hold them until today and then they go back into the system, and it could be months before she could reserve them again. So don't be mad. I'm going to the library, but I'll be home in plenty of time. In fact, it's probably the best idea. I'll get too nervous hanging around the house all afternoon. So, I hope it's okay . . . I knew you'd understand . . . love you . . . see you later, Mom."

By the time Vera Boyle and the *Dove Report* production crew arrived at the house, Nina had convinced herself that J.J.'s decision proved her daughter wise beyond her years. If she had come straight home from gym class, the afternoon would have dragged endlessly and had both of them bouncing off the walls.

Being alone allowed Nina to deal with certain necessary details. Such as what did a famous author-at-home-known-for-her-sexual-brashness wear when Prunella Dove called? Faded Calvins and a DKNY T-shirt? Too Hamptons. A slinky silk caftan over a naked body? Too St. Tropez. Her new Chanel suit with chains, quilted bag, and two-tone slingbacks? Too uptown charity.

What, then? If she really had guts, she'd answer the door as if she'd lost track of time and was deliciously frazzled to be caught in her preferred writing outfit, her "lucky" flannel nightgown. She had worn it her entire senior year at college while writing the sex and politics thesis that had launched her career. For nearly twenty years she had carefully washed it by hand, repaired the seams, and replaced the ribbon around the neck and wrists. Summers she'd worn it barefoot, using her toes to regulate the air conditioner. Winters she wore ski underwear under it and tennis socks a size too big.

Tempting but not a good idea. For tonight's interview she should wear something that she knew from experience always felt good and looked good. White pants, black turtleneck, diamond stud earrings, and bare tanned feet in black patent penny loafers. The two shiny pennies had been courtesy of Michael Ludovic the day he read her thesis and asked if she'd mind his putting his two cents in.

Next decision? Refreshments. If any. The delicate balance. Haul out the Georgian silver tea service? She and Michael had bought it in London on a whim and had yet to use it. Ice cream? Oreos? Madeleines? Nuts. Fruit? All too messy. Diet Cokes, Snapple, Perrier, and white wine would do the trick.

As for exactly where in the house Prunella would do the interview, Nina was determined the choice would be hers. Her workroom and bedroom were off limits since a certain French magazine had conned her into posing on her four-poster bed munching chocolates and lolling in a bubble bath with—unbeknownst to her—one breast exposed.

Vera agreed with her suggestion of the second-floor parlor with its original William Morris wallpaper and shelves full of books and memorabilia of Nina's career. Behind the cozy sofa French doors opened onto a small wooden porch that looked west across the Hudson River. By the time Prunella Dove arrived, the sun would be setting on the Jersey Palisades, purple, green, and red, nature at her most dazzling. The view would also be Nina's cue to point across the river at Weehawken, where Aaron Burr had killed Alexander Hamilton in their historic duel.

"It's an amazing coincidence," she explained as Vera Boyle took feverish notes. "We bought this house long before I decided to do a book on Hamilton and Burr. And would you believe it, after the duel Hamilton's friends rowed him back across the Hudson and carried him to William Bayard's house in Jane Street. Just around the corner from here. The house is gone, but"—she lowered her voice—"his ghost shows up every July twelfth on the anniversary of his death!"

"You've seen his ghost? Prunella will love that!"

"I didn't see him, but . . . I felt something last July. I was alone out back. There's a little garden and a tiny pool that's supposed to have been part of Aaron Burr's water system, and all of a sudden

I felt something whispering in my ear but I couldn't make out the words. Like it was some secret from the past trying to break through."

Vera's eyes shone with excitement. "You really think it was Hamilton?"

Nina saw that she had gone too far. In trying to divert Vera Boyle's attention away from the fact that J.J. had still not shown up, Nina was beginning to sound like some crackpot. Ghosts whispering secrets? That's all she had to say on network television. For all the vaunted eroticism of her biographies, her academic integrity was beyond question.

"Of course not," Nina laughed. "New York history is full of ghost stories, especially in this part of town. George Washington lived up the street at Richmond Hill when New York was the nation's capital. Someone's always seeing him and Martha in their coach on dark and stormy nights."

Vera shuddered. "I'm glad I live in a house with a doorman." She consulted her watch. "My God, it's after four o'clock. Where's J.J.? I thought she'd be here by now. I've got to pre-interview her so I can have the cue cards ready when Prunella gets here."

"Don't worry. She'll be here in plenty of time."

"You're sure she's responsible?"

"This may sound funny, but sometimes I think my daughter is too responsible. Her room is always neat as a pin. She always makes her bed and hangs up her clothes. I used to wish she was a slob like other kids. Underwear on the floor. Shoes under the bed. Pizza crusts, hair spray, candy wrappers, tape decks all over the place. I tell you, Vera, it drove me nuts. I was one mother who could never say, 'For God's sake, clean up your room!' "

Thus diverted, Vera nodded and made her notes. "That's a switch. Prunella will like that. An orderly child! Is that why you've hired her as a researcher?"

"Exactly. She's a terrier for detail, and she's inherited my instinct for what I call the 'Aha!' "

"The 'Aha!'?"

Nina explained. When seemingly unrelated facts, events, and people suddenly seemed to connect, a tiny voice in her head cried, "Aha!" J.J. had the same tiny voice. "She has an amazing mind, my daughter has. The other day she said she'd come to the conclusion that historical research was a form of archeology like digging for Egyptian tombs. You know *something* is there, but you don't know what it is until you dig it out."

"Prunella will love that, too." She closed her notebook in the time-honored journalist's trick of putting her subject at ease. The closed notebook signified a break and suggested whatever was said next would be off the record.

"Now tell me something, Nina—"

A danger signal flashed. Vera's studied nonchalance put Nina on the alert.

"As long as she's not here, let's be frank. Is J.J. as beautiful as you or does she have an ugly duckling complex like most daughters of great beauties?"

How to wreck a mother-daughter relationship with one bitchy question.

"As you will see for yourself, J.J. is not only touchingly lovely but is utterly unaware of it. She startles me at times when she walks in unexpectedly. Not a stitch of makeup. Skin flawless as satin. Glorious hair pulled back in a knot. Soft hazel eyes that melt your heart. To quote Byron, 'She walks in beauty . . .'"

Vera hesitated, her pen poised above her pad. "Byron?"

What did they teach where this dodo went to school?

"Lord Byron? You know . . ."

Vera bristled at the perceived crack. "Excuse *me*! I do know Lord Byron. But the *Dove Report* is not educational TV, you know. We're mass market all the way."

Nina hastened to smooth things over. "I'm sorry, Vera. I guess my nerves are on edge. You know how important this interview is for me. I just wish J.J. would get here so we can both stop watching the clock."

Clearly Nina had hit a nerve. Vera looked like a whipped puppy. "Why did you think I didn't know who Lord Byron was? Just because I didn't go to college? Who cares about poetry anyway! It doesn't put food on the table."

Nina poured them both a glass of wine. "I'm sorry, Vera." She raised her glass in a toast. "You've got one of the most glamorous jobs in television. Thousands of women would give their eye teeth to be in your shoes. Nobody realizes how demanding it is. Well, I do." She extended her hand. "Friends?"

Vera's hand trembled, her palm damp. "Friends. I'm sorry I snapped at you. Prunella will have my ass if J.J. isn't here. Now, let's talk about her, okay? She's, let's see, twenty-one? And you're thirty-nine?"

"I'd just turned eighteen when she was born."

Vera had recovered her cool. "Would you say she was a love child?"

Here we go. The pit bull mentality. Nina had recovered her cool as well. "Ah, Vera. Wouldn't you say every child is a love child?"

Gotcha. "I—I mean—"

"I know what you mean, and I know you're just doing your job—doing it well, I might add. But if you've done your homework—that piece about me in *People*, for instance—then you'd know I eloped with my high school sweetheart, Russell Drake, the night of the senior prom. I was seventeen and pregnant since our spring break in Florida. We were wildly, passionately in love. The world was ours. We would get married, have the baby, continue our education, and live happily ever after."

Vera was quickly taking notes.

"Am I going too fast?"

Vera shook her head no.

"A justice of the peace in Maryland married us. We spent the summer in a golden haze planning a golden future, but by the time J.J. was born we knew the marriage was a mistake."

"How did your family take it?"

Sorry to disappoint. "Both families were wonderful. They helped us work out an amicable divorce. Russ signed over full custody of J.J. if I agreed for her to keep his last name. He had visiting rights, but after a while he decided a clean break was best. He eventually married and moved to California."

"And you never heard from him again?"

"No." It was none of anyone's business. Russ had in fact written to congratulate her when her first book made the best-seller list. She had not answered. Nor had she acknowledged subsequent notes praising her books and telling her about his life. Only last week a letter had arrived saying he and his wife were planning a trip east and asking if he could see his daughter. No way. Not possible. As before, she had not replied.

"No alimony?"

"I didn't ask for any. His parents did offer to set up a trust fund for J.J.'s education, which was very nice of them. She used it at N.Y.U. Earned her degree in history just like her old lady, and a year younger than the average graduate."

Vera took a deep breath, the sign of a hard question before asking as casually as she could manage, "And so what about Mike? Will Mike be here for the taping?"

Mike? Could she possibly mean Michael Ludovic? If she'd done her homework she'd know he was one Michael who was never called Mike. Apart from which, who gave her the right to refer to him so familiarly when they'd never met?

Nina pretended to be perplexed. "Mike? I'm not sure who you mean. Unless . . . of course, how silly of me—you must mean Michael Ludovic."

Vera got the message. "I'm sorry. I meant to say Michael—Michael Ludovic, your publisher . . ."

"My publisher. My mentor. My lover and best friend. It's common knowledge, that I owe everything to him. We're a perfect match. I write the books. He publishes them. We live in harmony in this beautiful landmark house."

"Well, if it isn't too personal, why haven't you married?"

Definitely too personal. "Oh, dear. I thought we were going to discuss mothers and daughters. I didn't think you'd want to know about Michael's skills as a lover. Though I can tell you this. He's very, very good!"

Michael would love hearing that. It had taken

her five years to get him out of those drawstring pajamas and into a nightshirt and ultimately nothing at all.

Vera pressed on. "Is it because he's so much younger than you?"

So this was the way it was going to be! "Is *what* because he's so much younger?"

"Your decision not to marry, of course." An old clipping from *Publishers Weekly* slipped off Vera's lap and fell to the floor. Nina remembered it well, all about Michael Ludovic, the scion of an old, respected family publishing house who had inherited it at seventeen when his father died.

Instead of turning over the reins to hired help, he had left Choate and taken over. A year later, when the company was about to go belly up from years of bad management, he happened to attend a Young Historians seminar and heard twenty-four-year-old Nina Slocum's lecture on sex and politics based on her master's thesis.

Waiting until everyone else had left, his first words to her had been: "You've heard of 'publish or perish'? If you don't let me publish your thesis, my company will perish."

Her first impression of this slender young man was that he was wearing his father's clothes. Or maybe his grandfather's clothes. His three-piece suit and short hair were in marked contrast to the jeans and ponytails sported by the other young men. His seriousness touched her. More so when the waiter at Julio's in Little Italy asked to see his ID before he would serve them.

She had not laughed then or in the hours that followed as he convinced her that he was indeed a publisher and that he thought her views on sex and politics were provocative and controversial. The next day she had met with him at his Irving Place premises to discuss terms.

Vera pursued her inquiry. "How did it feel to be discovered by a teenage boy?"

Any compassion she might have felt for this cow disappeared. "Do you really want the truth?"

Clearly, Vera's entire being yearned for the truth."

"Michael Ludovic was not in his teens when we met. I know it's hard to believe, but he was only four years old. Just out of diapers. He looked at me with those grave, intelligent eyes. He wasn't a boy genius. He was a child genius like Mozart—and when he said, I'm going to make you a star, what could I do? I surrendered!"

"Very funny, Nina. For your own sake, I would not pull that on Prunella. She'll rip your throat out."

"I'm sorry. It's just that I'm sick to death of the Boy Genius story. How I robbed the cradle. Jokes about serving him baby food for dinner. For God's sake, I'm only six years older. It's no big deal. Besides, I thought the segment was about mothers and daughters."

"So where the hell is your daughter?"

"It's still early! She'll be here, I promise."

While Vera supervised the crew in setting up the lights and cameras, Nina excused herself. "I'm just going to change." What she was actually going to do, what she should have done hours ago, was to phone the library and track J.J. down in the Rare Book Room. A recorded message offered a list of exhibitions and the schedules of various departments but no living person. Appeals to the directory-assistance operator were fruitless. An inspired call to the library's executive office produced yet another recorded message.

There was nothing more she could do except switch on the classic movie channel to divert her while she changed. A vintage film buff, she prided herself on being able to recognize an old movie in an instant from whatever fragment of a scene was on when she tuned in. This afternoon's classic was a cinch. Katharine Hepburn in *Mary of Scotland*, 1936, directed by John Ford with Florence Eldridge as Elizabeth I.

This particular scene between Hepburn and Eldridge was wonderful except for one thing. Mary and Elizabeth had never met in real life. Nina often wondered whether old-time stars ever watched their early movies, whether at this very moment in her midtown brownstone Hepburn was watching herself and waiting for her famous death scene. Nina shivered at the thought.

"Nina! Open the door!"

Vera stumbled through the door. "You've got to do something. I just called Prunella to say everything's set. Lights and cameras in place. Cue cards ready. So what does she say? She'll be here at six-thirty instead of seven. No discussion. What if J.J. isn't here? I'm begging you. Do something."

There was nothing Nina could do. A deathly silence fell over the two women. As the seconds passed, Nina tried to think positively. "She'll get here and she'll probably come home with something scandalous she found in the archives. An exclusive discovery revealed for the first time on the *Dove Report!*"

Vera perked up. "About Hamilton and Burr?"

With effort Nina twinkled her eyes. "May be. J.J.'s a terrier."

Vera was thinking ahead. "Like maybe Hamilton and Burr were gay?"

"*Vera!* Come *on* . . ."

Vera defended herself. "Who knew Laurence Olivier and Danny Kaye were lovers? Men! No wonder I can't find a husband."

Six o'clock. Nina could no longer hide her fear. It did not take an hour to get home from the library. Something must have happened. Vera's mounting hysteria only made things worse. Suddenly the specter of J.J.'s corpse on a slab triggered flashes of maternal horror. Her precious child hit by a cab, raped on a rooftop, and hurled down an airshaft. Shot in a drug bust. Trapped between floors in an elevator. Crushed to a pulp by a cement mixer.

As if on cue the phone rang. Vera snatched it out of Nina's hand.

"Is this J.J.?" To Nina's imploring look she shook her head. It was not J.J. It was Prunella Dove calling from her limo in a tantrum directed at all the rush-hour peasants who had the gall to block traffic when she, Prunella Dove, was in a hurry.

"Let's have another glass of wine," Vera said as she hung up the phone.

But their relief at Prunella's delay was overshadowed by J.J.'s continued absence. "I wasn't kidding, Vera. This isn't like J.J."

Vera had an inspiration. "Maybe she's stuck in the same traffic jam as Prunella."

As the clock moved inexorably to seven o'clock, the two women were reduced to silent and private worst-case scenarios. Vera's focussed on Prunella's fury at being held up in traffic, compounded by J.J.'s absence and erupting into a violent temper tantrum, instant dismissal from her job and a new career as a bag lady. Nina's scenario was more graphic. Her daughter lying mangled on the street while pedestrians stepped over her with annoyance and a policeman giving her a summons for littering. Crazy? Not so crazy! Read the papers.

At last a familiar New York sound brought both

women to their feet. The shriek of brakes. A car door swinging open. A sputter of voices. Urgent footsteps pounding across the sidewalk and up the stone steps to the front door.

Chapter Two

J.J. sat in the hushed embrace of the Rare Book Room, staring at the material on the table before her, unable to bring herself to open it. She knew she should be home preparing to be on television. She knew that hundreds, thousands, millions of young women her age would give anything to be in her shoes and that she was an ungrateful wimp to be shaking in her boots, wishing she were dead.

For the first time in her entire life she could not confide in her mother. It wasn't just a matter of looks. J.J. could brush off Sally Morse's nasty cracks about gargoyles. Sally was nasty to everyone. J.J. knew she did not look like a gargoyle. She knew she looked like a fresh-faced American girl-next-door with even features and a good smile thanks to orthodontia.

It was fear, irrational, stomach-turning terror that had sent her into temporary hiding at the public library. She had tried unsuccessfully to laugh it off. Her mouth was too dry to laugh. The panic had been building for days. She had been sick to her stomach on her way to the gym. She had screwed up enough courage to call Nina intent on begging her mother to get her out of the interview. When the machine answered, she had lost her nerve and used the library excuse to give herself time.

She had hoped the panic would pass. That immersing herself in her favorite activity, historical research, would change her frame of mind sufficiently so that she could go home and fulfill her obligation. What would happen if she did not go home was for the moment beyond consideration. Trying once more for the balm of humor, she considered shaving her head and disguising herself as a Tibetan monk. The ultimate bad hair day!

By sheer willpower she opened the thickest of the dusty folders before her, muttering to herself her mother's oft-repeated approach to historical research. History did not evolve in a vacuum. Wars did not just start. Civilizations did not just end. "There are only two questions. What happened? And how come?"

"Here you are. Please be extra careful. They're the original clippings." The librarian placed before her the file of New York newspapers for the years 1799 and 1800.

Her hands trembled with anticipation as she opened the dusty folder and realized that the fragile newsprint was nearly two hundred years old.

She imagined herself as an ordinary New Yorker at the turn of the nineteenth century, sipping her mug of strong Jamaican coffee and munching a sweet currant bun while reading the *New York Daily Advertiser*.

The edition of January 4, 1800, reported the discovery of Elma Sands's battered body in the Manhattan Well. The next day's paper described the removal of the frozen corpse to her cousin's boarding house in Greenwich Street where frenzied mobs stormed the modest structure to view the remains. When the crowds got out of hand, the body was removed to the street and displayed to the public in an open coffin.

The subsequent arrest of the victim's lover, Levi Weeks, was reported in the colorful language of the day. He was charged with "being moved and seduced by the instigation of the devil" into beating and drowning the young Quaker beauty. The city prosecutor called her "a young girl of modesty and virtue, lively and cheerful" and was further quoted as vowing to "prove her virtue fell sacrifice to her lover's assiduity."

Without warning, a sudden wave of nausea engulfed J.J. The Rare Book Room whirled around her as if she were on a runaway carousel. Could it be the dust from the crumbling old newsprint? She felt her body go limp and pitch forward, her head as heavy as a bowling ball. Within the circle formed by her arms, her face came to rest on the library table like a first grader's during rest period.

"Are you okay?" The librarian loomed above her.

Only superhuman will brought J.J. upright.

"Sorry about that. Just an energy dip. I didn't have time for lunch."

The librarian consulted her watch. "It's almost two. Maybe you should go and get something to eat. I'll hold your material here."

J.J. didn't think she could move. Her entire body felt as if it weighed a thousand pounds and that her feet were nailed to the floor. "I'll be okay."

The librarian looked doubtful. "Well, take it easy. I'm going on my lunch break. Just return the material to the desk."

J.J. couldn't be sure, but she got the impression that the librarian whispered something to the man sitting across the table from her. He nodded and looked at her while pretending not to. His appearance reminded her of some of her professors; a 1970s throwback. Still wearing the denim shirt, the calico neckerchief, and the hair in a ponytail. She tried to distract herself by picturing the lower half of his body, the part she couldn't see because the table was in the way. Levi's, she was sure, the original 505s with the straight legs and the button flies, authentic Americana, no zippers. Levi Strauss's 49ers did not have zippers. She tried forcing herself to feel better, to disperse the invisible caul pressing tighter and tighter around her head. As for his feet—mustn't forget his feet, footwear definitely made a statement throughout history. This man who she could tell was watching her covertly, this man would be wearing cowboy boots she was sure.

She dropped a pencil on the floor to check. A bad mistake. As she bent down to retrieve it and to look at his feet, a tidal wave of nausea struck. She was unable to stop herself from sliding to the floor like a sack of meal.

He had her up and on her way out before anyone could offer to help. It was so stuffy in there, he explained. All she needed was some fresh air. He gathered up her things in one arm and held her firmly around the shoulders with the other, half carrying her along the marble corridor toward the elevators.

"I'm going to be sick."

He eased her to the wall. "Bend down. Head way down. Pretend you're tying your shoe."

She did as he said.

"Throw up if you have to. Don't worry. I'm here. Try to breathe deeply."

After a few deep breaths, her face dripping with perspiration, she rose unsteadily. "Ladies' room," she murmured. Fortunately, she knew where it was.

"Take your time. I'll wait outside."

She looked uncertain. He was holding her belongings.

"Trust me. I'll be here."

Out on the Fifth Avenue side of the library, he sat them down on the steps. "You're looking better. Have some of this."

The slender silver flask felt good in her hand. "What is it?"

"Brandy."

"I don't drink."

"Pretend you're lost in an avalanche and I'm the St. Bernard who's come through a blizzard to save your life." He gave her a reassuring grin and she almost smiled.

One sip acted like smelling salts. Her head snapped back. Color rushed to her cheeks. A voluptuous yawn filled her lungs with fresh cool air. "I don't know what hit me."

"I know. I was watching you in the library. It's happened to me. You were having an anxiety attack."

The very idea offended her. Who did he think he was? In bright daylight she could see the lines on his face. He must be forty if he was a day. Who gave him the right to decide what was wrong with her? "And what have I got to be anxious about?"

"You tell me. All I know is you were looking the way I feel before I face an audience. Call it stage fright. Call it anything else. What it boils down to is talking to strangers. Going to some party. Asking for a bank loan. Going to the doctor or the barber or checking into a goddamn hotel, you feel queasy as hell, you want to run for your life, anything to get away. I've been a performer for twenty years, and I still get sick as a dog."

"A performer?"

"Don't be embarrassed. I don't expect you to know me. I've been working in England and Europe, and I'm just getting started here. But we were talking about you. Why the anxiety? Are you an actress going for some audition?"

"What time is it?"

"Nearly three o'clock."

"Oh, my God, what am I going to do?" She knew she had upset her mother with her phone message. Nina would be frantic and furious, wondering where she was, wondering why she wasn't home so that mother and daughter could prepare for the interview as Nina had planned. The worst part of it was Nina's evident anticipation of an afternoon of girl stuff. Clothes. Makeup. Giggles. At one point Nina had wondered whether they should dress the same like sisters, an idea she herself had laughingly quashed before J.J. rolled her eyes in the negative.

She rose unsteadily to her feet. Nausea tasting of brandy crept up her esophagus. She sat down abruptly, her head between her knees. "I'm going to throw up."

New Yorkers mind their own business. As long as she was not screaming for help, those on the library steps chose not to see the tall gray-haired man brace himself against the young woman's back and hold her head as she heaved.

To lighten the situation he warned, "Don't get it on my boots."

Despite her distress, she hiccupped a laugh.

"What's so funny about that? They're Tony Lama's, five hundred bucks!"

The spasms had stopped. She explained about having trained herself to have an eye for details and how after seeing him from the waist up she had dropped the pencil in order to look under the table and see if she was right about jeans and boots. "It must be some kind of detail gene I inherited from my mother."

"What does your mother do? Read palms for a living?"

"She happens to be Nina Slocum." That would show him.

"Am I supposed to know who Nina Slocum is?"

"She's only America's most famous historian."

His eyes were scanning the Fifth Avenue traffic. "Time to go home, I think. In fact, you should really call your doctor. You may have a virus or something. Not just an anxiety attack."

"No, please, I can't go home. Please. Don't make me explain."

He shook his head. "Like the man said, 'No

good deed goes unpunished!' What would you suggest?"

Desperation made her reckless. "Do you live in Manhattan?"

"Are you crazy? Besides, I don't have an apartment. I'm staying at a hotel. And you are going home."

She looked up at him, her eyes pleading.

He shook his head again. "You promise not to cut your wrists in the bathroom?"

A musician friend in London had told Johnny Black about the Mohawk Hotel, "the poor man's Algonquin" and just down the street from the more famous hostelry. His room lived up to his friend's description as early Salvation Army. Attic-reject chest of drawers. Frayed chintz armchair. Heavy wooden bedstead with a clip-on lamp on the headboard. Clean and cheap, his friend had promised. Clean and cheap it was with the friendly smell of lemon oil reminding him of his Grandma Leah's house in Brooklyn before his father had moved them to England in disgrace.

The short walk from the library passed without incident. With her head on his shoulder and his arm propping her upright, Johnny worried that he might look as if he were abducting her. An elderly woman's indulgent smile made him realize they looked like lovers, an image confirmed by the desk clerk's blind eye.

Alone with her in his room, his uneasiness increased. He really didn't need this. His life was complicated enough without playing nursemaid to some waif who was afraid to go home. Why was it any of his business? The answer was a sublime irony. Among the demo tapes he had submitted to record producers was a version of John Donne's *No Man Is an Island*. The message? The importance of being involved with others, including this wan baby bird who was afraid to return to her mother's nest.

There was a coffee shop downstairs. He would leave her to freshen up while he got some hot tea and toast to settle her stomach.

He returned to find her on the bed with one of his pillows hugged in a close embrace. Her eyes were shut. What if she was dead? That was all he needed. More than forty years had passed since the McCarthy hearings. He was a child when his family had fled. This was his first time back to the States. All he needed was to get involved with the police.

Her even breathing reassured him. He settled in the armchair and slowly consumed the tea and toast. The steam heat from the ancient radiator and the distant sounds of traffic lulled him into the half sleep of nightmare losses and regrets. Haunting images of closed coffins and closed doors. Grim reminders of rejection and loneliness. And always the cold fact that this journey home was his last hope for achieving success and self-respect on his own terms.

"Are you okay?"

For a moment he didn't know where he was. The young woman standing before him was peering at him intently. With an effort he returned to the present. "The question is, are you okay?"

She touched his face. "You looked so sad in your sleep."

Her sweet, ingenuous sympathy unleashed a torrent of repressed emotion. With a deep sigh he stood and gathered her tightly to him. Her arms circled his neck. She buried her face in his shoulder. The closeness of their embrace cast a spell neither wished to break until J.J.'s gaze fell on her wristwatch and snapped her back to reality.

"Five o'clock!"

Energy danced through her entire body. She leaped away from him and cried, "Thank you, thank you. *Thank you!*" She knew about the eight-hour virus and the twenty-four-hour flu. What she had suffered was a one-day nervous breakdown! As quickly as it had come it had gone, and all because of Johnny Black's tender loving care.

She jumped on the bed in an exuberant little jig. "You saved my life. You're my guardian angel. I feel great. Don't you feel great, too?"

Something had happened between them. They had not kissed nor had they touched each other beyond the embrace, yet a bond had formed. A surprise to them both, a situation that demanded discussion but not now. J.J. had to get home and fast.

Johnny sat on the edge of the tub while she washed her face, combed her hair, and told him about the mother-and-daughter interview with Prunella Dove.

"I don't know why I was so frightened. I feel wonderful now!"

"You *look* wonderful. What a transformation from that pathetic little kid on the library steps. What time were you supposed to be home?"

"Two-ish."

"Well, it's six-ish now. Your mother must be frantic. Shouldn't you call to say you're on your way?"

"I'd rather surprise her."

"Should I put you in a cab?"

"Don't be stupid. You're coming with me!"

Nina had often chided her about all work and no play and regularly encouraged her to invite guys home. Wait till she got a load of Johnny Black.

Chapter Three

Please, God! Let it be J.J. Nina all but knocked Vera Boyle over in her haste to reach the front door. *I'll kill her! I'll strangle her with my bare hands. She damn well better have a damn good excuse. I'll break both her legs. I'll lock her in her room for the next ten years. Twenty years! On bread and water!*

"J.J.! Thank God!"

Vera rushed up breathlessly. "You sure had us worried. Your mother was ready to call out the army. What happened to you?"

Neither woman had noticed the man in the shadows outside the open door until he stepped into the light and put a protective arm around the runaway.

"I got sick at the library, I thought I was going to die. If it wasn't for Johnny, they might have called an ambulance or something. But Johnny saved me. He took care of me. He said I was having an anxiety attack, that's all."

The two older women exchanged knowing looks.

Was Johnny a doctor? Was that how he knew so much about anxiety attacks? Nina asked.

J.J. laughed and punched her rescuer's arm playfully. "Of course he's not a doctor. He's a musician. A performer. He knows all about anxiety attacks."

Nina turned to confront him. But Prunella would be arriving any minute. Nina would have to get to what happened between them after the interview.

He struck out his hand politely. "I assume you're her mother. My name's John Jacob Black."

For Nina courtesy was an automatic response. She shook his hand. "I'm Nina Slocum, and this is Vera Boyle, the producer of the *Dove Report*."

At any other time an attractive man like Johnny Black would have activated Vera's alligator instincts. She'd have snapped him up and swallowed him whole. What stopped her now was the imminent arrival of Prunella Dove.

"Is that an English accent? You look so . . . American." The way Vera said it, her comment was both a challenge and an insinuation, a technique that made guests guilty about hiding secrets they didn't know they had. Not so Johnny Black.

"That's very perceptive of you. I am an American, but I've lived most of my life in England, so I do have something of an English accent, I suppose. More mid-Atlantic, I'd say."

Nina interrupted. "Come on, J.J. It's a good thing Prunella's late. There's still time for you to change." And to tell Nina exactly what had happened, where she'd been, and who this aging hipster with the ponytail was. Had J.J. gone out of her mind? Wait till she got her alone!

Vera had other ideas. "No, wait! She's perfect the way she is. Beautiful! Look at her. I'd kill for that skin. She's glowing . . . or should I say blushing? Look at her, Nina."

Nina was indeed looking at her daughter's flushed glances at Johnny Black. She didn't have to be a mind reader to know something had happened that afternoon, and she was determined to find out what.

Charm personified, smile determined, Nina steered J.J. toward the stairs. "Just a little eyeliner and mascara. You know what the lights are like."

Vera was equally determined. "She doesn't need a thing. Believe me." She turned to Johnny for confirmation. "You two look fabulous together. Don't they look fabulous together? In fact, there's really only one small problem."

Now what? After four long hours with Vera Boyle, Nina was beginning to feel the kind of emotional exhaustion that she knew from experience raised dark circles under her eyes.

Vera explained, "You two look more like sisters than mother and daughter!" She waggled a mock menacing finger. "Prunella isn't going to like this!"

"Isn't going to like what, Vera?"

Prunella Dove's softly cooing trademark voice announced her arrival more dramatically than a blast of trumpets. Suddenly materializing in the doorway, she was a vision of loveliness in her trademark dove gray. She conveyed a waif vulnerability that made people want to protect her, to help her, and to disregard the many vicious things that were said about her.

Political sharks, corporate piranhas, seasoned talking heads, were always at first meetings convinced that this delicate porcelain figure with the goldilocks hair and raptly innocent blue eyes was a misunderstood victim of jealousy. Once before the cameras, they were totally unprepared when the cooing dove swooped like a vulture and pecked at their vital organs.

Without waiting for Vera's answer, she turned her attention to Johnny Black, "So you're Michael Ludovic!" Without waiting for his response, she switched her attention again to Nina, and said with a conspirator's grin, "Now I see why you keep him under wraps." It was well-known in intellectual circles that Michael Ludovic never went to media events. He left it to Nina to attend the various receptions and openings while he pedaled his basket of manuscripts home each night to read until she got back.

Nor could Prunella Dove be faulted for not knowing what he looked like. Photographers took the hint when he waved them away. Who the hell was he, anyway? The only photograph of him available from the publicity department was of him at seventeen when he first inherited the publishing house and first encountered Nina Slocum. There were traces today of that boyish creature in the three-piece suit, but for the most part his desired anonymity had been preserved.

The idea of a ponytailed Michael in jeans and cowboy boots revived Nina's spirits. Her panic over J.J.'s whereabouts disappeared. No, she explained, this wasn't Michael. It was Johnny Black. "A friend of J.J.'s," she added hesitantly. "They were both working at the library, and he was nice enough to see her home."

As Vera led the party toward the staircase, she called to J.J. "Perhaps your friend would like to wait for you downstairs."

No, Prunella countermanded. The presence of an attractive man was good for conversation, and that's what an interview was, wasn't it? Conversation? She smiled winningly at Johnny. "Unless, of course, you have another engagement."

Without waiting for his reply, she linked her arm through J.J.'s as if they were schoolmates, forcing Nina and Johnny to bring up the rear. "Am I right, J.J.? Is this your first time on television?"

"Yes."

Prunella halted abruptly in mid-staircase and turned her full blue-eyed battery at the younger woman. "Are you by any chance afraid of me, J.J.?"

J.J. looked to Nina and Johnny for the best way to answer. Nina shook her head no; Johnny nodded yes. J.J. returned Prunella's gaze without blinking. "I'm scared to death."

"An honest woman!" Prunella exulted, drawing J.J. closer to her side. "Everybody's scared to death of me. You're the first one with the guts to admit it. Don't worry. You'll be great!" She lowered her voice to a whisper that Nina and Johnny could easily hear. "It's your mother I'm not so sure of."

Divide and conquer, Nina thought. Michael was right, she should never have agreed to the interview. She didn't need it for promotional purposes. Vera had assured her the mother-daughter theme would be cozy and almost inspirational from the way she described it. Insights into the intimate private lives of high-profile women and generational relationships. Divide and conquer. She had to hand it to Prunella. With a few adroit words she had created a schism between J.J. and herself. Pitting mother against daughter doubtless made for better television. With the cold shock of recognition, Nina realized that Prunella would do her best to goad mother and daughter into ripping each other to shreds, leaving them to pick up the pieces after the lights and cameras had gone.

She should have listened to Michael. She had

allowed vanity to replace reason. Her daughter had the courage to admit she was afraid of Prunella Dove. She, with every fiber of her being, wished she had the nerve to abort the interview right then and there. Sorry, kids. No can do. Bad vibrations. Mercury in retrograde. Laryngitis. Sudden migraine. Another time perhaps?

Short of hurling herself down the stairs, there was no way out. As Michael had warned her, Prunella Dove could be a dangerous enemy. What's more, she realized that her daughter had been co-opted by Prunella's overwhelming assurances. The shy, insecure J.J. who had taken her fears to the library was now eagerly confident about making her television debut. If the show did not go on, she would forever blame her mother's jealous reluctance to share the spotlight.

VERA: Roll tape. The *Dove Report* with Nina Slocum and J.J. Drake in Greenwich Village, New York City.

PRUNELLA: Nina Slocum, is it really you?

NINA: No other.

PRUNELLA: And your beautiful daughter—

NINA: My beautiful and brilliant daughter.

PRUNELLA: It's hard to believe you're mother and daughter. You look more like sisters.

NINA: It's hard for me to believe, too.

PRUNELLA: Nina Slocum. You've been hailed as America's most controversial historian. In a word you have changed the popular perception of history by making it sexy.

NINA: I didn't make it sexy. It is sexy. In the history of the world, sexuality is the determinant. Sexual obsession. Sexual guilt. Sexual perversion. Sexual repression. Even sexual impotence. Think what the history of Europe would have been like if Henry the Eighth had not been riddled with syphilis. He would have had healthy sons. He would not have defied Rome and started the Church of England. He would not have chopped off his wives' heads in a fit of sexual jealousy—that's just one example. Think what the world would be like without uncontrollable sexual passion!

PRUNELLA: Speaking of uncontrollable passion, would that explain the birth of your daughter when you were only seventeen?

NINA: Eighteen, to be accurate.

PRUNELLA: You seem reluctant to discuss it. Is it so hard to talk about it even after twenty-one years?

NINA: Twenty-two years. It's personal history, of course, but all history is the same. It doesn't happen in a vacuum. Wars don't just start. Great inventions don't just happen. Civilizations don't just end. History is everything that has ever happened to all the people who ever lived, and it all boils down to two questions. What happened? And how come? And woven into the tapestry of humankind is the sexual component. What happened and how come? Try it and you'll see.

PRUNELLA: In a minute, but first let's get back to what I asked you about J.J. and use your formula. What happened and how come?

NINA: What happened? Why don't you ask J.J. if it's okay with her?

PRUNELLA: J.J.? Do you know what happened?

J.J.: Well, I guess . . . the usual thing happened because . . . well, here I am! It's okay with me.

NINA: What happened was spring break for a bunch of horny school kids. Fort Lauderdale. Sunshine. Bikinis. Beer. And a certain cheerleader who shall be nameless who wore wet T-shirts and had her own convertible and had her eye on my boyfriend.

PRUNELLA: Is this the first you've heard of this, J.J.?

J.J.: Mom? Is that the "how come" it happened?

NINA: It's how come *you* happened. Russ and I were pinned. We'd planned to go to college together and then get married. But Heather was coming on strong, and he was flattered as hell. I overheard her invite him to drive down to the Florida Keys, so I kept him occupied all night and until the next afternoon. She got tired of waiting. By the end of May we knew J.J. was on the way. The night of the senior prom we sneaked away and got married. Who knows what would have happened if we had waited? College changes things. We might have drifted apart and J.J. might never have been born. And I would not have her as my new research assistant.

PRUNELLA: Tell me about yourself, J.J.—and for heaven's sakes, what does J.J. stand for?

J.J.: Jennifer Joy. I've just finished my degree in American history, and now I'm planning to specialize in genealogy because ... because ...

J.J.'s sudden loss of concentration brought encouraging words from Johnny Black. "Because why, J.J.? Don't be shy. You're doing great!"

"Stop the tape!" Vera screamed. "My God, Prunella, I'm sorry. Jesus!"

"It's okay, Vera. We'll edit him out."

Johnny apologized. "I'm sorry. I don't know what got into me. It just popped out. Shall I leave? Maybe I'm making her nervous."

Prunella simpered. "You're making all of us nervous. Please stay. Only try not to make noise. Okay, are we ready? Let's get back to the subject of history. Roll tape."

PRUNELLA: Am I right in thinking there are ghosts in Greenwich Village?

NINA: No.

J.J.: Yes!

PRUNELLA: Whoa. One at a time. Do I detect a slight disagreement? J.J.? You first. Ghosts? Are there ghosts?

J.J.: Well . . . historically speaking I guess you couldn't consider that research. Mom wouldn't go for that, would you, Mom?

NINA: When it comes to research, we need all the help we can get. If you find a friendly ghost who can tip you off to some secret trove of material, go for it.

J.J.: Oh, Mom. It's not like I'm going to a seance or anything. It's just that I told a few people—like the man up the street who sits on the stoop—I told him about the new book and he said the ghost of Alexander Hamilton comes back to the neighborhood every July twelfth. That's when he died. Around the corner. In Jane Street. In horrible agony after Aaron Burr shot him. And Burr comes back, too. The guy swears it. He's seen them both.

PRUNELLA: Tell me, Nina. Aren't you taking a big chance doing a book about American historical figures? Most people think early American history is dull.

NINA: That's because of the way American history has been taught. George Washington and the cherry tree. Paul Revere getting saddle sores. Guys dressed like Indians throwing tea into Boston Harbor. Except for Jefferson and his black mistress we never hear anything about anyone else's love life. Hamilton and Burr were two of the smartest and horniest men in the early days of the republic. Maybe it was those tight pants and all that horseback riding. They were notorious in their private lives. Burr married a woman old enough to be his mother and had an incestuous passion for his daughter. Hamilton married into one of New York's oldest Dutch families and had an affair with his wife's sister until the day he died. Hamilton and Burr came from different backgrounds. Hamilton was born illegitimate in the West Indies and came to the mainland just in time to be part of the revolution. Burr's family was one of the original Massachusetts colonists. They were rivals in every way. And that, as I shall show—with J.J.'s help—is how sexual and political rivalry between these two men affected the future of this fragile young country—and what's more, it's my belief that if Aaron Burr had had his way, there would be no United States of America today. The North American continent would look like Europe—a bunch of small independent states endlessly fighting among themselves.

PRUNELLA: Whew! That's quite a theory. What will the academic community say about that?

NINA: Plenty, I'm sure.

PRUNELLA: And Michael Ludovic? How does he feel about your rewriting American history?

NINA: I haven't told him. We have a deal. He never asks how I'm doing. He never reads a word until I give him the finished manuscript.

PRUNELLA: Clearly a match made in heaven. So why in heaven haven't you married?

As if hearing himself being discussed, Michael Ludovic entered the room in a rush of energy. He stopped dead in his tracks with the startled look of a deer caught in headlights. "I'm sorry! I thought you'd be finished. Please don't let me interrupt."

"Stop tape!" Vera said.

"All my fault," Prunella gushed. "Rush-hour traffic. Gridlock. Took me nearly an hour to get here from midtown."

"So that's your limo blocking the street. You should ride a bicycle like me."

Prunella looked at her watch. "Let's call it quits for today, Vera. The crew are into overtime as it is. We'll see what we've got and then decide if we need to come back tomorrow."

Michael said, "Everyone looks like they could use a drink, Nina darling. Why don't I go downstairs and get out some ice?"

Prunella was fast on her feet. "Why don't I go with you? I've been wanting to meet you for the longest time. I've been thinking of writing my auto-biography. A real slice of Americana. 'Innocent young farm girl from the Midwest runs away from home and becomes a media superstar—' "

But Michael Ludovic was not listening. "Nina!" He pushed Prunella aside and dropped to his knees beside Nina's chair. "My God, darling! What is it?"

Nina's face was contorted with pain. "I—I was going to surprise you—" she gasped. Her body doubled over in spasms.

He cradled her in his arms as best as he could. Keeping his voice calm, he told J.J. to call the family doctor. "Tell his service it's an emergency."

Nina summoned sufficient strength to countermand his order. "No, J.J. Call Dr. Minkow instead."

"Your gynecologist?" Michael spluttered, the truth slowly dawning.

"Yes, darling. I found out this morning. I was going to tell you tonight. We're pregnant! Nearly three months, he said."

Tears coursed down her cheeks as she implored her daughter. "Hurry, J.J. Tell him the pains are like heavy menstrual cramps. Only worse!"

Michael held her close. "It's going to be all right, darling. I promise you. Just try to relax. J.J.'s on the phone. They'll beep the doctor wherever he is. I'm here, dearest. I love you. I won't let anything bad happen to you. I promise with all my heart."

It was then that he realized that he and Nina were not alone. He had seen J.J. usher Vera Boyle and the crew out of the room and assumed Prunella Dove had left with them. Now he was startled to find the woman was still there, watching them with an expression of naked jealousy, which sent a ripple of terror through his entire being. Clearly she hated Nina and wished her ill.

Instinctively, he shielded Nina's body with his own, placing himself like a protective wall between her and Prunella and gesturing toward the door until Prunella reluctantly responded. Before closing the door behind her, she lit a cigarette and inhaled deeply. In the exhaled cloud of smoke, she gave her final instructions. "Tell Nina I'll be in touch."

Chapter Four

Johnny Black was waiting for J.J. on the Fifth Avenue steps of the library, quietly playing chords on his Martin guitar. A week had gone by since the *Dove Report* taping, and J.J. had been practically living at the Rare Book Room since then.

The discovery that Nina was pregnant was both good news and bad news. The good news was the baby was safe. The bad news was Nina was having a very difficult time of it and would have to stay in bed for the next three months. "And that means I'll have to depend on you even more than we planned, darling," she'd said to J.J. "You're going to have to stop thinking of me as your mother and start thinking of me as a top sergeant. I'm going to be mad as hell lying in bed like some nineteenth-century heroine with the vapors. I won't be able to do much writing, but the research must go on! Have you got your notebook? Here's how I want you to work."

J.J. had been Nina's researcher for only a few weeks. Until now her assignments had been a haphazard mix of requests to look up this, find out that, track down the origins of these, them, and those, all on a one-at-a-time basis. Now Nina was to give her a crash course in the Nina Slocum method for organizing research material. File cards and folders stuffed with research were all very well. Pulling up data on the computer was useful. But what worked best for Nina were the walls of her office. She called it the War Room. Located behind the kitchen, it was Nina's sanctorum, off limits to everyone, including Michael. And J.J. until now. The windows were covered with heavy blinds so that the back garden could not be a distraction. The walls were lined with cork for soundproofing and, more important for Nina, floor-to-ceiling charts.

"Welcome to the War Room!" Nina stood regally in the open doorway, a queenly smile on her face as she extended her hand to her daughter. Both women recognized the solemnity of the occasion. For the mother it was the first official step of accepting her daughter as an equal; for J.J., it was the final transition from the sheltered life of the student to the adult world of the historian with all its pressures and responsibilities.

For J.J., crossing the threshold into the War Room was as symbolic as it was actual. Tears filled her eyes as Nina kissed her ceremonially on both cheeks. "This is one of the proudest moments of my life, J.J." She reached into her pocket. "To prove my love and confidence in your ability, here is your very own key to this room."

The key dangled from a chain necklace that J.J. recognized as one of her mother's favorite pieces of jewelry. Nina eased the chain over her daughter's head and carefully positioned the key in the space between her daughter's breasts.

An embrace, another set of kisses on both cheeks, and the ceremony was over. "On to business, J.J. There are some serious things we have to discuss."

Once they were seated, Nina went on to explain. "I can tell you quite candidly, Michael wanted to postpone the book. Or cancel it altogether. He wanted me to concentrate on having our baby without the emotional and physical stress of a new book. And what's more, he wasn't sure you were ready to take on the job of chief researcher. He knows how bright you are, of course, but also how inexperienced you are."

J.J.'s heart began to pound. What was Nina trying to tell her? That the project was off after all? Then why give her the key to the War Room? To make up for her disappointment? "Mom? What are you trying to tell me? Are we doing Hamilton and Burr or aren't we?"

Nina was flabbergasted by the question. "Of course we're doing Hamilton and Burr! What kind of a question is that? What have we been talking about all this time? Why have I given you the key?"

"But you said Michael wasn't sure I could do it!"

"Of course he's sure. You're my daughter, aren't you? A chip off the old block. Didn't I have my first book published when I wasn't much older than you? Haven't you followed in my footsteps? We're both supremely confident in you, J.J."

"Are you sure?"

"Of course I'm sure and so is Michael. Otherwise, why would we be going ahead?"

For the moment there was no reason to tell J.J. the truth about why they were going ahead with the book. Having announced to the book trade that Nina Slocum's next blockbuster was to be a sensational comparative biography of Hamilton and Burr, Michael was chagrined to learn through the grapevine that a new upstart publisher was planning a similar book to be published at the same time.

Imitation might be the sincerest form of flattery but from what Michael could learn, the other book would be a quickie, a cut-and-paste compilation of extracts from existing biographies and that the design of the cover would make it look like a Nina Slocum.

To postpone or cancel was out of the question, Nina felt and Michael agreed. The stress of risking her reputation would be far more dangerous to her pregnancy than going ahead with J.J.'s help. The time to start was now.

"The trick of doing a comparative biography is to be able to see how the comparisons evolve as the research evolves. Look in the closet and you'll find a stack of 11×14 poster boards and a carton of felt-tipped pens in all different colors. Use the poster boards to set up a series of chronological charts on Burr and Hamilton's lives. The poster boards are small enough to move them around on the cork walls. Now here's the point. Listen to me carefully, I can't do this myself. You have to do it for me. Are you listening?"

She knew her mother was stressed out, but she couldn't help laughing, "I'm *listening*, Ma! Honest! Cross my heart."

Nina tousled her daughter's hair. "Don't be smart. This is serious. I'm showing you how to become a world-class biographer. Pay close attention."

Nina explained her method with simplicity and pride. To start with, one wall of the War Room would be devoted to Aaron Burr, the opposite wall to Alexander Hamilton. A third wall would remain blank until the research progressed to the point that comparative data on each man's life could be collated under various headings for evaluation.

Nina warmed to her subject. "So you see what happens? I tack the charts to the wall, and then I start to move them around so I can begin to see the ever changing relationship between Burr and Hamilton. As the research accumulates under various headings, I can begin to make connections between what they did individually and in comparison with each other. And soon I'll be able to make assumptions and draw conclusions. Suddenly things will pop out at me. An illness here. A disappointment there. A death of a child. A passionate love affair.

"History is like Dickens and Shakespeare combined. Even the most insignificant character or chance circumstance can change the outcome of the story completely. Love turns to jealous rage. Ambition breeds conspiracy. Pascal said it in the seventeenth century: 'The heart has its reasons which reason knows nothing of.' Our job as historians is to dig out the reasons of the heart so that we may arrive at some valid conclusion as to why each man did what he did."

But wasn't that guesswork? J.J. wanted to know. All history was guesswork. "Educated guesswork!" Nina elaborated. "And everything depends on the details. Details. *Details!* Nothing is too trivial. Clothes! I want to know about their clothes. Did they wear silk underwear?"

J.J. was getting into the spirit of things. "Did they *wear* underwear?"

"Exactly! Did they use drugs? Did they pay for sex? Did they hate their fathers? Were they constipated?"

"Like Martin Luther?"

Nina smiled with satisfaction. "Remember, I'll be counting on you."

After grueling hours of squinting at printouts, J.J. emerged from the library, hoping against hope that Johnny would be waiting. At first she didn't see him. But then, suddenly, there he was, hunched over his guitar at the bottom of the broad marble stairway. He did not see her. She paused to savor her happiness. If only her mother would understand.

Soon after the Prunella Dove interview, Nina had confronted her daughter about *that afternoon*. J.J. was too forthright to play innocent. "You mean Johnny?"

"I most certainly do. He's old enough to be your father." Nina was reclining on her favorite colonial quilt, propped up by a mound of pillows. She removed the reading glasses she'd been wearing to go over the new material J.J. had brought and glared at her daughter.

"He's forty-six. What's that got to do with it? For months now you've been badgering me—"

"Never badger. I do not badger. I might show interest—"

"Okay, for months you've been showing interest by badgering me about my love life. I have not had a love life."

"And now I suppose you do have a love life with

this aging left-wing hipster. Are you sleeping with him? I hope you're having safe sex."

"You sound like a sitcom mom!"

"I am a sitcom mom. I'm only trying to protect you from sexually transmitted disease. You haven't answered my question. Are you—"

"Having sex? No, Mom. I'm a disgrace. I'm still a virgin."

"You said you went to his hotel room."

"Innocent until proved guilty."

"Are you planning to have an affair?"

J.J. looked hurt as well as indignant. "I've only known him a few days. That may sound naive, but as you've pointed out, I am naive. I'm not like some rap video. So you don't have to worry."

Nina considered her daughter with a sudden surge of maternal tenderness. "I can't imagine what it's like being your age today. AIDS. Herpes. God knows what else besides getting pregnant. Maybe this virtual-reality thing is the way to go. Totally safe orgasm in the privacy of your computer."

"You're not being fair to Johnny. You only met him for two minutes, and I could tell you thought he was handsome, too."

"Did he say that? That I was coming on to him?"

"Of course not! But I'll tell you who was coming on to him. Prunella Dove! She must have called his hotel a hundred times."

"Really? Is that what he told you?"

"He didn't have to tell me. When we got back to his room there must have been a hundred messages under his door."

"Back to his room?"

"Mom, please get off my case."

"You said his hotel room!"

"Remember what you once told me about you and Michael having sex in a phone booth? Johnny doesn't have an apartment and neither do I. Anyway, I've only been there once since the taping."

"Well, promise me one thing."

"Uh-oh!"

"Promise me you'll tell me if anything goes wrong."

"Promise."

"And remember, if you marry this elder teen, think about this. When you're fifty-one he'll be seventy-six and you'll have to nurse him through his dotage! Bed pans. Wheelchair. Alzheimer's!"

"I can't believe you said that, Mom."

Nina seemed genuinely startled. "Neither can I! Get your ass out of here. I want to have a private dinner with my husband. We're having a pizza picnic in bed. Besides, in case you've forgotten, we've got a book to do. Now scram."

Before J.J. could gather up her things, Michael entered the room holding a pizza box in his outstretched hands like a gift for royalty.

"Where are you going? There's more than enough for the three of us."

"No, thanks. Got to go."

Her smile of regret was lost in the bustle of preparation for the pizza love feast. Nina swept the magazines and other detritus off the bed. Michael opened the box and tore off the cover with elaborate care so that the pizza sat snugly in its own tray. To watch Michael and her mother you'd have thought the pizza was an exquisite banquet of caviar and Scottish salmon served on Sèvres china with crystal flutes of Dom Perignon.

Once in the upstairs hallway, J.J. felt hideously alone and abandoned. Not that she blamed them for wanting to be alone. They loved each other. They were going to have a baby. All was well and they were celebrating with a pizza.

The look of tenderness on Michael's face moved her beyond envy. Would a man she loved ever look at her like that? She went to her room and called Johnny Black's hotel. He was in his room writing a new song and had invited her to hear it.

Now it was the next afternoon. Gazing down at him from the top of the library steps, it gave her a dirty thrill to look at him without his knowledge. She took voyeuristic pleasure in the hard sculpted lines of his back and shoulders as he bent over his guitar. She longed to sit on the step above him and wrap her legs around his hips and press her face into the back of his neck.

After what happened the previous night she wasn't sure he'd show up. More to the point was what didn't happen! And why! There was an invisible aura about the man that reached out and enveloped her even before she tapped on his door. He was wearing his bathrobe, a striped blue and white terrycloth job that had seen better days. "I hope you don't mind. This is what I wear when I work."

Guitar music poured from his tape recorder, a plaintive sound made more so by its rendition on an acoustical rather than an electrified instrument. The bedside lamp had a small bulb and a peach shade. The soft light muted the signs of age in his face. The deep brackets around his mouth and the squint lines around his eyes disappeared. The sweetness of his smile conveyed the shy pleasure of the younger man he once had been.

There was an awkward pause as they stood together in the small space between the bed and the dresser. She could feel her breath pounding in her chest and prayed he could not hear it. She could feel his eyes asking her questions she was afraid to answer. Why did he just stand there? Why didn't he open the terrycloth robe and gather her inside it, holding her close and warm?

Or was he waiting for her to make the move? The music on the tape stopped abruptly, breaking the spell. She backed away from him and sat primly on the end of the bed. "Is that your new song? Where are the words?"

He removed the cassette, threw it into the air, and pretended to shoot it with his index finger. "Dead in the water."

"Is that the name of the song?"

Was she having him on? One look at her assured him she was serious. He had told her he was writing a song. What she didn't realize was that he couldn't write his way out of a paper bag. A wet paper bag. Was there anyone left on earth as sweet and honest as this girl? "You misunderstood. *I'm* what's dead in the water." He pulled the tape free of the cassette, all of it until it resembled a serving of whole wheat pasta.

"This isn't a song. It's garbage. If you want to hear a real song, I'll play you a real song."

The cassette was new, the song was old, written and recorded by his father, on an old 78 RPM acetate and transferred to tape. "He called himself 'Blackjack' Black. Not because he cheated at playing blackjack. He liked Black Jack gum. He could chew a whole pack at one time and park the whole wad in his cheek while he sang without anyone wiser."

"Where is he now?"

"Buried in London, in Highgate Cemetery with Karl Marx and the rest of the gang. Unfortunately, he died before he could become famous. He missed the boat and so have I. There's a small cult following but not like Hank Williams or Woody Guthrie."

Poor as the transferred soundtrack was, it could not diminish "Blackjack" Black's emotional yearning for better times, better loving, and better five-cent cigars. One folk music scholar had compared his fingering to Andrés Segovia and his dexterity to Chet Atkins. He could sound like an old-time settler in the Carolina hills with a three-string git-box made of a lard can and bring tears to your eyes. Or like a balladeer in the court of Henry VIII. J.J. was touched by how obviously proud Johnny was of his father.

Johnny lay down beside her on the bed and drew her close. She slipped one hand inside his robe and let it rest on his bare chest. He sighed and kissed her hair, nothing more, as his father's voice sent a gentle wave of contentment over them. Suspended between sleep and wakefulness she floated to a beach of purest, softest sand. Her clothes were strangling her. She had to pull them off or suffocate. A puppy gamboled onto the scene and licked her ear. It tickled. When she went to pet it, she found it was Johnny darting his tongue at a place inside her ear of such acute sensitivity, it was as if he had touched the core of her being, sending spasms of joy through her body.

She closed her eyes and the seashore imagery returned. They were the first beings to crawl out of the primordial ooze. The dry heat of the sun, the damp chill of water. The taste of salt. Clouds scudding and turning dark. Thunder rumbling in the distance and getting louder and louder. She sat up in a panic. Someone was pounding on the door.

Johnny cautioned her to be silent by pressing his finger to her lips. The pounding accelerated, louder and more insistent. A woman's voice screeched, "I know you're in there. Open the door. Nobody stands me up. I've been waiting for you in the Algonquin for over an hour, damn you."

The doorknob turned convulsively until it threatened to fall off. A body hurled against the door and threatened to break through the flimsy lock and chain. As a last resort Prunella Dove threatened to call the hotel detective.

Johnny grinned and whispered, "She's out of date. There are no more house dicks."

Prunella Dove finally gave up. "Okay. I get it. You've got someone there. Get rid of her. I'll be waiting for you at the Algonquin."

They dared not move or speak until they were sure she was gone. After several minutes Johnny crept to the door and opened it a crack with the chain left on. "The coast is clear. Sorry about this. Come back to bed."

J.J. swept up her belongings and locked herself in the bathroom. Her clothes refused to cooperate. Her knee-highs stuck to her toes, the zipper on her jeans broke, her T-shirt was inside out and ripped when she tried to turn it outside in. Bite marks dotted her neck. Her hairbrush jumped out of her hand into the toilet bowl.

What was Prunella Dove doing here? J.J. charged out of the bathroom and cried, "Don't try to stop me! I'm leaving."

He had dressed and straightened the bed. The room looked as it had when she arrived. "I would never try to stop you."

"Stand aside so I can get by."

"For God's sake, J.J., I'm not a rapist."

"I never want to see you again!"

"If that's how you feel, okay. But let's get one thing straight about Prunella Dove. Swoops like a vulture is right. She's been on my case ever since the taping. Phone calls. Notes. Invitations. A Ralph Lauren sweater, for God's sake. I sent the damn thing back. She came knocking on my door last night. I told her to get lost. It only encouraged her."

"What does she want? To make you a star?"

"Don't be a smartass. If I were for sale, I'd be staying at the Waldorf. I'm not stupid, you know. I know I'm old enough to be your father. I thought we had something. We're both misfits, you know, but we just might fit together."

She was compelled to ask, "Are you sleeping with Prunella, yes or no?"

"No. Are you satisfied?"

Tears filled her eyes. Why was she running like a scared rabbit? Why didn't he ask her to stay?

"I'm satisfied," she murmured.

Stalemate. She unlocked the door and turned the knob.

"What are you doing tomorrow?" he asked.

"I'm not sure."

He knew and she knew he knew that she would be back at the 42nd Street library. Suddenly she wanted to see Michael. She needed to talk about Johnny with another man. Someone she could trust.

The kitchen light was on.

"Michael—? You there?" Rather than risk waking Nina in her fragile condition, he had switched his bedtime reading to the kitchen table. Before slipping out of the house to see Johnny, J.J. had left a note under their bedroom door. "I've gone out. Be back soon."

But the kitchen was deserted. Propped against the Lazy Susan in the middle of the table was a note addressed to her. "In case nobody fed you, there's cold chicken and salad in the fridge."

Gypped again. She had gone to Johnny in hopes of finding the love light she'd seen in Michael's eyes when he looked at Nina. Confused by what had happened, she had returned to the nest for comfort and advice only to find a closed door.

At least there was cold chicken and salad. Alone at the kitchen table, she turned her attention to

Aaron Burr and Alexander Hamilton, making her list of the research she hoped to cover tomorrow.

Drifting off to sleep, she conjured up her favorite fantasy. She would be in an abandoned corner of the library, poking through some unmarked files when suddenly, in a shaft of sunlight streaming from a high window, she would find a box of historic treasures that had been hidden from view for two centuries. Julia Sands's letters to her family in Cornwall-on-Hudson. An angry exchange of letters between Hamilton and Burr discussing the trial of Levi Weeks. Ezra Weeks's deathbed confession of how and why he and Levi murdered Julia.

"Oh, it was nothing, really. Any good historian could have done the same thing!" was how her fantasy always ended as she accepted the Mayor's Medal of Excellence on the steps of City Hall, with Nina and Michael smiling at her from the crowd.

Chapter Five

Nina had tossed and turned until dawn.

"Michael?"

He stirred in his sleep and automatically reached for her.

"Are you awake?"

Good-natured as ever, he said, "I am now." Suddenly remembering her condition, he sat bolt upright, his face clouded with concern. "Are *you* all right? Nothing wrong, is there?"

Of course she was all right. It was worrying about J.J. that had kept her up. "I didn't hear her come in. I think she stayed out all night."

Michael seemed amused. "So? You've been nagging her for months to find herself a man, and now she's found one! She *is* of age, you know."

"I meant someone her own age. A student. Someone with a future. Not someone old enough to be her father."

"Calm down. I think your new maternal hormones are raging. She's not marrying him. She's just spending the night with him. *If* that. Let me check and see if she got home before we jump to conclusions."

He returned moments later, grinning. J.J. was sleeping the sleep of the innocent. Work folders and Xerox copies of library material lay scattered on the floor. "It looks like your wayward daughter worked far into the night until she couldn't keep her eyes open. Okay?"

Unmollified, Nina clung to her suspicions. "Well, she left us a note didn't she? 'I've gone out.' Out where? Where else but Johnny Black's hotel room!"

His grin was more telling than a verbal reproach. She had to laugh. "You're right. She's a grown woman. She could probably tell *me* about safe sex. Then maybe this wouldn't have happened." She patted her belly.

He looked stricken. "You're still not sure? It's not too late to change your mind." She could see the pain that the suggestion cost him, and instantly regretted her teasing.

Of course she was sure. Of course she wanted the baby.

"In fact, Michael, I've been thinking."

"About . . . ?"

"Us."

"And?"

"Remember Mary Wortley Montagu?"

Of course he remembered. Among his early gifts

to Nina was a collection of the famed eighteenth-century noblewoman's letters and poetry. "So?"

She quoted her favorite lines from memory,

"Be plain of dress and sober in your diet/In short, my dearie, kiss me and be quiet!"

Assuming her to be playful, he swept her into his arms with exaggerated concern for her delicate condition and was about to obey her command when the look on her face stopped him. "Darling? Are you trying to tell me something?"

With a sigh of tender exasperation, she drew him close and whispered, "The time has come, the walrus said, to talk of many things."

"There's only one way I know of to shut you up." And he did, with a long, luxuriant kiss of the kind usually enjoyed by new lovers.

When at last they came up for air, Nina said, "I've been trying to say, 'Yes! Let's get married!' "

As simple as that. His heart cried out for roses and diamonds and mounds of Beluga and champagne by candlelight. But his body was paralyzed with happiness, absorbing his joy like a giant sponge. Violins? Trumpets? Shouts of glee from the rooftops? He could not move. Nor did he wish to. What he wished was to spend the rest of their lives lying quietly in their bed with Nina's head on his shoulder and her body pressed sweetly to his in perfect harmony.

They slept the sleep of contentment until J.J. tapped on the door to announce that she was leaving for the gym and would be home for lunch and that she had something very important to discuss with Nina.

"I'd better get up, Michael."

"You stay right where you are. Remember? You're staying in bed for the next three months."

More than most things, she hated being told what to do. Michael had never tried to bully her before. She wondered if this was a harbinger of things to come.

"Then how are we going to get married if I have to stay in bed?"

They'd work it out, he promised. Now that she'd actually agreed to marry, that was enough for him. Keeping her healthy was top-priority. The marriage license and the ceremony could wait.

"What if I change my mind?" This kind of bitchiness was not her style. What'd got into her? she asked herself and instantly answered. The baby, that's what. This was not a time for teasing. "Forgive me, darling. I didn't mean that."

"I know you didn't. But . . ."

The dangling "but" always meant Michael had something difficult to say and was having trouble spitting it out.

"Let's have it, partner."

He hesitated, then plunged. "I think we should push the book back until you're up and about. That way you can relax and think baby thoughts and not have to worry about deadlines. Doesn't that sound practical?"

It sounded brain-damaging in the extreme. Her body might need to rest; her mind, her inquisitive, acquisitive mind needed to work, to absorb information and find out *what happened* and *how come*.

"Don't be silly, Michael. J.J. will be doing all the legwork. She's already started. I can read in bed, can't I? I can use my laptop, can't I? Madame Recamier spent her life on a chaise longue, didn't she? And she didn't have J.J.! The girl's good. A fast learner. She's already shown me how she can sniff out details another researcher or even I might skip right past."

Truth to tell, Michael Ludovic had not been too enthusiastic about the Burr-Hamilton book in the first place. Compared to Napoleon and Nelson, they were a big yawn. Most people didn't know who they were except that Burr had killed Hamilton in a duel. To test his reluctance, he had asked a young summer intern at the office what she knew about Alexander Hamilton. The young woman was studying film history. She asked if he was related to Vivien Leigh in *That Hamilton Woman*.

Nina's passion for her subject had steamrolled him into submission. How could he argue with the woman he adored and whose earlier books were still best-sellers?

"All anyone knows about Hamilton and Burr is that Hamilton's picture is on the ten-dollar bill and Burr killed him in a duel. Period. They're boring. And if they weren't boring, they're perceived as boring."

"All the more reason for this book. They were not boring. Like I keep pointing out, they were two of the brainiest and horniest men in American history. Maybe it was the tight pants and all that horseback riding, how do I know? They were notorious. They chased women. Got themselves into trouble. Had the same mistresses. But more to the point, they both wanted to be president of the United States. Burr hated Hamilton's guts. He was purple with jealousy because Washington picked Hamilton to be his personal aide and sent Burr away. He hated Hamilton because Washington made Hamilton secretary of the Treasury and left Burr out of his government entirely. Burr hated Hamilton so much he set him up as a patsy in the first big sex scandal in American governmental history.

"Tell me, Michael, did you ever read about that in school? Well, neither has anyone else! Burr paid a beautiful woman called Marie Reynolds to seduce Hamilton and then had her husband threaten him with accusations of stealing money from the American treasury. He didn't totally get away with it, but he stopped Hamilton from being president.

"And then Hamilton not only got even personally. He probably changed the entire history of the United States by preventing Burr from beating Jefferson for the presidency in 1800 and—four years later—destroying any possibility of Burr being elected to high office by forcing him into the duel and sacrificing his own life for the sake of his country."

Months ago Michael had precipitated the only major quarrel they'd ever had by asking in what Nina regarded as a flippant tone, "Where did you read that?"

Where? Nowhere! That was the point. She had read all of Hamilton's papers. All of Burr's papers. Every book about each of them. Nobody, not one biographer or historian, past or present, had come anywhere near her theory. Yes, they had related what had happened to each man but no, they had not answered what to her was the essential question. *How come?*

In a sublime example of being in the right place at the right time, the two men were inexorably destined to get in each other's way. They could not escape. In Nina's view, nobody would ever know what each might have achieved if the other had been stillborn. In fact, Nina was slowly coming to the conclusion that without Hamilton, there might not even be a United States of America.

That was one of Nina's ideas that Michael had

a hard time accepting. "How can you say such a thing?"

"I won't say it until I can back it up. But remember, Michael, when Washington died in 1799, the individual states were really like separate countries. They were weak. The federal government was weak. There was no unified sense of cooperation. There was bickering over interstate tariffs. The north and south were contemptuous of each other. If France and Spain hadn't been so busy with their own internal problems, they could have sailed across the Atlantic and wiped us out, state by state."

"Didn't the British try it in 1814?"

That war was later, of course, after Hamilton's death and after Burr had been tried for treason and lived the remaining quarter century of his life as a figure of contempt.

What excited Nina most was the way the fates had conspired to entangle the destinies of two men from such diametrically different backgrounds: Hamilton, the illegitimate son of a whore and a dissolute Scottish aristocrat, born in the West Indies, tutored by a rabbi, reduced to working in a general store until the combined efforts of an older woman and a Protestant missionary sent him to the North American colonies to continue his education just as revolutionary fever was spreading.

Among his letters of introduction were several

to the leading colonial families such as the Jays and Livingstons asking for their hospitality and suggesting that young Hamilton and young Aaron Burr be brought together.

Burr's family was among the early settlers of the Massachusetts Bay colony. His grandfather was the famed "Great Awakening" preacher of the eighteenth century, Jonathan Edwards. His father, also named Aaron Burr, had been the president of Princeton University.

Both men were handsome, ambitious, and reluctant to meet each other.

When Washington set up headquarters in New York, he appointed Hamilton as his youngest aide. This fueled later rumors that Hamilton was actually the general's son, sired during the general's 1752 visit to Barbados, ignoring the fact that Hamilton had been born on the island of Nevis five years later. Other Hamilton rumors included an intimate friendship with South Carolina aristocrat John Laurens and its implications of homosexuality, and his twenty-five-year love affair with his wife's sister Angelica Church that ended with both women at his deathbed.

Burr also served on Washington's staff but not for long. Washington reassigned him to General Putnam's staff, where he acquitted himself well. He liked actresses and the lower orders until he married the widow of a British officer ten years his senior and became a more or less dutiful husband until she died. He was rumored to have been sexually obsessed with his daughter Theodosia. In his later years he was the quintessential dirty old man who married one of America's richest women, the infamous Mme. Jumel. The marriage soon ended when she caught him selling her property, stealing her money, and consorting with barmaids.

"Wait till the halls of academe get a load of this!" Nina cried, rubbing her hands together in anticipation. "Publish or perish? I'll publish. They'll perish!"

Michael's suggestion that the book be delayed troubled Nina. "Are you saying postponed? Or are you saying cancel?"

Michael was constitutionally unable to lie. "Well, I'm just worried about your health—and the baby, of course."

"You just listen to me, Michael. This is not an either or situation. It's not either the baby or the book. It's the baby *and* the book!"

"And me, I assume."

She couldn't believe it. Her agreement to marry had deteriorated into a petulant argument. "Are you saying you won't marry me unless I cancel the book?"

"I said no such thing. I think that after all these years of refusing to marry, you're still not sure that's what you want to do."

Could he be right? Having said yes, was she doing everything in her power to pick a fight?

"Let's deal with this one thing at a time. Yes, darling. I want to marry you. I want to tell the world we're getting hitched. Starting with J.J. when she comes home for lunch. I want her to be the first to know."

"I would wait if I were you." He was not smiling.

"A minute ago we were so happy. Why are you acting this way?"

"I have wanted to marry you since the first minute I saw you. Standing on that dais. Talking about phallic symbols. I will not have you treat this frivolously. Your life and the baby's life are more important to me than any book."

"Oh, Michael. Are we suddenly strangers? If this is your ultimatum, if this is a deal breaker, I'm warning you. If you force me to give up my book, I'll wind up hating you and the baby! Why do you push me to that?"

He looked at her with the saddest expression she had ever seen. "I say we go on as before and think seriously about the next step. You will follow the doctor's orders and stay put for as long as he says. J.J. will do the legwork and set up the War Room the way you want it until you're ready to write the book. In the meantime you can use your tape recorder and the laptop."

"In other words, you don't want to marry me."

"Not so. Think about it, Nina. When push comes to shove, are you sure you want to get married? We'll talk about it later. Now, promise me you'll take care of yourself."

She smiled to herself. She had often thought New Year's Eve was a wonderful time for a wedding. Michael Ludovic didn't know it, but that was when they were going to tie the knot. She closed her eyes and began to make plans.

When J.J. returned home for lunch, Nina sat up with a start. "I wasn't asleep! Just resting my eyes," she said.

"Oh, Mommy, I'm so glad you're home!" In the emotion of the moment, J.J. regressed from calling her mother Nina to the child's cry for solace.

Tears flowed as mother and daughter embraced. Nina realized it was her first born she held in her arms while her next born was growing within her. "You don't mind, do you, J.J.?"

"Mind what?"

"It won't embarrass you to have a baby brother or sister more than twenty years younger?"

"Oh, Mommy. I'm already planning to take it for walks and teach it dirty words."

The thought had occurred to Nina that the news about the baby might have sent J.J. into the arms of that cowboy. Blaise Pascal's words again made the point. The heart did have its reasons that reason did not know.

Contemplating her daughter, she felt a rush of love mixed with pride in this creature she had borne and raised and was now depending upon as a professional colleague. She kissed the tip of her nose. "Enough of this. We have work to do. Now, what's all the excitement? Tell me what you've found."

The words spilled out. She'd been examining the files on Aaron Burr's nefarious Manhattan Water Company. As was well documented by other historians, the charter he had pushed through the New York state legislature was a cynical joke. New York City's water supply was dangerously contaminated and unsafe to drink. While Aaron Burr's company promised to supply pure water through a series of wooden pipes and wells, the text of the charter allowed him to raise money and use it any way he chose.

"In other words, the Manhattan Company wasn't a water-supply company. It was a bank. And eventually became the Chase Manhattan Bank, as we all know!"

Nina's medication was making her sleepy. "I'm sorry to be a grouch, but please, J.J., get on with it. What did you find?"

"I'm getting to it. Remember what you always say. Details. Details. Details."

To show good faith, Burr did lay down a few miles of wooden pipes and sank a well in the Lispenard Meadow at what's now the corner of Spring Street and Greene Street, in the heart of Manhattan's trendy SoHo. It never provided an ounce of drinking water, but it did achieve notoriety when the bruised and battered body of a beautiful young Quaker woman was found in it just after the New Year 1800.

According to the *New York Daily Advertiser* of January 4, 1800, the victim was Gulielma Sands, and the discovery of her frozen body created as much of a sensation in the New York of that time as the murder of Nicole Brown Simpson in 1994. For several days thousands of the curious mobbed Greenwich Street, where the body was on view in the rooming house where she had lived with her cousin Catherine.

The crush of sensation seekers was so heavy, her open coffin was moved outside onto the cold winter street for further viewing. Local gossip pointed to a handsome young carpenter, Levi Weeks. He was known to be her lover and thought to have proposed marriage. The younger brother of the city's most successful builder, an early day Donald Trump, Levi's family connections might have enabled him to avoid arrest. But feelings ran too high. He was brought to trial at the end of March amid a continuing circus atmosphere and was acquitted by the jury in less than five minutes.

J.J. paused suspensefully. "Now, here's the point, Mom. Here was a murder case like the ones in the paper every day. A guy is on trial for killing his girlfriend. But what makes this intriguing is the defense team of lawyers. Do you know who they were? Aaron Burr, who owned the well, and his arch political enemy, Alexander Hamilton! The two of them. Working together! To get this guy acquitted of murder! Don't you see?"

Nina stifled a yawn. She and her baby needed a nap. "I do remember reading a little something about the Levi Weeks trial. Nothing much. I can't really remember."

"Exactly, Mom! I've checked the index of every book ever written about Burr or Hamilton. Most ignore the trial completely. A few mention it in passing, and when they do"—she paused again for effect—"they say *what* happened. But nobody has asked your favorite question, 'How come?' "

To J.J. it was as if Kennedy and Nixon had postponed their debates in order to skip hand in hand into court to defend the accused in an ordinary manslaughter case. Or Clinton and Bush, both lawyers, leaving the campaign trail in 1992 for a similar reason.

"See what I mean? In the few books that mention the trial, I kept turning the page for a follow-up. How come Burr and Hamilton joined forces? Nobody has given it a second thought. Was there some kind of cover-up? Were both men in some way involved? And did this terrible secret become so intolerable that it led ultimately to the duel?

"I tell you, Mom, I checked everywhere. Every book. Every article in magazines and newspapers dating back to 1800. Nobody asked, 'How come?' "

Nina's eyelids struggled to stay open. "Maybe

it's because most historians were men. At least in the past. The murder of an obscure young girl didn't interest them."

"Well, it sure interests me. One source calls the Levi Weeks trial New York's first recorded murder case. It's still on the books as unsolved. Well, guess what? I'm going to solve it!"

She *alone* was going to solve it? Despite herself, Nina felt a pang of envy over the rush of wild excitement in the chase that had once been hers alone.

Having J.J. follow in her footsteps was fine. She welcomed it with open arms. She was ready for a nap. She was not quite ready to pass the torch.

Chapter Six

The phone rang just as Johnny Black finished zipping Prunella Dove into her dress with a kiss on her neck as an apology for his poor performance.

"Johnny? It's me! I know I'm early, but I'm downstairs. You haven't forgotten, have you?"

He had at least for the moment forgotten that J.J. had asked him to accompany her to the Friends Society Library in Stuyvesant Square. She had made an appointment to examine some material about Quakers in New York during and immediately after the American revolution. Her fingers-crossed hope was that there would be some information about Gulielma Sands, the murdered girl in the Manhattan Well and any possible links her family had with Hamilton, Burr, or both.

"You sound funny, Johnny. Are you okay? I picked up some bagels and coffee. Okay if I come up?"

Shades of French farce. The situation would be funny if it wasn't so sad. Of all the people he'd met so far in New York, the one he most wanted to think well of him was J.J. Drake. He could not let her know he'd been seduced like some bimbo by a bigtime TV producer who might help his career.

"Stay where you are. The maid's doing the room. I'll be right down and you know what? It's a beautiful morning. We'll go over to Bryant Park and have our breakfast in the sun."

Since Prunella's entire world revolved around herself, she assumed Johnny was protecting her reputation. "Thank you, darling. We don't want any little items in Liz Smith, do we? Now run along." She would wait ten minutes before leaving. He did not like the idea of Prunella Dove alone in his room and going through his things as she surely would. But he had no choice.

Waiting for the elevator, he mentally catalogued his scant belongings: clothes, some old 78 records of his father's. A ballad he had begun to compose about J.J.'s girl in the Manhattan Well. And—his heart sank—his passport bearing his real name. He had hidden it by habit under the paper lining in the bottom dresser drawer with his pathetic supply of underwear and socks on top. Women like Prunella and his ex-wife had an instinct for finding things. *Que sera, sera.* Performers frequently took stage names; the worst thing she would find out was that he had sliced five years off his age.

If only he could get his life together. Last night when Prunella had called and coyly said she happened to be in the neighborhood, he had nearly wept with gratitude. His father had once written that loneliness and failure were his only friends. Johnny thought he had left them behind in Britain, but they had followed him to New York and moved into his shabby room.

Earlier last evening he had tried to cheer himself up by strolling through Times Square. A heavyset man in a pinstripe suit and carrying an attaché case had asked him the time. He didn't realize until the man fell into step beside him and was plainly wearing an expensive gold watch that he was being picked up. He had cut and run back to the hotel and was seriously wondering if he could possibly cut his wrists with a nail clipper when Prunella Dove called.

A beam of morning sunlight danced on J.J.'s hair, reminding him of his daughter the last time he saw her, waving good-bye at Victoria Station in her new school uniform. He had enjoyed feeling a paternal responsibility for Miriam. He recognized something of the same protectiveness toward J.J. He liked the fact that she fancied him—what man wouldn't?—but he had made up his mind to keep her at a distance. The intimacy of her visits to his room had stopped short of sexual. But barely.

Seated on a bench in Bryant Park, J.J. positioned her backpack between them, covered it with paper napkins, and served their breakfast as if presiding over a children's tea party. "Thanks for coming downtown with me."

He'd been thinking about what she'd told him about the Girl in the Well. Killed on her wedding night. By the man she was supposed to be marrying.

Nina had reluctantly agreed that the murder should be treated with more depth than in previous biographies, but for the moment other things came first. Last night she had given her daughter a long list of questions about the women in Hamilton's and Burr's lives.

It wouldn't take long, J.J. assured him. For one thing, she wanted to find the murdered girl's actual name. Little had been written about her, yet she was variously referred to as Elma, Alma, Elmore, Juliana, and Gulielma Sands. What she hoped to find at the Friends library was not only her name but any original data about her family background, the murder and trial of Levi Weeks, and where she was buried.

The name Gulielma had seemed strange to her. Yet in reading about the Quakers in colonial America and in the early years following independence, she had come across it many times. William Penn's first wife was Gulielma. If it wasn't exactly as popular as names like Catherine and Elizabeth, Gulielma was nonetheless in common usage.

She explained all this to Johnny. "So what do you think?"

"About what?"

"About forgetting Gulielma altogether. And calling her—Julia. Julia Sands. That sounds right to me. I'll bet that's what everyone called her. Julia Sands."

Her certainty made him laugh. "How do you know they called her Julia Sands?"

As they got off the bus at Stuyvesant Square, J.J. grinned impishly. "As Nina would say, 'How do we know they didn't?' "

Stuyvesant Square is today a pleasant four-acre park bisected by Second Avenue a few streets north of the bustle of Fourteenth Street. Its name dates back to the seventeenth century, when New York was New Amsterdam. It was part of a huge land grant given to Governor Peter Stuyvesant by the Dutch West India Company. Known and feared as "Peg Leg" Pete because of his wooden leg, Stuyvesant ran the small colony with an iron hand, restricting the use of alcohol and imposing compulsory Sunday worship at the Dutch Reformed Church. His autocratic ways turned the colonists against him. Formerly friendly Indian tribes threatened rebellion. When the English fleet sailed into the harbor under the leadership of the Duke of York in 1646, Stuyvesant surrendered without firing a shot.

Not that Old Peg Leg returned home to The

Netherlands. He liked living in America and spent his remaining years on his farm. Some two hundred years later his property had passed down to successive family members until in 1836, the present Stuyvesant Square was given to New York City for the enjoyment of its citizens.

Much of the Victorian character of the square had survived. Walking through the wrought iron gates was to magically exchange the bedlam of traffic for the hush of elms, gingkos, sycamores, and ailanthus and the perfume of manicured grass. To the west was Rutherford Place and the Society of Friends Meeting House and Seminary. As a reminder of the man who introduced the first Quakers to the American colonies, a granite hitching post that once stood in front of William Penn's house in Philadelphia has a modest place of honor outside the building.

On the bus going down Second Avenue, Johnny had asked J.J. what she hoped to find waiting for her. The born researcher's equivalent of sugar plums danced in J.J.'s head like a greedy child's montage of gumdrops and pizza and Tootsie Rolls. Stanley finding Livingston. Carter finding Tut. Jennifer Joy Drake knew exactly what she *hoped* to find in the archives of the Friends Society Havilland Record Room.

Treasures of nearly two hundred years ago hidden in what mystery writers called plain view:

- A portfolio of pen-and-ink drawings made by an unknown artist at the trial of Levi Weeks, including individual portraits of Hamilton and Burr, the accused Levi Weeks, his brother Ezra, the murdered girl's Quaker relatives, and citizens of the town dressed in their finest. Ideally, on the back of each drawing would be the artist's personal observations of what happened.

- A bundle of letters preserved in a battered tin box, some written by the murdered girl to her family in New Cornwall, saying how much she missed them, how happy she was living on Greenwich Street with her cousin Catherine, and how she had had an offer of marriage from a fine young man named Levi Weeks and hoped to pay a visit home with her new husband. Some of the letters would brag about Levi's older brother, and the fine houses and hotels he had built.

- Last but not least, burial records for January 1800, when the murdered girl must surely have been interred. "Was she buried in New York or did her cousin ship her back to the Sands family plot in New Cornwall?" J.J. wondered aloud.

Johnny was incredulous. "You really expect to find that? After all these years? And wouldn't other researchers have found out already if it's possible to do so?"

"Not if they weren't looking. Nobody's ever cared about the girl in the Manhattan Well until I got on the case. Who knows what's stashed away on those dusty old shelves?"

As it turned out, not much. Not that J.J. in her wildest dreams really expected to find sketches and letters. But there was one important item, the Monthly Meeting Book for January 1800. There in brown ink in a graceful hand was the name Gulielma Sands followed by the brief notation of her interment on January 8 in the Friends burial ground on Liberty Place. Period.

"Isn't it sad?" J.J. sighed. Whereas all the other listings of the dead included the names of their parents, siblings, spouses, and other family members, the murdered girl's name was pitifully alone. There was no mention of the date or place of her birth or of her parents or of any relatives.

"Not even her cousin Catherine Sands Ring!" J.J. observed mournfully. "It's crazy. She lived with Catherine and her family in Greenwich Street. It's like Catherine was ashamed of her."

"Maybe she was," Johnny said. "Maybe she was a disgrace to the family. The scandal and all. Maybe they did their duty and got her buried and washed their hands of her."

J.J.'s face suddenly lit up. "What about the gravestone? There's got to be a gravestone! 'Here lies Gulielma Sands, born so-so-so, died December 22, 1799. Beloved daughter of so-so-*so*. Rest in peace!' "

Foiled again. Until the middle of the nineteenth century, the Society of Friends had a "strong testimony" against the use of gravestones. Bodies were consigned to the earth with no distinguishing marks. What's more, the Friends Meeting House and its burial ground on Liberty Place had been sold in 1825. All of the remains were moved to a new burial ground in an area near the Bowery where Houston Street is today.

"You mean she's buried somewhere underneath Houston Street?" Johnny wondered.

Not quite. A quarter century later, in 1849, the Houston Street burial ground was sold and the remains of those interred were again moved, this time to their final resting place in Brooklyn. "In the middle of Prospect Park, as a matter of fact," J.J. discovered.

"A cemetery in the middle of Prospect Park?" Johnny's father had grown up in Brooklyn. During the early years of the family's exile in London, father and son would often leave their shabby flat to play catch and have an ice lolly in Hyde Park. "Beautiful as it was, my dad always said it couldn't compare with Prospect Park. What a place to put a cemetery!"

J.J.'s grin alerted him to the fact of his having said something dumb. "What? What'd I say?"

With a young person's glee at an older person's stupidity, she pointed out that there had been no Prospect Park in 1850, that the Friends cemetery was there before the park was created.

"And that's where Julia's bo-o-o-ones are buried!" She fluttered her fingers at him like an apparition. "Maybe her ghost is still there. Maybe she can't rest until she tells someone what really happened that co-o-o-o-old December night in 1799."

"You really want to know?" he demanded, the imperious schoolmaster challenging a bright but slap-happy child.

"Yes, oh yes! I really want to know."

"Then let's go to Prospect Park."

They were racing hand in hand along 14th Street toward the subway when J.J. stopped dead in her tracks. Her body slumped like a puppet with broken strings, her chest constricted so that her voice was an anguished gasp. "I can't! I'm supposed to be at the 42nd Street Library. I've got a list of stuff a mile long. Nina will kill me as it is! How about tomorrow? We can go tomorrow."

"There is no tomorrow. It's a figment of speech. Because when what we think of as tomorrow comes—it's not tomorrow! It's today. This day. Have you read Saul Bellow?"

Her eyes brightened. "*Seize the Day?*"

"Seize the day!" He pointed at the subway entrance. "See what it says? Brooklyn."

When they emerged from the subway at the Brooklyn Museum, the vast parkland stretched out as far as their eyes could see in a shimmer of sunlight. With growing exuberance they skirted the Botanical Gardens and half ran through the Long Meadow to the park's southern extremity where, sure enough, there it was. The Friends

Cemetery, a fifteen-acre private graveyard surrounded by a chain-link fence.

The entrance gate when they found it was locked. They could see in the near distance a low-lying building but no sign of anyone in attendance. A man walking his dog stopped to explain. There was rarely anyone there. Every so often he saw landscape people pruning trees and repairing the pathways. Occasionally there was a funeral, he said. Montgomery Clift, the movie star, was the most recent one that he could remember.

How could they get in touch with whoever was in charge?

The man shrugged and moved on.

J.J. rattled the fence. "She's in there, I tell you. And she knows what happened!"

Johnny Black got caught up in the spirit of the occasion and joined her at the fence. "Julia! Julia Sands!" he bellowed.

In an instant they were chanting in accelerated rhythm, "Jul-ia, Jul-ia! Julia Sands. Julia Sands!"

"Are you there?" J.J. cried. "Tell us what happened! Tell us who did it! And why!"

"Was it Hamilton? Was it Burr? Tell us, Julia! We love you, Julia! Tell us, Julia! Tell us."

The guitar on his back was so much a part of him, it looked and felt as if it were attached to his body. As J.J. rattled the chain-link fence in time with her repeated cries of the dead girl's name, Johnny Black's fingers pulled a thunderstorm of chords from his father's old Martin until a blast of ice-cold air knocked them off their feet. It was gone as abruptly as it came.

J.J. rolled exultantly in the grass. "She heard us!"

"Don't be silly."

"She wants me to find out what happened."

He pulled her to her feet. "All this gives me a great idea."

"What?"

"I'll tell you on the way back."

He waited until they were settled into their seats on the Manhattan-bound subway. With his guitar at his chest, he strummed softly. "I'm calling it 'The Ghost of Julia Sands.' It's still rough. It's all in my head. But Julia herself is helping me with the words."

Because the train was traveling into Manhattan and against the rush hour, the relatively few other passengers listened with varying degrees of interest. One woman pushed back her head phones and moved a few seats closer.

The Ghost of Julia Sands

It happened on a Sunday night
In Seventeen and Ninety-Nine
Fair Julia said she'd soon be wed.
And life would be so fine.
She never heard the wedding bell
The man she loved betrayed her

He threw her in Manhattan Well
The man she loved, he slayed her.
The ghost of Julia Sands does roam
The Village streets at night.
The darkness is her only home.
Injustice is her plight.

At the City Hall station, the woman readjusted her head phones. As she left the train, she stuffed a dollar bill in Johnny's pocket. "Good luck."

He waved the dollar bill in the air. "This is the first time I've ever made money from writing a song!"

By now it was too late for the library. J.J. decided to bite the bullet and tell her mother what had happened. The fact of the Quaker girl's bones being moved from place to place before finding a final resting place lent even more poignancy to her death.

But still, J.J. did not want to face Nina alone, so she insisted Johnny Black come home with her.

"I don't think your mother likes me."

"Of course she likes you." She needed backup when she told Nina how she'd spent the day instead of being at the library. Her mother could hardly blow her top in front of him. What's more, she wanted Johnny to play some of his new song for her. She knew Nina would be knocked out when she heard it.

"Ni-na? I'm ho-ome!" J.J. called out as she bounded up the staircase to the parlor floor.

"In here!" Her mother's voice came loud and clear through the parlor door.

"Wait outside a second, Johnny. In case she's not dressed for company," J.J. whispered before opening the door. Because of her pregnancy, there was a chance Nina would be in her favorite old terry robe and tennis socks.

What greeted her was the exquisite sight of her mother in Michael's latest gift, an apricot silk caftan. From her reclining position on the chaise longue, she stretched out her arms in theatrical welcome. "Don't stand there in the doorway. Come in."

Satisfied that her mother was more than ready to welcome a guest, J.J. pulled Johnny Black into the room with her. "Guess who I've brought home for a drink."

It was then that they noticed a fourth person in the room. Curled up like a naughty kitten in the wing chair opposite Nina was Prunella Dove.

Chapter Seven

The terrified look on Johnny Black's face instantly changed Nina's mind about him. Her suspicions about his motives had clearly stemmed from a mother's fears about this aging hipster with a ponytail coming on to her daughter and ruining her life. Poor, insecure baby, his eyes ablaze with panic, trying to smile and make small talk, his forehead gleaming with sweat, his hands ice-cold clammy when he shook her hand.

In a situation like this she had to remind herself that she was a famous writer and that the woman seated across from her was the equally if not more famous television star Prunella Dove. Pretty fast company for someone who looked as if he could use a good meal.

"Come in. Both of you. J.J., fix the two of you a drink while I do the introductions. Johnny, I'm sure you remember meeting Prunella Dove the night we taped her show?"

Johnny stumbled on an area rug. The guitar

slung across his back slammed into a table lamp. Prunella deftly caught it and restored it to its place. With a merry laugh that conferred humor on his klutziness, she extended her hand. "Of course he remembers, don't you? Come sit by me." She indicated the floor beside her chair.

He recovered sufficiently to say, "I'll try not to knock over anything else."

Nina swung herself into a sitting position on the chaise and beckoned her daughter to join her. "I'm glad you're here. Prunella was asking about you. She didn't get everything she wanted the first time. So we're going to set up another session. After all, things have changed."

"You mean we're not doing mother-and-daughter?"

Prunella intervened. "Of course we're doing mother-and-daughter, but the story's better than ever now that Nina's pregnant and about to be married! Do you suppose you could have the wedding here? This room is so pretty. And J.J. as your maid of honor, of course," she concluded brightly.

"You're getting married?" J.J. turned to Nina with startled eyes.

Damn Prunella! Why couldn't she have kept her mouth shut? Of course Nina had wanted to break the news to her daughter herself. In fact, in her private scenario she had planned to tell J.J. the instant she got back from the library, to describe how she had come to her senses that morning and phoned Michael at the office and how he had raced home with daisies and roses.

"You were right, Michael. How could I have been so stupid?"

"You were right. I'm the stupid one."

"You still want to marry me?"

"Any time you say."

"New Year's Eve? Start the new year right?"

"Whatever you say, darling."

"And I've been thinking about the book and what you said. Maybe I should put it on the back burner."

"That would be breach of contract. I would be forced to sue. That would lead to all kinds of unpleasantness."

"You mean you want me to go ahead?"

"I want you to do whatever makes you happy."

"You make me happy, Michael. Everything else is gravy."

Somehow the rest of the day had run away with her. Michael had wanted to stay home after lunch but was scheduled to speak at a seminar. And then the phone rang, and it was Prunella asking if she could drop by to discuss the taping. And somehow when Prunella gushed over how beautiful she looked, Nina had let it slip that she and Michael had decided to tie the knot.

With a withering glance at Prunella, Nina took her daughter's hand. "Forgive me, darling. You were going to be the first to know. I planned to tell you the minute you got home. You must believe me."

Prunella chimed in, "It's all my fault. I wouldn't dream of making trouble between mother and daughter. It's too precious a relationship. I know. I mean, everyone knows my own daughter refuses to speak to me. So I'm really sensitive to the subject. I'm really so sorry to cause you any pain. I'm really, truly—"

J.J. stood up. "It's okay! Don't make such a big deal out of it. It doesn't matter who told who first. I'm not a child, you know. Michael Ludovic is the only father I've ever known. I love him. I love my mother. I'm really happy they're finally getting married. Now, let's change the subject, okay? Want to know what Johnny and I did today?"

Nina's heart ached for her daughter's obvious feelings of rejection. What had become such a beautiful day for Nina, one to cherish forever, had somehow in a matter of seconds turned tense with anxiety. Never in a million years would she make her daughter unhappy. What was it about Prunella Dove that insinuated doubt and chicanery into an otherwise happy situation? A spoiler was Michael's name for people like Prunella. She gratefully agreed to J.J.'s desire to change the subject. "Of course I want to know what you and Johnny did today."

Come to think of it, she had thought J.J. was spending the day at the library checking out certain details about Dr. David Hosack. From Nina's original research she'd learned Hosack was a famous botanist who figured prominently in the lives of both Hamilton and Burr. In reviewing her notes on both men, she had found that Hosack popped up frequently. He was in Philadelphia in 1793, when the Hamilton family was stricken with yellow fever, and saved their lives when hundreds of others died. He was the attending physician at Weehawken when Hamilton was shot and at Hamilton's deathbed at the Bayard house on Jane Street. Ironically, he was also at Burr's side when he died on Staten Island thirty-two years later.

And there was more, a tiny factual gem that she knew would excite her daughter given her fascination with the murder of Gulielma Sands and the subsequent trial of Levi Weeks. When the young Quaker girl's body was examined by the coroner to establish the cause of death, the coroner was guess who? The very same Dr. David Hosack. David Hosack the lifelong buddy-buddy of both Hamilton and Burr. And what was Dr. Hosack's conclusion after examining the poor girl's bruised and battered remains? That she had been beaten to death before being tossed into the pure water of the Manhattan Well, and that rumors to the contrary, she was not pregnant. Or was she? And if she was, who was Dr. Hosack protecting? New York was a small town in 1799. Everyone knew everyone. Since Hamilton and Burr defended Levi Weeks, they must have known him and his brother Ezra well. Logic suggested they also knew the pretty young Quaker girl he was known to be courting.

Nina would save this little tidbit until after the others had left. Of course, it would have dovetailed with the information she had asked J.J. to find on Hosack at the library. No matter. J.J. could go there tomorrow. It was obvious that she and Johnny had spent a wonderful day together. J.J. had been flying high with news of where they'd been and what they'd done, only to be shot down by Prunella.

Why wouldn't her daughter be hurt and upset to find that she had told a perfect stranger about her marriage plans before telling her own child? Later when they were alone, she would again apologize. They would kiss and make up and discuss the wedding. And *then* Nina would read her the riot act regarding their professional relationship. There was one boss and Nina was it. No arguments. Henceforth Nina would set the schedule and J.J. would keep to it.

For now, however, she was enjoying the pleasure on her daughter's face as J.J. recounted the day's adventure. It didn't surprise Nina to learn that J.J.'s fascination with Gulielma Sands had led her to call the Friends Society Library and make an appointment to see their archives. J.J. smiled timidly at her mother as she explained that she hadn't been expecting to find too much but that she felt compelled to go anyway. Historians were detectives, weren't they? Same as archaeologists. You never knew what you were going to find under the next sand dune.

The sparsity of records saddened rather than angered J.J. The burial records and the Encyclopedia of American Quaker Genealogy were limited to the simple basic fact that Gulielma Sands had been interred on January 6, 1800. There was a copy of a clipping from the *New York Daily Advertiser* dated January 4, 1800, that referred to the victim as Guliana Elmore Sands. It said the circumstances attending her death were "somewhat singular" since she had left Greenwich Street with her lover "with the intention of going to be married."

J.J. grinned with delight as she read aloud the final sentence of the newspaper report: "Strong suspicions are entertained that she has been willfully murdered."

Prunella appeared to be mesmerized. "And then what happened? What did you find out? Why is history supposed to be dull? This is the kind of murder case that could happen today. It's got everything. An innocent young girl. Big political names. What else did you find out? You could be an investigative reporter for TV!"

Not if I have anything to do with it, Nina promised herself. TV journalists looked for dirt, and what they couldn't find, they manufactured. Historians looked for truth or at the very least explanations and reasoned interpretations. She included Johnny Black in her next remark. "So then what did you two do? It was such a beautiful day. I wouldn't blame you for goofing off."

J.J. pretended to be hurt. Of course she hadn't goofed off. The Manhattan burial ground had been moved by the wagonload to Brooklyn in the middle of what was now Prospect Park, and that's where they'd gone!

"And what did you find?" Prunella Dove nearly fell off her chair.

The fit of giggles that choked the younger woman was contagious. In a moment they were all laughing, Nina, Prunella, and Johnny, until J.J. was finally able to gasp the word, "Nothing!" The Quakers didn't believe in headstones. All the remains were in a mass grave surrounded by a chain-link fence.

"We started shouting through the fence for Julia, which is what I call her. And then, you're not going to believe this, Mom. Johnny was playing chords, and suddenly there was this blast of cold air that sent us flying. She heard us, Nina. I'm sure of it. She wants us to find out what happened!"

Nina had heard enough. J.J. was supposed to be at the library! Not gallivanting around with Johnny

Black! But with Prunella Dove in the room she was helpless to do more than pretend her daughter's adventure in Prospect Park was nothing more than a charming escapade on a bright sunny day. Her reputation for scrupulous if unorthodox scholarship had to be protected at all costs. The barbarians in the historical establishment would love to hear that her researcher was trying to communicate with a ghost in Prospect Park.

It was all Johnny Black's fault, she decided, a truly bad influence on an impressionable and for the most part sheltered young woman. J.J.'s interest in him was added to the list for discussion later that night. For the moment she tried to switch everyone's attention to her guest with an elaborate gesture of concern. "Prunella, dear. How rude of us to keep you. Didn't you say you were having drinks with Donald and Marla?"

Prunella was not to be manipulated. She leaned back and crossed her arms. "They can wait. This is so fascinating. I want to know what happened next."

Nina's warning look toward J.J. did not connect. "The most exciting thing. On the subway ride back from Brooklyn, Johnny wrote a song, a ballad. 'The Ghost of Julia Sands.' Can you imagine? Isn't it wonderful?"

Nina did not think it was the least bit wonderful. Prunella did. She glowed with wicked enthusiasm.

"Can we hear some of it?"

"It's still rough," Johnny protested.

"Please. Just a little bit," Prunella begged.

Nina rose and planted herself between Johnny and Prunella. "I'm sure Johnny wants to work on it some more before letting us hear it."

"Oh, Mom. Please! Wait till you hear it."

Defeated by forces she could not have foreseen, Nina gave in to the inevitable. Arranging herself in Madame Récamier splendor on the chaise longue, she assumed an air of affectionate condescension toward her daughter and this intruder into her well-ordered and highly disciplined life.

She sensed danger. Michael had once laughingly called her a control freak. She had burst into tears because it sounded so hard and ugly. He was right, of course. If you don't control your life, others will control you. Johnny Black's introductory chords and melody were better than she expected, Elizabethan in feeling, reminding her of English ballads she and Michael enjoyed in concerts. Her pleasure was again short-lived.

Her daughter's delight was compounded by Prunella Dove's cries of pleasure. "Wonderful," she trilled. "Brilliant!" Without so much as a glance at Nina, Prunella asked Johnny Black if he would sing his ballad when she returned with her crew to tape the new segment.

Powerless. Was it her pregnancy that was sap-

ping her warrior strength? All of her skillfully ac-
quired techniques for controlling her life were
deserting her. Could nature's hormones be turning her inward, transforming her into a protective
cave around the new life growing within her?

Or, as she was convinced from her field of
study, history was an accident. Empires rose and
fell. A bullet here, a plane crash there, an earth-
quake, a shipwreck, a plague, a revolution. All
pieces in history's jigsaw, but the underlying invisible glue that held the pieces together was sexuality in all its forms.

Seated within, yet apart from, the small group
assembled in her parlor, she could feel the sexual
vibrations. Prunella Dove could not keep her
hands off Johnny Black's arms and shoulders as
she congratulated him and made plans to pre-
interview him before the taping. J.J. beamed with
proprietary joy at the way things were going.
Johnny Black was going to be on television because of her, singing a ballad about Julia Sands.
Nina herself could admit to a surge of lust for
this self-styled balladeer, an erotic longing for a
wild and passionate collision that could also be
attributable to her pregnancy.

Watching the two other women fluttering
around him, she felt an ugly desire to slam them
against the wall, claim the prize for herself, and
then, like ancient queens, use him for her pleasure and have him executed at dawn.

Greeting cards proclaimed, "Today is the first day of the rest of your life."

Only this morning she had thought of her life as a bed of roses. She had agreed to marry the man she loved and who loved her even more. She was about to have their child. Her books were a success. Her reputation controversial. J.J. was turning into a lovely and responsible young woman with her own brilliant career ahead of her.

In a matter of hours, everything seemed to have changed. Prunella. J.J. Johnny Black. All had seemed amenable to fit themselves into her agenda. Suddenly, without rhyme or reason, the kaleidoscope had turned. All the pieces she had thought were in place had fallen askew to form a new pattern. Prunella's idea for a segment on Nina's decision to marry the father of her expected child and to tape J.J.'s reaction to a sibling more than twenty years her junior had expanded to include Johnny Black's ballad. J.J., the devoted and obedient daughter, had cut the umbilical cord without ever having realized how tightly attached she had been. Nina had tried to train her to be original of mind and independent of thought. The result? An afternoon of shouting at ghosts with Johnny Black.

Her plan to have a heart-to-heart talk with her daughter when the others had left was aborted when Johnny invited J.J. to have dinner with him at a midtown bar where they played folk music and Prunella offered to drop them there on her way to Trump Tower.

Michael would be home in an hour or so. In the meantime she would try to answer the two questions that she could not for the moment answer.

This morning everything had seemed perfect.

What had happened? And how come?

Chapter Eight

Failing to sense her mother's growing displeasure, J.J. had accepted Johnny's invitation to a folk music club where he'd given an impromptu performance of "Pretty Polly," an early English ballad about a naive young girl murdered by her lover.

Just like Julia Sands, she had thought, but knowing Nina's feelings about the girl in the well, she had decided to keep the thought to herself. On her arrival home, she found a furious Nina waiting up for her and an ashen-faced Michael trying to keep her calm.

"Sit down, J.J., and don't say a word!"

"But . . ." Why was her mother so angry?

Michael eased J.J. into a chair facing Nina. The younger woman felt like Joan of Arc on trial. "I'd do as your mother asks," he murmured.

"I've canceled the Prunella Dove show. Michael was right. The woman is dangerous. After you all left, she telephoned to say she wanted to include footage of our wedding in the interview, and she planned to have Johnny Black sing 'The Ghost of Julia Sands'! Can you believe that?"

Only the fury in Nina's expression stopped J.J. from smiling and saying it sounded great to her. The false-hearted lover was after all in the old tradition of "Pretty Polly." A warning glance from Michael reduced any other response to a nod.

"Now, as for you, J.J., I must tell you how disappointed I am in your attitude. This is my book, J.J., and it will be researched and written my way. If you weren't my daughter and if I didn't believe in your ability and loyalty, I would fire you on the spot. Do you understand?"

J.J. did not understand. Her shocked silence was interpreted as a willingness to listen.

Nina leaned toward Michael and took his hand. "Michael wanted me to drop Hamilton and Burr until after the baby was born, but I talked him out of it. As you know, the doctor says I have to spend the next few months in bed or at least confined to the house. I will go ahead with the book only if I can count on you to do exactly and only what I ask of you. And to obey certain ground rules. Do you agree?"

J.J.'s head was whirling. "It's okay by me! I didn't want to do Prunella Dove in the first place. Just the thought of it made me sick to my stomach! Remember? That's how I met Johnny!"

Nina continued, "Which brings me to the ground rules. We have a lot of hard work ahead of us, and I want to repeat that I have every confidence in you but—! There are three subjects that are never to be mentioned or discussed in any way, shape, or form. Prunella Dove. Johnny Black. Julia Sands."

Nina's face softened. She beckoned her daughter to stand before her. Taking the younger woman's hand, she lowered her voice. "Bear with me in this, darling. Tell me you agree?"

J.J. had acceded to her mother's wishes. In the three months that followed, she kept her promise never to mention Prunella, Johnny, or Julia. According to the *New York Times,* Prunella had canceled the mother-daughter series with no explanation. The *National Enquirer* blamed it on problems with Vanessa Redgrave and Natasha Richardson. Reluctance from Carrie Fisher and Jamie Lee Curtis left Vera Boyle and the rest of the *Dove Report* staff with J.J. and a pregnant Nina, who vehemently refused to be taped in bed and at the private wedding ceremony uniting her with her longtime mentor, publisher, and lover, Michael Ludovic.

Prunella's suggestion that Johnny Black sing the song he'd written about Julia Sands was never mentioned. Not even between J.J. and him during their many clandestine meetings. What Nina didn't know couldn't hurt her. J.J. dutifully never mentioned Prunella in Nina's presence. Or

Johnny Black. But there was no harm in seeing him. She felt she owed him some consideration after Nina's dismissal of his Julia Sands ballad. It wasn't Johnny's fault. J.J. had put him on the spot, insisting he sing it. Of course it was rough. He'd only started composing it on the subway coming back from Brooklyn. When Prunella insisted on taking them uptown in her limo, J.J. was amazed at her suggestion that Johnny work on it some more.

It was during that trip that Johnny Black explained about the music documentary he was developing for the BBC. The American Revolution from both sides of the Atlantic. Marching songs. Ballads. Love songs. Laments. Both from the British and the American point of view. It was then that J.J. learned that Johnny's development deal was contingent on a matching deal with an American media company. Or else the whole project would fall apart.

An indignant Prunella Dove was not about to let that happen! Pressing her card on Johnny, she appealed to J.J.'s influence on him. "I'm counting on you to make him call me, J.J. I'm sure I can open some doors."

Taking her responsibility seriously, she kept asking Johnny whether he had called Prunella and taken her up on her offer to open some doors. Drop it, he said. Didn't she realize Prunella's offer to help was an ego trip of the moment, the same as the way some people said, "Why don't you come to dinner sometime?" But never said when?

Maybe it would be better if they didn't see each other, he said. He knew Nina didn't approve. He did not know the mention of his name had been banned. J.J. was not especially given to analyzing behavior beyond the obvious. She'd had very little reason for teenage rebellion in her life. She was born sensible. Her mother was generous and loving. Michael was more of a father and brother than most of the girls at school could brag. She was old enough to vote. Therefore she was old enough to have a friend of whom her mother did not approve.

As for Nina's sanction against Julia Sands, J.J. obeyed her mother's wishes. This did not dampen her passion for the hapless Quaker girl; rather, it redirected it into her own secret archives of facts and speculation as they arose from the main body of Hamilton-Burr research that was fast accumulating in the cork-lined War Room. When push came to shove, Nina would have to pay some attention to the trial of Levi Weeks for her murder and the joint involvement of Hamilton and Burr in the young man's acquittal.

Three months went by very quickly. Nina was feeling better. Wonderful, in fact. The morning sickness gone and the stringy hair with it. Thanks to Nina's direction and J.J.'s tireless energy, the bulk of the research was in place. In another few weeks the serious organization and writing could begin. By then J.J. felt she might choose the right moment to reopen the subject of Julia Sands. Or maybe wait another couple of months until the baby was born.

For now, J.J. led her mother down the stairs for her first view. Because Nina's condition had kept her upstairs until now, the two had held daily conferences on how to assemble each new piece of research, following which J.J. would set it up in the War Room.

The cork walls were arranged as they had been for Nina's previous comparative biographies. Hamilton and Burr faced each other from opposite sides of the room with portraits, maps, and poster-board charts highlighting the categories of each man's life. Supporting each category was a waist-high bank of swivel files containing the substantiating material from sources that included letters, diaries, memorabilia, newspaper clippings, magazine articles, speeches, and computer printouts.

Following Nina's instructions, J.J. had left the two intervening walls blank, where material from each of the two men's lives could be arranged and if necessary rearranged to provoke Nina's insights that might never have occurred to her if not for seeing them in front of her on a large space.

By Nina's calculations, the separate Burr and Hamilton walls provided facts. The walls in between provided the proving ground where she could use her skills as a historian to make connections between facts and events and judge the ironies, coincidences, and fatal inevitabilities of their lives.

As with Napoleon and Nelson, the lives of Hamilton and Burr would have been totally different if either had never lived or if one had been killed in battle. If. If. If! It was the detective-story aspect of historical figures that most excited Nina. Putting herself into their boots. And their beds.

"Well, Mom. What do you think?" By way of a surprise, J.J. had hung enlarged portraits of Hamilton and Burr above their respective cork walls and had strung up an enormous paper banner painted with Nina's familiar WHAT HAPPENED? AND HOW COME?

She expected a giggle or a shriek. Instead, she felt her mother suddenly grasp her arm. Was something wrong? Had she hurt herself coming downstairs? "Mom?" Turning to see what was wrong, she found herself in a convulsive embrace with Nina's face streaming tears.

"It's okay. I'm okay. I'm more than okay. I'm so proud of you, J.J. You've done more than I thought possible. I can see the whole book jumping out at me. Everything. Everything we discussed! Where would I be without you?"

Happiness suffused the younger woman.

"Where would I be without you? Who else would give me a job like this?"

Nina's emotional binge had run its course. "You're damn right. And don't go thinking the job's over. Like I said, it's time to review what we've got and figure out what else we need. Let's start with the basic charts."

She settled herself in a leather armchair with a lined yellow pad at the ready. "Now compare the birth and childhood of each man for me, and remember, I want details, *details*! We've got all the time in the world. Michael's playing backgammon and won't be home until late. We can send out for pizza if you like."

Pizza was the magic connection between mother and daughter. Any other night J.J. would have welcomed the chance of intimacy generated by take-out food. But not tonight. Tonight she was supposed to meet Johnny Black at the Spring Cafe, where he was auditioning for a New Year's Eve gig. She had to remind herself that Christmas was just around the corner. Hard to believe the way the weeks flew by when you were engrossed in work.

Not that she'd seen much of Johnny lately. She'd phoned him a few times. And sent him a silly cartoon. She had had no choice but to tell him Nina didn't want her to see him because she was too young. They agreed he could write her notes as long as he didn't use a return address.

His note about the audition begged her to be there. To give him courage.

The approaching holidays made her wistful. Working on the book had effectively isolated her from former school friends. No party invitations had come her way. Nina and Michael would be staying quietly at home. Christmas week was probably as good a time as any for catching up with work. Parties were a waste of time. She wasn't much on drinking at any rate.

She really wanted to attend the audition. Even if Johnny Black did get the New Year's Eve gig, she wouldn't be able to be there. That was the night of Nina and Michael's wedding.

"Remember, Mom. You're still supposed to take it easy. Michael will skin me alive if I let you work too long."

Chapter Nine

For J.J. there were times when Nina seemed to be more than a mother, when she seemed more like a movie star, a figure of dazzling, irresistible glamour. This was one of those times. Having survived the early months of a difficult pregnancy, Nina was once again in high spirits and radiant with energy and enthusiasm.

Grateful to be back once more in her beloved cork-lined workroom, she eased herself into the battered leather armchair with a happy sigh and stretched her legs voluptuously on the matching footrest. "J.J.?"

"Yes, Nina."

"Astonish me, darling. Dazzle me with your erudition." Under her mother's encouraging gaze, J.J.'s shyness fell away like a discarded snakeskin. She felt a wild rush of confidence in herself and her ability to hold her audience of one spellbound. The hundreds and thousands of facts and fancy she had assembled suddenly sprang to life in meaningful patterns. Funny what a mother's love could do. An overhead light fixture cast a glowing circle in the middle of the room. J.J. stepped into it and began to talk about Aaron Burr and Alexander Hamilton.

"They couldn't have been more different. Or more the same! They were practically the same age. Born less than a year apart. But more than five thousand miles apart. And worlds apart in terms of family and background. Burr was an American aristocrat! A fifth-generation descendant of Jehu Burr, one of the original English settlers of the Massachusetts Bay Colony in 1630. The family became wealthy New England landowners. One of his grandfathers founded Princeton University. Another grandfather was the Reverend Jonathan Edwards, a kind of eighteenth-century Billy Graham who led the great religious awakening of the 1730s. And his own father? He was the first Aaron Burr. A minister and the president of Princeton.

"In other words, when he was born just across the Hudson in Newark, New Jersey, in February 1756, it was to a family of wealth, privilege, and the most respected intellectual and religious standing. He was the only boy in his immediate family. A beautiful infant with perfect features, a sound, healthy body, and obvious intelligence and curiosity. All of which sounds like a great start to a charmed life. Until tragedy struck when he was two."

J.J. paused for dramatic effect before continuing. "Meantime, thousands of miles away in the Caribbean, Alexander Hamilton was born on the island of Nevis. The date of his birth, January eleventh, seems certain, but the year has never been verified. According to some sources it was 1755. According to others it was 1757. There were no birth certificates in those days on Nevis. In all of Hamilton's thousands of papers he never mentions his birth date directly. It's possible that when he arrived in North America in 1773, he decided to say he was sixteen instead of eighteen. But that's getting ahead of the story."

In stark contrast to Burr, Hamilton was illegitimate. His father, James Hamilton, called himself a merchant but seems to have been a drunken ne'er-do-well. He claimed to be the son of a Scottish laird in Ayrshire, but J.J. had been unable to find any records in Scotland to substantiate the fact.

His mother, Rachel, made a mess of her life. She was married to a wife beater, and when she left him he refused to give her a divorce. And then when she took up with James Hamilton, the husband had her arrested and jailed as a prostitute. Her father was another loser. He was a doctor and a plantation owner but somehow managed to lose it all. And then, after giving birth to two boys—Alexander and his brother—Hamilton upped and walked out on her.

She was so destitute, friends and neighbors pitched in so she could open a little shop with little Alexander working behind the counter while she drank herself to death. Not exactly a promising start, but that's when fate stepped in with the first link between Hamilton and Burr that led ultimately to the dueling ground in Weehawken, New Jersey, more than thirty years and a revolutionary war later.

The fateful link was a traveling Presbyterian minister, the Reverend Hugh Knox, who visited St. Croix in 1772 and was deeply impressed by the accomplishments of the young Alexander Hamilton. Despite his poverty the lad had mastered Greek and Latin, wrote brilliant prose and poetry, and proved to have such an inborn gift for finance that a leading merchant put him in charge of his warehouse when he was fourteen. All this with little formal education.

The situation changed when a group of local families raised money to send the young man to the North American colonies to further his education. Knox, in his youth, had been a close friend of Aaron Burr's father and still mourned his untimely death. Knox saw in the Hamilton boy the same charm and brilliance as was evident in the Reverend Burr's son, Aaron.

The two young men must meet, Knox decreed.

Among Hamilton's belongings when he set sail from Christenstedt in 1772 were a series of letters from Knox to the leading families of New York and New Jersey, including the Livingstons, Boudinots, and the young Aaron Burr.

"You two boys should get to know each other!" Knox said. Hamilton was willing but not Burr. He regarded the newcomer with jealous suspicion and avoided meeting him for more than three years until they met face to face as members of General Washington's staff. Right from the start Burr had reason to be jealous. Washington preferred Hamilton and soon transferred Burr to General Putnam's staff.

And that was when Burr's deep hatred of Hamilton really took seed. As the War of Independence progressed and finally ended in victory, Burr's grievances accelerated against this nobody who had succeeded where he had not.

Point—Hamilton ended the war as a general, Burr was a colonel.

Point—Hamilton was among the authors of the Constitution and the *Federalist Papers*. Burr was not.

Point—Hamilton was asked to serve in Washington's presidential cabinet. Burr was not.

Point—On the day the New York state legislature ratified the Constitution, the citizens of New York City held an enormous parade in honor of

Hamilton, who had helped get the necessary votes. Burr was nowhere to be seen or heard.

"And that's what started me thinking along psychological terms, Nina," J. J. concluded triumphantly.

Her mother smiled gently. "Since when did you become a psychiatrist?"

"Didn't you know? Everybody's a psychiatrist. What drove Burr crazy is obvious. He was obsessed with getting rid of Hamilton. Pulling all kinds of dirty tricks. Hamilton was naive. He didn't see what Burr was doing until it was too late for both of them."

"Explanation, please. And don't hold back. I'm enjoying this, J.J."

"Okay. Both men wanted to be president. In the first instance, Hamilton was hot. He was brilliant, handsome, articulate. He created the federal monetary system, the federal bank, the strong standing army that the new country would need to defend itself if any European aggressor decided to invade. He seemed destined to be Washington's successor until Burr set him up in a sex scandal involving Burr's friend Maria Reynolds and the subsequent attempt by her husband to smear Hamilton in a scheme to defraud veterans of the Continental Army.

"Hamilton cleared his name by writing a juicy confession of his affair with the luscious Maria while denying any plot to line his own pockets.

His fiscal integrity was preserved, but he was seen as a pushover for a pretty face."

Nina tapped her fingernails on the leather armrest. "Are you saying Hamilton didn't realize that Burr had sent Maria Reynolds to his house in the middle of the night begging for help when Burr knew that Betsy Hamilton and the children were away and he was alone?"

"Maybe he did. Maybe he didn't. Maybe he was too embarrassed to admit it even to himself when the truth did dawn on him. The point is, nowhere does Hamilton write about Burr's trickery or the fact that Burr was the Reynolds' lawyer and family friend."

Nina allowed herself a wry laugh. "I keep thinking of Burr as a kind of mosquito that Hamilton kept swatting but couldn't get rid of."

"A burr in his side?" J.J. smiled.

"Go to your room for that! No milk and cookies for you. What I was thinking was Burr as a kind of annoying shadow. After the war Hamilton studies law in Albany. Burr studies law in Albany. Hamilton opens a law office in Wall Street. Burr opens a law office in Wall Street. Hamilton is one of the founders of the anti-slavery movement in New York. Burr starts a splinter group. Hamilton starts a bank, and what does Burr do? He starts a bank, too, the Manhattan Bank."

Mention of the Manhattan Bank caught them both unaware. Each recognized the touchiness of the subject and its implications. J.J. had scrupulously kept her word regarding the Manhattan Well murder and the trial of Levi Weeks. A thick silence fell between them.

Nina affected an obviously fraudulent yawn. She rose and embraced her daughter warmly. "Let's start again tomorrow morning. Mother-to-be isn't as strong as she thought. I think a little nap is in order before the lord and master gets home."

J.J. was relieved the subject of Julia Sands had been avoided for the moment. But just for the moment. Nina could not really plan to finish the book without some discussion of the Levi Weeks trial and why Burr and Hamilton had defended the accused.

There would be time for that. For now the procedure was this. Nina and she would continue to review the research and discuss the implications. Once Nina was satisfied, she would begin to write the first draft of the manuscript. J.J. would then be given the nerve-wracking task of reviewing the draft and tagging it with Post-its for factual queries, logic, and inconsistencies. A daunting task for anyone working with Nina and more so for her daughter.

This first session in the War Room had taken more of an emotional toll than she had expected. She felt drained but gratified. Nina had seemed pleased, her parting hug more eloquent than any words.

"Just going out for a bit," J.J. whispered a while later from the bedroom doorway.

Nina stirred in a half sleep. "It's supposed to snow. Put something on. Don't be too late."

"Yes, Mother darling."

"Don't 'Mother darling' me! Where are you going?"

"Out!"

They both laughed in fond recollection of J.J.'s teen years.

Nina would not have laughed if she had known J.J. was on her way to meet Johnny Black.

Chapter Ten

The Christmas season had crept up on J.J. while she wasn't looking. After spending the day indoors with Nina, she welcomed the cold night air and decided to walk to her rendezvous with Johnny Black. Greenwich Village resembled a stage set. An ink black cloudless sky sparkled with silver stars. Wreaths and candles, styrofoam snowmen and solemn Nativities filled the windows of private houses and brownstone apartments. Decorated fir trees could be glimpsed in living rooms. Swags of greenery crisscrossed the intersections. At one corner J.J. really had to laugh. Someone had managed to hang a bouquet of mistletoe from a traffic light, and a couple on a motorcycle had stopped underneath it for a kiss.

The Christmas spirit became more commercial along Greenwich Avenue and Eighth Street. Jolly animated Santas and reindeer. Angel choirs singing carols. Dickensian tableaus with Scrooge and Tiny Tim. Mouth-watering displays of food and drink in festive settings of china, crystal, and silver. And then there were the toys and housewares and clothes and untold treasures calling out: "Buy me. Make someone happy."

So intent had she and Nina been on their labors that there had been little discussion of Christmas except that it would be quiet. As for shopping for gifts, a sign in one boutique brought J.J. up short. ONLY THREE MORE DAYS TO XMAS. Sure enough, X's marked off the days of the December calendar up to today, December 22.

December 22? The date in 1799 when Julia Sands set off from her cousin Catherine's house in Greenwich Street to marry Levi Weeks and wound up beaten to death in Aaron Burr's Manhattan Well. Not only had J.J. done her best to put all thoughts of the murder aside at least temporarily but in agreeing to meet Johnny at the Spring Café she had managed to "forget" the actual site of the Manhattan Well still existed in a narrow alley where Spring Street met Greene Street.

What had been the bleak, dark marshes of the Lispenard Meadow the night of Julia Sands's murder had become the SoHo of trendy galleries, boutiques, and high-energy bistros. J.J.'s terrier research had uncovered a 1957 feature story in the *New York Times* that placed the well at 89½ Greene Street, about a hundred feet north of Spring Street. The address, if it was still there, was no longer visible, but weeks before she had paced out the hundred feet and found a rickety wire gate leading to the back door of a pizza parlor. She could see a weatherbeaten cellar door that might be covering the well, but the gate was padlocked and she had lacked the courage to ask the pizza parlor proprietor if there was indeed an old well behind the store.

The night had turned cold with a giddy promise of snow. The icy wind invigorated her. At the corner of Spring and Greene, she could see the mellow lighting of the café just ahead. It would be warm and cozy, and Johnny Black would be waiting. She had been working so hard and so intensely she had forgotten how it felt to be young and on her way to an evening of music and laughter with a man whom her mother had forbidden her to mention.

Still, she hesitated. Not because of Nina. Strictly speaking, J.J. had promised not to mention him; she had not promised not to see him. It was the alley that was pulling her into Greene Street like an invisible magnet. Was the gate to the alley still padlocked? Johnny had laughed when she told him about another newspaper clipping that said the murdered girl's ghost had been seen in the area several times. Maybe that's why Julia had not answered J.J.'s cries in Prospect Park. She was in SoHo, Johnny had said.

A light snow began to fall. She turned into

Greene Street and paced the hundred feet to the gate. In contrast to the activity on Spring Street, Greene Street seemed dark and deserted. "Julia?" she whispered scaring herself with the sound of her own voice. She pushed tentatively at the gate. Its squeak reacted on her spine like a fingernail on a blackboard and sent her scurrying toward her original destination.

Johnny had been watching for her arrival from the bar and reached her side as she struggled out of her huge down coat. "You're shivering!" He rubbed her hands.

"I'm fine." He handed her coat to the checkroom man and gathered J.J. close. "Let me warm you up. I'm so glad you're here."

"Me, too." Gladder than she thought possible to be snug as a bug in a rug with his arms around her and his warm face fragrant with tobacco and aftershave pressed against her cold cheek.

They stood locked in a time-out-of-time reluctance to separate until a juggernaut of holiday makers shoved them apart in their haste to check their gear.

"Guess what, J.J. I've got a surprise for you."

"You've got the gig for New Year's Eve. You've got the grant from Washington. You've got the record deal. You're doing the documentary. You—"

Prunella Dove was where Johnny Black had left her. Seated at the bar, her sable coat draped

around her shoulders, Johnny's guitar held posses-
sively at her knee. "J.J. dear, how lovely you look.
Let's get you a drink. There's so much I want to
tell you."

"Johnny—?" What was going on? He knew Nina
was furious with Prunella. Was her appearance at
the café a strange coincidence, or was something
fishy going on?

Johnny had the grace to look slightly embarrassed as he explained, "Wasn't it nice of Prunella
to come all the way downtown for my audition? I
need all the help I can get."

Prunella patted his arm. "You'll be wonderful,
Johnny. Won't he, J.J.?"

A queasy feeling threatened her equilibrium. If
she had any brains, she'd get out of there and
fast. Sneaking out of the house to meet Johnny
Black was one thing. Nina wouldn't be crazy
about it, but she would probably understand. Sitting at the bar with Prunella Dove was something
else, a fundamental betrayal. Yet how could she
leave without seeing Johnny perform? And if she
did leave, then what?

Wander the holiday streets alone with nowhere
to go except home? No friends to be with? No
loving arm around her shoulder? No cold nose
nuzzling her cheek? No plans for Christmas Day
or New Year's Eve? Not that it was anyone's fault
but her own. She had cut herself off from her
classmates in order to devote all her time and en-

ergy to Hamilton and Burr. The calls to meet for a beer or hang out at the coffee bar had dwindled to silence. There had consequently been no invitations to tree-trimming parties or ice skating at Rockefeller Center.

Her self-pity turned to guilt when she realized, too, that she had not been called to volunteer in toy collection and distribution for the terminally ill children's wards. All was not lost. There were still a few more days, including Christmas Day. First thing tomorrow morning she would make some calls and see where she could be of help.

Prunella was demanding a reply to her question. "Won't Johnny be wonderful, J.J.?"

"I—" J.J. looked wildly around, wondering how she could escape.

Johnny Black intruded himself between the two women, his back to Prunella, his hands cupping J.J.'s cheeks. "I hope you'll think I'm wonderful. Your opinion means everything to me."

"I . . . need some air. It's so hot in here."

He was instantly concerned. "Is it like that day at the library? Let me take you outside."

A drumroll from the bandstand intervened. The master of ceremonies announced a special holiday treat. "The first New York appearance of an international recording artist coming to us direct from London, England—Johnny Black. Let's give him a warm Spring Café welcome! He-e-e-e-re's— Johnny Black!"

A nearby drunk yelled, "Who the hell is he?"

In the hush that followed, Johnny faced his attacker with a smile and a bow. "I guess I'll just have to show you who the hell I am!" His silver ponytail glistened; the weathered contours of his face conveyed the suffering and sexuality of a battle-scarred veteran of the eternal war between lovers.

A woman cheered as he elbowed his way through the crowd to the bandstand.

Whistles, catcalls, hoots of anonymous derision, only seemed to increase his amiability. Poised and relaxed as a veteran politician, he pressed the flesh and exchanged banter until he reached the bandstand, where a woman in black satin jumped up beside him and pressed herself against his thigh.

"Season's greetings! I've got a present for you," she purred into the microphone. A hush of expectancy fell over the audience. Was she part of the act?

"And a merry Christmas to you." Johnny smiled and bowed as he had to the heckler, without a hint of the sexual innuendo the audience might have expected. With easy grace he dislodged her from his hip and turned her to the sea of eager holiday makers. "Isn't she lovely? Maybe I should write a ballad about her. What do you say?"

Amid the cheers, he tried to help his admirer off the bandstand without success. "Kiss me!"

Half sob, half shriek. "That's all I want is one goddam lousy kiss." Her desperation was as fragile as it was naked.

The audience held its collective breath. What would he do? J.J. could see that whatever he did, he could wind up as the villain. If he brushed her off, he was a pompous bastard. If he kissed her, he was taking advantage of a poor thing who'd had one too many.

Johnny Black took the young woman's hand in his and addressed the audience. "I ask you. Could any man refuse a kiss from such a sweet and beautiful creature as this?"

A group of young women at the bar sighed in unison as Johnny Black gently embraced his tormentor and kissed her full on the lips. Audience applause swelled. The kiss went on. A rhythmic clapping erupted spontaneously and spread, the sound accelerating in tempo and intensity until at the point where J.J.'s heart was pounding so hard she thought she would faint, Johnny released the young woman and helped her off the bandstand into the arms of her companions.

He did not acknowledge the wild applause that followed, choosing instead to pick up his guitar as if he were alone and concentrate on tuning the strings. A cascade of single notes, some fancy fret work, a blues riff by way of Chet Atkins, a hint of Segovia. A pause that demanded pin-drop quiet and he was ready.

"My name is John Jacob Black. I sing ballads and I play an acoustical guitar. I was born right here in New York—Brooklyn, as a matter of fact—but I have lived for many years in Britain. I sing ballads about love gone wrong. Love turning to hate. Love leading to betrayal. Love turning deadly and ending in murder.

"Love is a powerful emotion. Strong. Passionate. Possessive. We all know it can end violently. We all know the celebrity cases. But what about those of us here tonight?"

His eyes swept the room. "How many of you are in love?"

Nervous laughter. "Okay. I see it's the women who are in love, right?"

"Right!" several women shouted. Their escorts looked sheepish.

"Okay. Now, how many of you are convinced you're the exception? You're the ones who are going to live happily ever after?"

One couple kissed passionately.

"Okay. That's one happy couple. Now, the ballad I'm going to sing for you tonight was written in the early 1770s, but it could have come from the *National Enquirer* or the six o'clock news. A young man falls in love with a fair young maiden. And she with him. And all is fine until she becomes—you guessed it—pregnant. And he? Well, he—he panics!

"Who is this bitch trying to trap him into marriage and fatherhood, right? He's too young to die. He's got things to do. This woman he thought he loved is trying to trap him. He wants out. He wants to get rid of her. And fast.

"It happens every day. He waits for her in the parking lot and shoots her down. He sneaks up on her in the subway and shoves her in front of a train. He throws her off the roof. He stabs her in the bathtub. He drowns her in the lake.

"The love that once overwhelmed him with tender passion now overwhelms him with hatred and a passion to escape.

"I, too, am a man who has felt this gut hatred. This desire to destroy. Every man here tonight has probably felt it, too. But we are civilized men, are we not? And we have controlled this murderous passion. The man in my song has not. It's called 'Pretty Polly,' but it's not a pretty tale, as you will see."

He embraced his guitar, held it for a moment to his bosom as if it were a sleeping woman, caressing its curves as if awakening it from a lover's sleep. His right hand beat a slow, funereal tattoo. His eyes closed and his body tensed as if in dreaded anticipation of the gory deed that lay ahead. His lips barely moved yet from somewhere deep in his soul came the silent cries of grief and remorse until finally unable to contain himself, he began to sing in a balladeer's voice from another time and place.

"He courted Pretty Polly the live-long night.
He courted Pretty Polly the live-long night.
Then left her next morning before it was light . . ."

The guitar became a second voice, a voice of a young girl's ecstasy in the throes of first love.

"Pretty Polly, pretty Polly, come go along with me
Pretty Polly, pretty Polly, come go along with me
Before we get married some pleasures to see.
She jumped on behind him and away they did go
She jumped on behind him and away they did go.
Over the mountains and valley below.
They went a little farther and what did they spy?
They went a little farther and what did they spy?
A freshly dug grave and a spade lying by.
He throwed her on the ground and she broke
into tears
He throwed her on the ground and she broke
into tears
She throwed her arms around him and trembled
with fear.
He stabbed her in the heart and the blood it
did flow.
He stabbed her in the heart and the blood it
did flow
And into the grave pretty Polly did go . . .
He covered her with dirt and started for home
Covered her with dirt and started for home,
Leaving no one behind but the wild birds to moan.

With that, John Jacob Black shrugged his shoulders with indifference. "What did she expect? Did she really think he was going to marry her?"

The song concluded with the same funereal tattoo with which it began, getting softer and softer as if disappearing down the road away from the graveyard.

"And what did her killer expect? Did he really think he was going to get away with murder?"

Female voices rose in vindication.

"Son of a bitch."

"Got what he deserved."

"Kill all the rat bastards!"

He calmed the crowd with a preacherly gesture, palms raised. "The message is, a four-letter word. Love. Not lust. Love! In little more than a week a brand-new year will begin. Let's all make a new year's resolution to love each other. Starting now!"

"More!" They wanted more. They pounded the tables with their glasses and their fists. "More. More! More!"

As Johnny prepared to leave the bandstand, the master of ceremonies leaped to his side.

"He'll be back, ladies and gentlemen. On New Year's Eve. Make your reservations now! John Jacob Black at one minute after midnight right here at the Spring Café on New Year's Eve. John Jacob Black, ladies and gentlemen!"

J.J. turned to Prunella. "Wasn't he wonderful? And that song. It sent chills right through me. Wasn't he fab?"

Prunella Dove was not smiling. Ignoring J.J., she snapped her fingers at the bartender for another brandy and knocked it back with a single gulp.

What's eating her? J.J. wondered. Couldn't Prunella see how the crowd loved him? How they screamed for more, more, more?

"Looks like I got the New Year's gig!" Johnny joined them at the bar and embraced them both.

Prunella pushed his arm away. "You broke your word. You didn't sing it."

"Sing what?" J.J. wanted to know. Why was Prunella so pissed off?

"You tell her! It involves her, doesn't it?"

"Tell me what?"

"It's the song I wrote about Julia Sands. Started to write. But it still needs work. Please, Prunella. Not now. Let's discuss it later."

"Not later. Now."

"Please, Prunella, another time."

"Shut up, Johnny. He was going to introduce 'The Ghost of Julia Sands' tonight. December twenty-second. The anniversary of her murder. And that's where you come in, J.J. I know all about your obsession with Julia and who killed her and whether Hamilton and Burr were involved. And I know that Nina told you to cool it, to never mention Julia Sands or the Manhattan Well ever again. Isn't that so?"

"Johnny! I told you that in confidence."

"Never mind that, J.J. I'm offering you a chance to be an instant television star. 'The murder of Julia Sands. New York's oldest unsolved mystery.'

"You and this story are just what I want. You're young. You have your credentials as a historian. It doesn't hurt that you're the daughter of Nina Slocum. The story is young, too. Julia Sands was young and naive and foolishly romantic. She believed what men said." This last was a gibe at Johnny. "And she paid for it with her life."

"But, Prunella—" J.J. could barely speak.

"Let me finish. What I see is a one-hour special prime time with Johnny's 'Ghost of Julia Sands' as the theme and you as the narrator telling the facts that are known. The arrest and acquittal of the man Julia thought she was going to marry and your theory—based on months of research—as to what really happened."

"But what about Nina?" J.J.'s head was spinning.

"Your mother has her career. Her books appeal to an older audience. People who read books. You're part of the television generation. Young audiences want young people to teach them about history, and in a way they understand—the electronic media. Don't you see? This is your big chance. Julia's story has all the modern-day ingredients. An innocent young farm girl comes to the wicked city to seek her fortune and find a husband. She falls in with fast company, winds up dead, and famous men conspire to cover up the truth."

J.J. turned to Johnny. "Is this why you asked me here tonight? You want me to double-cross my own mother? What kind of creep are you? I—I thought I loved you, Johnny. I'm young and stupid, aren't I? Just like Julia Sands. Well, both of you can go straight to hell!"

In her blind panic to leave, J.J. failed to notice the exchange of glances between Johnny and Prunella before he followed her out into the street.

The predicted snow flurries had become a raging blizzard. A fierce wind flailed at J.J.'s down coat, buffeting her from side to side. The air-filled fabric billowed around her, threatening to lift her off her feet and carry her high into a night that seemed made of wet confetti. The driving snow filled her nostrils and clogged her lashes.

She had lost all sense of direction. She felt trapped in a Victorian paperweight. Her first thought on leaving the Spring Café had been to find a cab and get home as fast as possible. She could barely see her hand in front of her face as she tried to shield her eyes so that she could open them.

She could hear distant sounds of automobiles but could see nothing. Christmas lights gleamed dimly through glazed shop windows. Any thought of finding shelter in a bar or restaurant was doomed. The shops were closed. Not a sign of a bistro or even an all-night deli.

Was it her imagination or was someone calling her name?

"J.J.! Wait up! Please. I'm sorry."

Johnny! She turned away from the sound of his voice and began to run as fast as she could in the swirling drifts. A pothole tripped her and sent her flying against a mailbox.

"J.J.! Thank God I found you. Are you okay? Anything broken?"

Just her heart. "I think you've got some explaining to do."

That was exactly why he had asked her to see him perform and why Prunella had been there and why he had run after her. To tell her everything. The snow had abated somewhat. He took her arm. They began to walk while he explained all that had happened since the day they had gone to Prospect Park in search of Julia Sands's grave and he had written the first draft of his Julia Sands ballad on the subway ride home to Greenwich Village.

J.J. did not need to be reminded of Prunella Dove's presence in Nina's parlor and Nina's annoyance when J.J. insisted he sing his new ballad. Prunella had spat nails when Nina decided not to appear with J.J. on the *Dove Report*. Nobody rejected Prunella Dove.

She had tracked Johnny down. After all, she

was a top television producer, wasn't she? How could he be rude to her? Before he knew it he was telling her about Nina's refusal to let J.J. pursue the Manhattan Well murder case. "So from Prunella's point of view, the Julia Sands story is public domain and up for grabs. Like she said, it could happen today. It does happen today. And that's why she had me finish the ballad and why she wants you to tell the story in a one-hour TV documentary. Can't you see? You'll be your own person. And we? We'll be working together. Won't that be great?"

A few cars moved slowly past them. No cabs. Johnny seemed to know where he was taking them. "Does this look familiar?"

She recognized the wire gate leading to the narrow alley where the Manhattan Well lay beneath a cellar door. The rusted padlock broke off in his hand. He opened the gate. "Those stories about the ghost of Julia Sands being seen in this area. The bartender said she appears every year on the anniversary of her murder—"

In a barely audible voice J.J. said, "That's tonight. December twenty-second."

"Several people have said she wears a billowing cloak with a deep hood that hides her face, and she moans piteously, repeating over and over, 'Justice! Jus-tice!' "

The outline of the cellar door could be seen in the snow. Johnny fell to his knees and brushed it clean. He pulled with all his strength on the metal knob until with a squeal like chalk on a blackboard the door opened and the smell of dank water assailed them.

Could this be where the murder most foul happened? Contemporary sketches of the Manhattan Well had shown it enclosed by a thick stone wall several feet high. Logically, of course, the wall had been knocked down years before when New York City moved northward and the damp marshes of the Lispenard Meadows became commercial streets lined with factories, livery stables, and mercantile ventures of every kind.

The well might have been a danger to citizens and animals and was doubtless covered over to prevent accidents.

Johnny explained he had done some research on his own. In a 1921 article in the old *New York Sun*, a man living in Spring Street had reported seeing the ghost of Julia Sands on the night of December 22. "Right here, J.J. At the well. She was wearing a cloak with a hood so he couldn't see her face and she was moaning, 'Justice! Justice!' "

From somewhere in the thickly falling snow, a woman's voice sobbed, "Jus-tice. Jus-tice!"

J.J. clung to her companion's arm. "Did you hear that?"

"Hear what?"

"A woman's voice. Crying for justice!"

He laughed indulgently. "You're too suggestible. I shouldn't have told you about the ghost."

"But I distinctly heard a woman's voice."

"Probably somebody trying to get a cab. Which is exactly what I'm going to do. You stay here. Out of the wind. I'll be right back."

Before she could stop him, he was gone and she was alone.

"Julia, are you there? Gulielma! Elma! Elmore! Whichever name you like—are you there?"

"Gulielma. But I know you call me Julia." At the open gate leading to the alley stood a shadowy figure wrapped in a voluminous hooded cape.

Was she seeing things? Seeing what she wanted to see? Could there really be ghosts? That day in Prospect Park with Johnny she'd only been half kidding when she called out to Julia. Or had she been half serious?

In a choked voice J.J. said, "Jul-ia?"

"It's nearly two hundred years since the murder, and you are the only one ever to ask who did it and why."

J.J. held her breath. "Who did it, Julia? And why?"

"Levi did it. Levi and his brother Ezra. But why? I don't know why!"

"Were Hamilton and Burr involved in the cover-up?"

"A cover-up? What is a cover-up?"

"A conspiracy to get Levi acquitted."

"His brother made him do it. Right here in the Lispenard Meadow on December 22, 1799. Please—please find out why."

"I'll try."

"Promise?"

"Promise!"

As if to clinch the deal, J.J. pulled off her glove and extended her hand in a gesture of friendship. The cloaked figure stepped forward, hesitated, and then rapidly backed away, disappearing in a curtain of white. "Julia . . ."

Another figure burst through the open gate. "J.J.? What's wrong?"

"Didn't you see her?"

"See who?"

"Julia! Julia's ghost! She was here!"

He gathered her to him and pressed his lips to her forehead. "You're burning with fever. I've got a cab waiting at the corner. Hurry before somebody steals it."

"But I saw her. It was Julia."

"Tell me about it in the cab. I'd better get you home and into some dry clothes before you get pneumonia."

Except for the carriage lamps at the front door, the house was dark. She had not uttered a sound in the cab. Trembling from both the cold and her experience at the well, she had collapsed against him like a rag doll and squeezed his hand convulsively.

"It's all right," he said, stroking her face as he had the first time he'd brought her to his hotel room.

With a deep sigh she guided his hand through the opening of her coat and pressed it against her breast, which swelled to his touch despite the layers of wool and cotton shirts. After the cab pulled away, she took his hand again as if he might disappear and led him to the side of the house and in through the kitchen door.

Michael had left a note for her on the kitchen table. *If you haven't had dinner, cold chicken in the fridge. See you in the morning. Important news! M.*

"We'll take it to my room," J.J. said, again leading the way, giving him no choice but to follow. The stairs creaked. They stopped, still as statues. Not a sound. At last they reached the top of the house, originally servants' quarters and now J.J.'s private domain that had changed as she had changed from toddler to grown woman. The walls were covered with what she called her magpie memorabilia. She never threw anything away. Photographs. Souvenirs. Certificates ranging from Good Posture to Young American Historians. Drawings. Collages. Valentines. Hats. Beads. Scarves. A map of New York City dating back to the Dutch when it was New Amsterdam.

"And a fireplace, too! One of the things I miss most in London. Okay if I light it?"

Romantic situations were new to J.J. In movies women said things to provoke men, sarcastic but not really sarcastic, keeping them off balance. "As long as you know what you're doing," was what she said when what she really wanted to say was more like "You can light my fire anytime."

With a platter of cold chicken and a bottle of chablis on the hearth rug between them, J.J. turned her attention to a rack of CDs. "Rock? Or Bach?"

"Bach if you please. Segovia if you have it."

"As a matter of fact, I do have it." Nina had taken her to Segovia's final New York concert in 1986, and she had been hooked on classical guitar ever since.

The food, the wine, the music. The crackling fire the sole illumination. The windows glazed with ice. Distant warning sounds of fog horns on the Hudson River. All the ingredients of a sexy movie but with one major problem. John Jacob Black held her in his arms like the brother she'd never had, his hands discreetly avoiding her breasts or any other intimacy.

Her mind was in direct conflict with her body, a desperate struggle between her need to tell him about the apparition she may or may not have seen and her need to feel his kisses and his hands and his naked flesh in hers. Which was more important, her need as a historian to solve the riddle of Julia's murder or her need for this man's love by firelight and Bach? Had Nina faced this dilemma at J.J.'s age? Had her career come first? Her mother had once remarked that her elopement with Russell Drake was the only time she had let her heart rule her head.

"Kiss me, Johnny."

He extricated himself and scrambled to his feet. "I thought you wanted to talk about Julia's ghost."

Why was he rejecting her? Did he have somebody else? Prunella Dove, for instance? Was that why she wanted to produce that documentary? How could Johnny think J.J. would do anything behind Nina's back? Okay. If he wanted to talk about Julia's ghost, they'd talk about Julia's ghost. "I saw her, Johnny. At the well. Wearing a cape and a hood. She said in nearly two hundred years since the murder I'm the only one—the only one, she said—who ever asked what happened. And why."

"Did she tell you?"

"She said Levi and Ezra killed her but she didn't know why, and when I asked her if Hamilton and Burr were involved, she said she didn't know. And then before I could ask anything else, she disappeared. In the snow. Do you think I really saw her ghost?"

"What do you think?"

"I think . . . I want you to kiss me!"

This time he did not back away. This time he did as he was told, kissing her sweetly at first and then harder and rougher, crushing her lips and then once again backing away. "I'm too old for you. And that is that."

I'm in heat, she thought. Hot, crazy heat. Bach might be in the background; her thoughts were rock 'n' roll. Set me free. Fill me up. Make me shriek. Who did he think he was, turning her on and then turning her off? As he bent to put on his shoes, she knocked him flat on his back and fell hard on top of him, pinning his arms to the floor.

"Give up?" She was more surprised than he at her aggressiveness. The sex articles in magazines always said women had the right to ask for what they wanted.

As it turned out, she didn't have to ask. Her challenge stirred his erotic core.

" 'Give up?' Did you say, 'Give up!'! Before I finish with you, miss, you'll be the one to give up!"

He pulled off her turtleneck sweater. "Give up?"

She countered by tearing off his flannel shirt, ripping the buttons in her haste. "You give up."

He lunged at her jeans, grappling for the zipper while she unbuckled his belt, threw it over his shoulder, and scraped her knuckles on the open teeth of his zipper.

They fell shrieking to the floor, wrestling with all their strength to see whose jeans would be the first to go. Johnny swung hers around his head like a lasso. "Give up!" His were around his ankles. She butted him in the midriff, again knocking him flat, and swung his jeans around her own head in triumph. "Me give up? Never."

Well matched in cunning and in lust, they stripped each other garment by garment, underwear, socks, until she was brazenly bare as a toddler on the beach and the last bit of covering on his body was the calico kerchief around his neck. He did not resist when she untied the knot and tied it around his eyes as a blindfold. "Now do you give up, Johnny?"

He stretched himself luxuriously on the tattered old quilt she'd had since childhood. Because his eyes were covered, she felt a voyeuristic thrill in candidly exploring his nakedness. She had seen few men naked and none as old as John Jacob Black. His arms and legs were muscular, his belly flat but not hard as a young man's. The dark hair on his chest and at his groin was mixed with gray.

The canola oil for their neglected salad captured her attention. Starting with the soles of his feet, she oiled his body as if it were a fine piece of bronze sculpture, slowly working her way up the muscled contours of his legs and thighs to his manhood, the part of a man she had on previous encounters on dates touched and felt but only glimpsed.

Now she examined it with an anthropologist's curiosity, watching it react to her ministrations, both fascinated and aroused to a wonderment she had never known. Raising her head to look at his face, she found he had pushed back the blindfold and was watching her with a tenderness that moved her to tears.

"Johnny!"

"Give up?" He had her in his arms, the oiliness of his skin sealing them together.

"Only if you give up."

He murmured into her hair. "I give up."

When at last sleep overtook them, they lay exhausted and entwined like the magician's link puzzle that can't be pulled apart. The music continued like an invisible blanket that covered their nakedness with a sound barrier against the outside world.

They did not hear the knock on J.J.'s door or Nina's voice calling through it. "You still up, darling? I can hear the music! I've got something wonderful to tell you. Okay if I come in?"

Chapter Eleven

Always a respecter of her daughter's privacy, Nina knocked on the door again. Ordinarily that would be that. A closed door was a closed door. But not tonight. Tonight she was bursting with news. Assuming J.J. had fallen asleep, Nina decided she would break the rule just this one time. "Wake up, darling! I've got something wonderful to tell you."

Shock.

Followed by panic.

Followed by blind fury.

J.J.! My God! At first glance in the dim light there appeared to be only one naked body sprawled lifeless before the fireplace. Had she committed suicide? She'd looked a little depressed tonight when she left the house. Holiday blues, maybe. Nina being too tough on her, maybe.

Panic froze her in the doorway. More and more young women were committing suicide. Young women like J.J. with nice homes and loving families and good educations and everything to live for. She tiptoed closer to the fireplace, whispering as if fearful of disturbing the dead. *Please, God, no!* "J.J. Darling? Are you asleep? Let me cover you."

It was then she saw that her daughter was not alone and blind fury took over. Like the mother whose child swings too high and falls on its head, her fears disappeared in a raging desire to kill.

Forgotten was her rule about respecting privacy. Forgotten, too, were her many discussions with Michael about J.J.'s love life and how she worried about her seeming lack of interest in anyone. What about that Johnny Black? Michael had asked. J.J. seemed to like him. Johnny Black was much too old, Nina had scoffed. She should have a boyfriend her own age like whoever this was with her.

Her daughter was not dead. Common sense told her to turn around and tiptoe out before she was discovered.

"Mom?" Too late. J.J. sat up.

Nina retreated. "Forgive me, darling. I—I didn't mean to intrude. Your private life is your own business. See you in the morning."

She had backed her way to the door when J.J.'s companion stirred and raised himself up on one elbow. His eyes shut as if reluctant to awaken, he kissed J.J.'s shoulder. Nina lingered for a moment—what a sweet romantic young man, she thought, content that her daughter had found someone to love—when some embers burst into flame and she saw who he was.

"Johnny? My God! Out! Get out of here before I call the police."

Like Adam and Eve in the Garden of Eden, the lovers scrambled to cover themselves with the quilt.

"Well, I'm waiting. I told you to leave!"

"It's none of your damn business, Mom. I happen to be in love with him."

"Sure, and I suppose he's in love with you."

Both women turned their attention to the figure crouched under the quilt. He sat up and reached for his plaid shirt.

"As a matter of fact, I am in love with her. All of my life I've been looking for a woman who would make me honest and keep me honest and where did I find her? At the New York Public Library! I love her and if she'll have me I want to marry her and make a life together. But first I've got to get something off my chest."

Nina was fighting a losing battle but could not stop. "See, J.J.? He's probably married and has six kids. No money. No career. What are you going to do, sing on the street corners while J.J. passes the hat?"

J.J. interrupted. "That shows how much you know. You should have seen him tonight at the Spring Café. It was an audition. He sang just one song. The crowd went wild."

"And what song was that? 'The Ghost of Julia Sands,' I suppose. Can't you see he's just using you, J.J.?"

"It was a ghost ballad, but it wasn't about Julia. It was an old English ballad about a girl named Pretty Polly. She was just like Julia. She trusted her lover and he killed her! The oldest story there is. The innocent young maiden and the false-hearted lover. And then the most amazing thing happened."

"Please don't, J.J.!" Johnny pleaded. He had to talk to her. Alone!

Despite her anger Nina had to concede that J.J. fairly glowed with the proprietary tenderness of new love as she pressed a finger to Johnny's lips. "First I want to tell Nina about the ghost. I saw Julia Sands's ghost, Mom. During the snowstorm. Around the corner from Spring Street. On Greene Street. The old Manhattan Well is still there. Under some metal doors. I know it sounds crazy, but it was exactly the way it was in that old clipping. From the *New York Sun*? This man who lived in Spring Street who kept seeing the murdered Quaker girl's ghost wearing a cape and a hood and moaning and crying for justice?

"Well I swear to you, Mom. There she was. Tonight was the anniversary of the murder. December twenty-second. And she said Levi and his brother killed her but she didn't know why. She begged me to find out the truth about Hamilton and Burr and whether they were involved. And then she disappeared in the blizzard."

Nina sighed with muted exasperation. "And I suppose Johnny here saw the whole thing?"

J.J. defended him. "He was getting a cab. But I saw her, I tell you. Are you calling me a liar?"

"I'm calling you an idiot. You're obsessed with this ridiculous murder. It's driving me crazy. Maybe working on this book is too much for you. Maybe I was wrong to get you involved with no experience. Maybe I'd better get someone else to help me finish the book."

"Fine! Go ahead and fire me. I don't need you. I've had another offer." J.J.'s voice trembled. It was the first time she had ever openly defied her mother.

"What?"

She took a deep breath. "If you must know, Prunella Dove wants me to do a TV special on the girl in the well with Johnny's ballad as the theme music and me as the writer. I told her to shove it, but now I just may do it! Right, Johnny? In fact, I can leave right now. With Johnny!"

As if to shut out the nightmare that had begun when she burst into J.J.'s room unannounced, Nina covered her ears. "I don't want to hear another word. I must be going crazy. If I have a miscarriage, it's all your fault!"

Dressed now, John Jacob Black stepped between them. "There's something I've got to get off my chest. I was going to wait to tell it to J.J. when we were alone, but now I think you both better hear it and then let J.J. decide if she still wants me."

All that had happened last night was a hoax. Prunella Dove had not taken Nina Slocum's rejection lightly. Johnny's ballad about Julia's ghost had given her the idea for the special. What better way to stick it to Nina than to hire her daughter to write the script and promote her as one of the new generation of young historians?

And the scene at the bar when she talked about Julia's ghost and tried to convince J.J. that her mother was jealous of her and wanted to hold her back and how J.J. went racing out of there and Johnny followed her? All a setup. All a part of the plan.

The snowstorm had proved to be an unexpected bonus when he left her in the alley, ostensibly to find a cab. The ghost of Julia Sands was Prunella Dove! Johnny thought he could go along with it. He was desperate to work in America. Prunella promised him the world. His name above the title. A record deal. All kinds of doors open to him. But now he realized he couldn't go through with it.

After a long silence J.J. asked, "Was making love to me a setup, too?"

"I'll spend the next hundred years proving to you it wasn't. I promise."

"And what are you going to tell Prunella Dove?" Nina asked.

"The truth. In fact, I'm going to call her right now."

"At this hour?"

He allowed himself a wry grin. "I promised to let her know what happened. She's probably waiting at the phone."

Prunella Dove's unmistakable voice picked up at the first ring. Mother and daughter pressed close to hear both sides of the conversation.

He made an uncomprehending face. "Forgive you?"

"I did what we said. I put on the cape and waited ten minutes like we said and then I—I'm not sure what happened. It must have been my boots. I slipped and fell in the snow. My limo driver saw me and took me to St. Vincent's. It's my ankle. It's broken. I'm in a cast. I'm sorry, Johnny. I never got there. I never made it to the well."

Chapter Twelve

J.J. lashed out at John Jacob Black. "First you tell me you and Prunella set me up! That the ghost of Julia Sands was really Prunella. Then Prunella says no, she slipped on the ice and never made it to Greene Street and that I couldn't have seen anything even though I know what I saw. What the hell am I supposed to believe?"

She was wrapped in her cherished colonial quilt, and her nakedness reminded her of their lovemaking and added to her desperate sense of loss and vulnerability. Her eyes cast down, the quilt half covering her head, she rocked back and forth like an American Indian squaw in a frontier painting.

Johnny answered haltingly. "You're supposed to believe that last night changed my life. I was a failure. I was for sale. Prunella bought me. She was going to make me a star, make up for all the years of rejection and at the same time she was going to get even with Nina."

"What kind of a whore are you?" Nina demanded.

"Believe it or not, I was a flop at that, too. I couldn't go through with it, and when J.J. brought me here and put her sweet arms around me, I knew that I had a chance for happiness."

"So why didn't you tell her the truth before you took advantage of her?"

His poise deserted him. In a choked voice he tried to explain. "We were so happy. I kept waiting for the right moment and then we fell asleep. And then—"

"And then I barged in." A hint of apology softened Nina's voice.

Johnny allowed himself a smile. "You sure know how to barge in."

J.J. staggered awkwardly to her feet, clutching the colonial quilt around her. "Stop changing the subject. I've told you I saw the ghost of Julia Sands at the old Manhattan Well on the anniversary of her murder. You say Prunella Dove was supposed to be there masquerading as Julia's ghost, but she slipped in the snow and I couldn't have seen anything because there wasn't anything to see! Are you saying I made the whole thing up?"

"It's way after midnight, J.J. Time for sleep. Put something on and go to bed. We'll talk about it in the morning."

J.J. disappeared into her bathroom.

"Am I allowed to stay?" Johnny asked.

"The guest room's on the first floor. You're welcome here, but remember, the stairs creak."

J.J. emerged from her bathroom dressed for the weather. "No sleep for me till I see Prunella face to face."

"It's after midnight!" Nina repeated.

"It's only nine o'clock on the West Coast!" J.J. countered.

Despite herself, Nina laughed. "What do you have in mind, a snowball fight at dawn?"

J.J. ignored her mother's limp attempt at levity. "You know where she lives, Johnny, don't you?"

He nodded sheepishly. "Two East Seventy-Third Street."

"That's where I'm going right now. She says her ankle is swollen like a basketball. If it isn't, I'll know she did show up on Greene Street."

"And if it is swollen?"

"Then I'll know I did see Julia's ghost."

"You're not going without me," Johnny said.

"Or me," Nina added.

The snow had stopped. Manhattan's sins lay covered in coconut icing, an old-fashioned Christmas card illustration, silent and pristine until the morning rush. The lateness of the hour had not deterred the jubilant snow people who came dancing out of their caves with skis, sleds, and toboggans to declare dominion over the quiet, empty streets.

"Nina, you're crazy!"

While Johnny went to find a taxi, Nina lay down in the middle of the street wrapped in an old full-length mink she hadn't worn since an animal activist threw paint at her.

"I'm making angels in the snow." With her arms gaily outstretched she pressed them into the snow in a semicircle from above her head to her thighs.

"Moth-errr!" J.J. pulled Nina to her feet.

"Oh, so you want to play!" The older woman scooped up a pillow of snow and pushed it into her daughter's face.

With the snow fight in full shriek, Johnny pulled up in a cab and was pummeled by both combatants.

"What's got into you?"

"It's Mom. She's gone ballistic."

"It's battle fever. I can feel it in my bones. I'm going to tear that woman apart. I'm going to give her a face lift without surgery! I'm going to feed her to the squirrels in Central Park! Anyone who does dirty to my little girl has to answer to me!"

Once settled into the cab between J.J. and Johnny, Nina patted his hand companionably, adding in the sweetest possible voice, "And that means you, too."

The doorman at Nina's apartment house was helping two of his young tenants build a snowman. His instant grin of greeting was not lost on Nina and J.J.

"Good evening, Mr. Black. Should I buzz Miss Dove?"

"It's okay, Fred. It's a surprise. I've got the key."

Once in the elevator, Nina observed, "How convenient that Johnny's got the key. Now we won't have to go through the terrible strain of ringing the doorbell."

The door to Prunella's apartment opened quietly. Except for the pale streak of light from the outside corridor, the interior was dark and heavy with musk. A sudden sliver of light revealed a partly open door at the end of a long hallway.

A slurred voice called out. "Johnny, darling? Is that you? I knew you'd come! I knew you couldn't stay away from me. We belong together, darling. That little bitch can't do for you what I can do for you. Hurry, angel. Momma's waiting."

Johnny moved cautiously toward Prunella's bedroom door, signaling the two women to stay back. Confronting Prunella Dove was something he had to do alone.

The voice emanating from the bedroom rose in volume, tinged with the sound of breaking glass. "If you don't get in here this minute and kiss me, I'm going to cut my wrists! There! I warned you I'd do it. There! There!"

Johnny bounded through the door, the two women at his heels. Prunella Dove lay back against a mountain of pillows on her king-size bed, holding a bottle of wine in one hand and the broken glass in the other. With a practiced gesture she gulped the remaining wine and tossed the bottle aside. She flourished the jagged shard and pressed it to her wrist. Her bravado collapsed in a paroxysm of piteous sobs. It was obvious she had been drinking for hours, her always perfectly groomed hair hanging in sweaty clumps, her always perfectly applied makeup a muddy smudge.

It was obvious, too, that in the dim light of her pink-shaded bedside lamp, she was too groggy to see Nina and J.J. until they stepped from behind Johnny.

Nina got straight to the point. "Show us your ankle!"

Prunella's eyes bulged with terror. She dragged the broken glass across her wrist, exerting just enough pressure to draw a line of red. "I'll kill myself!"

"Go ahead. That's one way to make the six o'clock news."

Prunella stacked her pillows around herself like a fortress against attack. "Haven't you done enough? I lost my show because of you. My only hope was that stupid daughter of yours."

"Because of me? What did I do?"

"You canceled out on the mother-daughter series, and you got the others to cancel out, too! Don't think I didn't know that."

"Now wait just one minute. I don't even know

Vanessa Redgrave or Natasha Richardson or any of the others."

"They were looking for an excuse to get rid of me, and this was just what they were waiting for. I was losing my clout, they said. The Redgraves wouldn't turn down Barbara Walters, would they? Or Diane Sawyer. But they turned me down. Once you lose your clout, you're finished. They throw you out with the garbage."

She pointed the piece of glass at J.J. "That idiot daughter of yours was my last hope. Controversy. Sex. Crime. Ghosts. American history. I got the idea the day Johnny sang us his song about the ghost of Julia Sands. I thought it would make a great prime-time special. I was going to have J.J. swear she'd met the ghost of Julia Sands on the anniversary of her murder and then make a fool of her—and you, Nina—by exposing the hoax."

Nina was genuinely baffled. "Why would you want to do that?"

"Headlines. *Entertainment Tonight*. The talk shows. Exposing you, the famous historian. And Johnny"—she made a futile attempt at sending him a kiss—"I'm mad about him, Nina. I thought if I could help his career—well, it was all working out. And he was part of it, weren't you, lover? You agreed to the whole thing, didn't you?"

Nina was interested in one thing.

"Did you or did you not show up on Greene

Street wearing a cape and pretending to be the ghost of Julia Sands?"

Prunella turned coy. "No comment."

Nina sprang at her, tossing aside the broken glass. "Goddammit. Let me see your broken ankle!"

Three against one, the pillows and blankets flew in all directions until only a sheet covered Prunella's huddled figure. Enjoying her final moment of triumph, she kicked away the sheet. "Go to hell, all of you!"

Her left foot and ankle were encased in a cast.

J.J. gasped. "Then she was telling the truth. She did fall in the snow. It really was the ghost of Julia Sands."

"In a pig's ear!" Nina snapped. She took hold of the cast and began to twist Prunella's leg. "Where's the cape? Tell me or I'll break your other ankle!"

"Over there! In the corner."

Lying in a heap was a voluminous cape.

"Put it on!" Nina commanded.

"I—I can't stand up."

"I'm warning you!"

Prunella complied.

"Stand over there in the shadows so J.J. can't see your face."

The three visitors fell silent at the sight of the hooded figure. Nina quietly asked her daughter if this was the ghost of Julia Sands she had seen the night before on Greene Street.

J.J. burst into tears. "Why did you lie about being there?"

"I wanted to make a fool of you. I could see Johnny was crazy about you. I was jealous. Haven't you ever been jealous?"

Johnny had been quiet. Now he asked, "Is the broken ankle a fake, too?"

"It happened afterward. On my way back to the Spring Café, where the limo was waiting. They did patch me up at St. Vincent's."

"Now what?" Johnny wanted to know.

Nina surveyed the battleground like a victorious but disappointed general faced with deciding what to do with the vanquished and helpless enemy. "I guess you'd better put her to bed. I'm going home."

J.J. linked her arm through Johnny's. "I'll help clean up the mess, and then we can go back to your place."

"I'm afraid not, J.J. You're going home with your mother. I've got some things to take care of here."

J.J. held fast. "But you love *me*. You said so."

Nina put her arm around her daughter. "Come on, darling. We're all totally exhausted."

J.J. allowed herself to be led away. At the bedroom door she turned toward him with the heartsick plea of all rejected lovers. "When will I see you, Johnny?"

"I don't know. I'll have to call you."

"Bastard!" Nina repeated at intervals on the journey home. "Dirty, dirty bastard. You're lucky to be rid of him."

"No, I'm not!" Tears poured down J.J.'s face.

Nina wiped them away with her glove. "One good night does not a lifetime make."

"How could he, you know, be with me and then go back to her?"

"It's a question women have been asking since time began. Like I always say, 'What happened and how come?' You can search for clues, but when it comes to men, there's no guarantee you'll find the answer. Assuming there is one, which I sometimes doubt."

J.J. rolled down the taxi window to let the cold air strike her face. "I feel sick to my stomach. I don't think I'll be able to work tomorrow. Or ever again. Maybe I should go back to school or something. You can get someone else to finish the research. I may just stay in bed and sleep for the next five years."

"You mean that?"

"Every word."

"That's really too bad, because I have a brilliant idea that will make you almost as famous as I am."

"What?"

"You say you're too emotionally exhausted to work."

"Tell me! Or I'll teach the new baby a four-letter word!"

"Promise?"

"*Tell* me!"

"I'd like you to write your own separate chapter on the girl in the Manhattan Well. We'll call it 'A Young Historian's Theory about New York's Oldest Unsolved Murder.' "

Nina wanted J.J. to describe how she had first become intrigued by Julia Sands and how Nina had fought her tooth and nail, dismissing her questions as trivial and how J.J. had persisted in defying her mother and mentor in her pursuit of truth.

"I can't do that!"

"It's perfect! Can't you see? It's a totally new take on mother-daughter hostility. We can thank Prunella Dove for that. And this isn't about 'Go clean up your room.' This is about a young woman's professional rite of passage. How she asserts her values as a woman and her integrity as a historian.

"Think of it. Every mother and daughter in the country will want this book. But like you said, you're too broken up about Johnny Black. You'll probably need a year at least to get over him."

J.J. took her mother's hand while continuing to look out the window. "Can I say exactly what I want about Julia and Aaron and Alex?"

"You can say whatever you like! It's your chapter."

J.J. suddenly remembered why Nina had burst in on her and Johnny. "Was that the big news you wanted to tell me?"

"I talked it over with Michael. He said it was okay with him if it was okay with me."

"Well, it's sure okay with me!"

"And, oh, I nearly forgot. There was something else. The guy from the Weehawken Society called. Everything's set. He's dying to meet us."

The Weehawken Society was a group of history buffs who had agreed to re-create the Hamilton-Burr duel expressly for them on the twenty-seventh, two days after Christmas. Even though the actual duel had been fought in July, Nina had talked them into it despite their concern that the Jersey Palisades high above the western bank of the Hudson River would be treacherous in winter. The book couldn't wait for July.

It was no problem, Nina said. They would cross the Hudson by boat and follow Hamilton and Burr's footsteps up the side of the cliff.

"You're pregnant, Mom."

"So what? I'm a mountain goat."

"You could fall."

"Not unless somebody pushes me."

Chapter Thirteen

"Try to imagine what it was like on that hot summer morning." Hal Williams, president and founder of the Weehawken Society, welcomed Nina and J.J. to the motor launch moored as close as physically possible to the foot of Horatio Street, where Alexander Hamilton had set out for his "interview" with Aaron Burr just as dawn broke on July 11, 1804.

The snow had gone as quickly as it had come, leaving behind a post-Christmas gift of mild temperatures and a pleasant breeze. Michael had objected strenuously to the excursion. Nina was pregnant and should not be bouncing around in a motorboat. Furthermore, her excuse about her need for authentic research was like saying she would have to cross the Alps on an elephant if she decided to write about Hannibal. Bowing to her determination, he prepared a thermos of strong coffee laced with brandy for the two women to take with them, and J.J.

promised to call him the minute they returned to Manhattan.

Once clear of the Manhattan shoreline, the little boat headed north and west toward the Jersey Palisades. Williams prided himself on the wealth of historical material he and the society had amassed in their archives. These included copies of both Hamilton's and Burr's original correspondence that led to the duel and firsthand accounts of those who witnessed the duel and its aftermath.

He had given this tour before but never to as distinguished a guest as Nina Slocum. "Of course, there were no powerboats or steamships in those days. Just sailboats and men with oars. Ignore the great ships you see. Edit from your mind's eye the buildings and cars on the Jersey heights and the George Washington Bridge to your right. Envision the Palisades as a wall of primitive greenery, for that's how Alexander Hamilton and Aaron Burr saw it that fateful morning."

Mother and daughter knew most of what had happened that fateful day but nonetheless smiled in encouragement to their host, who was obviously enjoying himself. As he explained with relish, the etiquette of the day required the two principals to arrive at the appointed place separately, each with his second. A fifth person would be a doctor who would not witness the actual duel but would wait within call several yards away. By this convention he could never be called to bear witness in law to something he could honestly swear he had not seen. Yet he could be summoned instantly if his medical services were needed.

"As I was saying, Burr and Hamilton made their way to Weehawken separately. The route we're taking is Hamilton's. The boat was small. His close friend, Nathaniel Pendleton, was his reluctant second. He sat close beside Hamilton with the scarred leather case that held the Wogden dueling pistols that had been borrowed for the occasion. The pistols belonged to Hamilton's brother-in-law John Church. And ironically, Church had also used the pistols in an earlier duel with Aaron Burr."

"And the doctor, the famous Dr. David Hosack? Did he cross the Hudson with Hamilton or Burr? Or in a third boat?" J.J. wanted to know.

Hosack was not only a brilliant young physician of the times but was a close friend of both opponents. As history would show, he had saved the lives of the entire Hamilton family during a cholera epidemic and was the attending physician at Hamilton's deathbed as well as on Burr's demise some thirty-two years later. Students of botany knew of his research in the medicinal use of herbs, and students of New York City urban development could discover that Dr. Hosack's botanical gardens had covered the land now occupied by the New York Public Library and Bryant Park.

J.J. could not help herself. She felt compelled to whisper in her mother's ear, "He was also the city coroner who testified that Julia Sands was not—*not* pregnant! Get it, Mom? Hamilton's friend? Burr's friend? Part of the cover-up!"

Her mother's pursed lips reminded her that Nina had made one condition to her writing her own chapter on the Manhattan Well murder and that was Nina did not want to hear another word about it until it was finished.

Their guide was answering J.J.'s question. "Hosack rode with Hamilton. He and Pendleton both had a dark premonition of the outcome. Hosack's medical bag contained bandages, laudanum, spirits of hartshorn, some sharp surgical instruments for digging out bullets, and a strong herbal anodyne of his own invention. But he knew his limitations. If either man was shot in his vital organs, there was not much an eighteenth-century doctor could do except to try to lessen the pain."

The high spirits with which mother and daughter had begun the journey turned somber. Williams continued, "Pendleton and Hosack tried once more as the Palisades loomed above them to get Hamilton to change his mind. 'I have made my decision,' Hamilton said. 'I will hold my fire. I will give Colonel Burr the first shot.' "

The point was this. Because duels were illegal and the idea of killing or being killed had lost much of its glamour, many men seeking satisfaction would meet on the dueling ground and fire wide. In this way honor would be served and they could bury their differences over a hearty breakfast at a popular coffee house.

For the idea to work, both men had to agree, albeit secretly. Burr knew nothing of Hamilton's plan. Pendleton pleaded with Hamilton for permission to tell him. Hamilton forbade it. "I'll never understand why!" Williams said dolefully.

"I understand why!" J.J. murmured under her breath but just loud enough for Nina to hear and ignore.

Williams tied up the boat. "It may be winter, but one thing's the same. It's seven o'clock, exactly when Hamilton, Pendleton, and Hosack landed. There were two landing places then. Separated by thick vegetation so that the duelists could not see each other arrive and depart. The dueling ground was up there, about twenty feet above us. Just a grassy ledge about twelve yards long and two yards wide."

Nina looked upward in dismay. "How do we get up there?"

He reassured her. "By road."

"How did they get up?" J.J. asked.

The dramatic edge returned to their guide's voice. "When they stepped ashore, they could see the stern of another boat a short distance away. Burr and his second, William Van Ness, had arrived first. As prescribed by the code, Dr. Hosack silently shook hands with Hamilton and positioned himself so that he could hear the shots and any calls for medical help. As he watched the rising sun burn away the remains of the morning haze, he prayed his services would not be needed by either gentleman that day.

"Nat Pendleton preceded Hamilton up the rocky facade, carrying the pistol case on one shoulder. When he reached the grassy promontory, he found Burr and Van Ness clearing away branches. 'So as to make a fair opening, sir,' Colonel Burr explained.

From Williams's description, Hamilton and Burr acted as if they'd run into each other by chance at some social event. "They acknowledged each other with formal bows before retiring to the sidelines to await instructions. Acting in concert, Pendleton and Van Ness measured off the required ten paces and loaded the two Wogden pistols with elaborate concern for each other's mutual approval. When each was satisfied, the pistols were given to their respective principals.

Lots were cast for position and for the honor of calling. Pendleton won.

" 'Gentlemen, are you prepared?' "

"As each nodded, he continued, 'Gentlemen, take your places!' "

Williams led them to the promontory and the bust of Hamilton that peered down at the river.

"Is this where it really happened?" J.J. asked in a hushed voice.

"Afraid not, ladies. The ledge is long gone."

The gentlemen obediently did take their positions, the prescribed ten paces apart, and stood facing each other, their pistols at their sides pointing down.

"Pendleton cleared his throat. 'Gentlemen,' he cried, loud and clear. 'Pre-sent!' They raised their weapons. 'Fire!' "

Nina cringed as if she could feel the shots.

"Mom. You all right?"

Nina hushed her daughter. Williams was working himself up to the dramatic finale. "The gentleman from St. Croix raised his arm and fired high and wide into the air. He watched Colonel Burr slowly and deliberately take aim. He heard the report and saw the trajectory of the bullet roar toward him and crash into his right side.

"He sighed and pitched face forward on the grass in a pool of his own blood. He could hear Nat Pendleton's frantic shouts for Dr. Hosack. What he could neither see nor hear was the hasty departure of Burr and Van Ness."

"Where's that flask, J.J.? It's time for that coffee and brandy."

J.J. proposed a toast to Hal Williams.

"A pleasure, I assure you. And by the way, I hope you didn't mind about Page Six."

"Page Six? What do you mean?" Nina asked.

"Last night's *Post*. You know. The newspaper Hamilton founded?"

"Get to the point! Of course I know Hamilton founded the *New York Post*, 'America's oldest newspaper.' What about it?"

Williams was clearly disappointed. "You didn't see it? Like I said, I didn't think you'd mind. I gave them an item about your visit. You know, good publicity for the Weehawken Society. How I was re-creating the Hamilton-Burr duel for the famous historian Nina Slocum. I was sure it would be okay. And as a matter of fact, some TV reporter left a message on my machine last night. Said she was going to be here this morning to cover the story. Isn't that great?"

At that moment a familiar limousine screeched into view, followed by a New York City yellow cab with its horn honking. Prunella Dove jumped from her car waving a butcher knife.

"Nina Slocum!"

Nina turned at the sound of her name.

"Here's your Christmas gift, bitch!"

In the mini-second it took Prunella to hurl herself at her prey, John Jacob Black all but tore the door off the yellow cab in a flying leap at the shrieking assailant.

Chapter Fourteen

The demented act of a dying woman was the only way Johnny could explain what had happened. As he and Michael waited in the obstetrician's office for word on Nina's condition, Johnny repeated for the umpteenth time that he had arrived at Prunella's just as she was leaving the building. "Out of my way" was all she'd said, pushing past him and getting into her limo. As it pulled away from the curb, she tossed a crumpled piece of newspaper into the street. "Thinks she's so smart! I'll show her who's smart!"

The crushed paper was Page Six of the previous night's *New York Post* with the item about Nina and the Weehawken Society circled in lipstick. There was no doubt that's where she was heading. The first cab he stopped demanded a hundred dollars to go to New Jersey.

"Only if you don't lose that limo!"

Michael roused himself from his misery to thank Johnny for his quick thinking and physical bravery. "If it wasn't for you, we'd be at the morgue."

"I couldn't let anything happen to Nina. Or J.J. And if anything's gone wrong with that baby, it's all my fault. I knew Prunella was a little nuts. High-strung. Caught up in that kill or be killed atmosphere of television reporters. And then getting the bad news from the oncologist! All that medication must have pushed her over the edge."

It was only by accident that Johnny had learned the seriousness of Prunella's illness and the extent of her denial. The day of his guest appearance at the Spring Café, he had been in Prunella's living room waiting for her to finish dressing when the phone rang. Would he get that? she'd called out. A chirpy female voice had asked if this was the husband and without waiting for confirmation had gone on to say the lab report had come in.

"The doctor's away, but I thought you'd like to know. It's bad news, I'm afraid."

Some dingbat nurse with bad news? "Who is this?" he had demanded.

The sharpness of his voice made her realize she might be making a mistake. "I'm new here. I just thought you'd want to know."

"Of course we want to know. Is her chart there? What does it say under Prognosis?"

"Oh, my God! I don't think I'm supposed to— the doctor's going to kill me. I was just trying to be efficient." Gasp. Click. Dial tone.

Who was it? Prunella asked. "My doctor? If I listened to him, I'd have been dead a year ago. Zip me up!"

The dress was the one she'd been wearing their first night together at his hotel. It was now that he saw how loose it was, how much weight she had lost, how drawn she looked, and how she popped a handful of pills into her mouth and washed it down with vodka.

When Nina and J.J. and he had broken in on her, she seemed to have deteriorated in the few hours since the ghost fiasco. Whatever she had said and done, one look at her had convinced him he could not desert her like a dying dog. Whatever her motives of hatred and jealousy of Nina, she *had* tried to jump-start his career. His guest shot at the Spring Café had been arranged by her and had led to the New Year's Eve gig. Trying to involve J.J. in a television special would never have worked, but the lady had tried.

And most important, he had tried unsuccessfully to reach J.J. by phone, hoping with all his heart she would hear him out and try to understand.

Speaking of J.J., what was happening in the examining room? Why hadn't J.J. come out? He knew he should be wondering about Prunella's condition as well. After pulling her off Nina and knocking away the knife, he had shoved Prunella into the limo with instructions to the driver to lock the doors so she couldn't jump out and take her directly to her doctor's office.

Nina had remained calm and insisted she was well enough to walk to the yellow cab by herself and even managed to quip, "Who says you can't find a cab when you need one?"

What was taking so long? Had she lost the baby? Where in hell was J.J.?

"J.J.?" Both men jumped up and rushed toward the young woman, stopping short at the invisible barrier that separates the seeker of truth from the giver of news.

"Everything's fine. She's fine. The baby's fine. I'm not so fine." She sat down heavily on the nearest chair and began to sob, all the while gesturing at them to keep their distance.

Did she want some water? Coffee? Anything?

"The doctor'll be out in a minute."

"How does she feel? What did she say?" Michael asked.

J.J. looked at Johnny as if noticing his presence for the first time. "She wants to thank you for saving her life."

"Sure."

She reached out an imploring hand. "I want to thank you, too."

"That's nice of you!" he snapped.

She was perplexed. "What do you mean? Why the sarcasm?"

"I've called you a dozen times. Christmas Eve.

Christmas Day. Yesterday. Last night. Nina said you were out. You were working. You were sleeping. You were washing your hair—"

Even more perplexed, J.J. turned to Michael for an explanation.

"Nina was only trying to protect you."

"J.J.?" Nina called out from the inner sanctum. The nurse popped her head into the waiting room. "Your mom wants to know if you have a lipstick and comb."

"Be right there."

Johnny blocked her way. "Please, J.J., listen to what I have to say."

"Nina was right. You're as dangerous as Prunella. Ever since you came into our lives, there's been nothing but trouble. Haven't you done enough? Just stay away from me!"

"All I have to say is this. I meant everything I said to you that night. I mean it even more right now. I love you, J.J. You're the most precious thing that ever happened to me."

"J.J.? Where are you?"

"Be right there!"

She hurried through the door to the examining room just as the doctor was coming out. He told Michael that Nina was fine. "I wanted to give her a mild tranquillizer. No deal. Didn't want to jeopardize the baby. I said it couldn't jeopardize the baby. And you know what she said?"

Michael laughed. "I can't imagine."

"She said even if I had to amputate her leg, she wouldn't take anything that would jeopardize the baby."

"Johnny?" J.J. had returned to the waiting room with a message from Nina.

John Jacob Black had slipped quietly away.

"Where'd he go? Mom wants to see him."

The strain was beginning to show in Michael. He looked around the waiting room as if expecting to find Johnny hiding behind a piece of furniture. "He's . . . gone."

"It's all my fault. Why was I so rotten? He saves Mom's life, and I treat him like shit!"

"Michael, darling!" Nina embraced him tenderly. "You're really all right?"

"Really and truly."

A shudder coursed through his body. He held her away from him, his hands trembling as he grasped her shoulders. "Why didn't you listen to me? I warned you not to have anything to do with Prunella Dove. I told you she was dangerous. She tried to *kill* you! I—I—I want to shake you till your teeth fall out and your bones rattle, but—but . . ."

His hold on her loosened. His arms fell to his sides. She gathered him to her. "I know, darling. I know. You'd like to beat me to a pulp, but you don't want to jeopardize the baby."

They stood in silent embrace as J.J. and the doctor pretended not to notice.

"What's new in contraception, Doc?" J.J. asked casually.

"Why not come and see me and we can talk about it."

"What's that?" Nina asked.

"None of your business, Mom."

"Listen to her, Michael. Is that how a daughter speaks to her mother? I give up. Why am I having another child?"

"Because we love each other and we'll teach her good manners. Now let's go home."

"I'm hungry."

"We'll have something at home. You need some rest."

"Doctor, do I need rest?"

"Get her out of here, Michael. She's fine. I've got to go and deliver some babies."

Nina gathered up her things and checked her appearance in the mirror. "I think we deserve to have lunch at the Plaza!"

Michael would have agreed to lunch in Katmandu.

"Okay with you, J.J.?"

"I've got work to do. See you at home."

Nina ignored her excuses. "They have that salad you like. With the pine nuts? And after lunch . . . ? What shall we do after lunch, Michael?"

She had bullied and teased his spirits to rise. "Whatever milady wishes."

"Your lady—your very pregnant bride-to-be—

wishes us to stroll lovingly from the Plaza down Fifth Avenue to Tiffany's to buy us matching wedding bands! You haven't forgotten, have you? We're getting hitched in four days."

J.J. tried without success to join in the celebratory mood. The salad she liked was on the menu, as Nina had predicted. J.J. managed one forkful. Her mouth was so dry she had to wash it down with a Diet Coke. Same thing with another childhood favorite, the pineapple sorbet. One spoonful.

At Tiffany's, Nina tried again to involve her, asking her opinion on the various wedding rings presented on the traditional blue plush trays.

"Whatever you think" was the younger woman's listless response.

Nina asked Michael for a quarter and gave it to her daughter. "What I think is you better call Johnny Black before you go up in smoke."

The desk clerk at the Mohawk Hotel informed J.J. that John Jacob Black had checked out an hour ago and left no forwarding address. He hoped J.J. would take his word for it. Some other woman had been calling him every five minutes, threatening to blow the joint up if she wasn't connected.

"I told *her* fifty times and now I'm telling *you*. He's *gone* and he didn't say where!"

Chapter Fifteen

In the euphoria of the remaining few days before the New Year's Eve wedding, only one thing marred Nina Slocum's happiness. Her daughter's pervasive melancholy. The younger woman tried valiantly to hide her sadness. She chattered inanely at breakfast. She hugged Nina and Michael at every opportunity and thanked them again and again for giving her the opportunity to write her own chapter about Julia Sands in the Burr-Hamilton book.

There was no doubt in Nina's mind that J.J. was genuinely and lovingly thrilled about the wedding and was doing her best to join in the preparations with all the energy and enthusiasm she could muster. But whenever the phone rang, she could feel her daughter's expectation that it might be Johnny Black. J.J. had told her about the phone call from Tiffany's. Nina herself called the Mohawk Hotel, pretending to be a business associate with important news. The desk clerk and the manager both insisted that John Jacob Black had left no forwarding address.

The overall theme for the wedding was simplicity, an intimate candlelight ceremony at home limited to the bride, the groom, J.J., and Judge Graham and his wife, Molly. That Nina and Michael were an established couple was an old story. They had lived together for more than fifteen years. Most people assumed they were already married. Most people had plans for New Year's Eve.

The wedding vows were a symbolic as well as legal confirmation of their commitment to each other in the new year and the years to come. In a few weeks they would send out a simple engraved card announcing the marriage of Nina Slocum and Michael Ludovic on New Year's Eve. Later in the spring after the baby was born, they would have a huge open house for friends and family to help them celebrate both happy events.

Like many successful men in New York, Michael enjoyed a wide circle of business associates, health club acquaintances, and backgammon cronies, but no relative or friend close enough to be his best man. Being an only child whose interests were books rather than sports, he had quit prep school at seventeen to take over his late father's publishing house; he had no brother or roommate to call upon.

Much the same could be said of Nina. Her relationship with her mother was based on mutually courteous estrangement. It had taken Nina many years to realize Celia could never forgive her for skipping the expensive graduation party Celia had arranged by eloping with Russell Drake. She had also disapproved of Nina's refusal to have an abortion, her decision to get a divorce, and her successful career, all without discussing a single aspect or asking a scintilla of her mother's advice.

They spoke ritually by phone and remembered ritually birthdays and holidays. She had not informed her mother about her new pregnancy or of her wedding plans. In any case, Celia and a group of other widows who played golf together at the country club were somewhere in the Caribbean on a Christmas cruise. Nina would call her with the news on her return.

Furthermore, Nina knew full well that Celia loathed coming to the city. Every time there was a power blackout or hostage situation, Celia would phone to make sure Nina and Michael were okay. In answer to Nina's ritual invitations to visit for a few days, Celia could always be counted on to say she was scared stiff and wouldn't come to New York on a bet.

Years ago she had driven in for Nina's first book party, a gala bash at the New York Historical Society. Expecting to share in her daughter's glory, she had resented being brushed aside by networkers seeking more useful connections than the author's mother. Although always invited to subsequent celebrations of Nina's new books, she had always found reasons not to attend.

By the time Judge Graham and his wife arrived in the late afternoon of New Year's Eve, Nina and J.J. had transformed the parlor into a bridal bower. Nina had ordered baskets of paper whites for their beauty and exquisite aroma. And also because their name symbolized the printed pages of the books that were at the heart of all their lives. Gleaming silver candlesticks fitted with tall white candles had been placed on the mantelpiece, ready to be lit when the lights were turned off and the ceremony began.

"Champagne?" Michael's hands were shaking so hard, Judge Graham relieved him of the bottle and poured glasses for his wife, the nervous groom, and himself.

For a frantic moment Michael could not find the florist's box that contained the boutonnieres for the two men and the corsage for Molly Graham.

Judge Graham pointed at the large white box on the sideboard. "Is this what you're looking for?"

"Nerves. It's this suit. Nina made me get it. I feel like some tango dancer in a thirties movie. A damned gigolo. Nina told the salesman at Bergdorf's I was her boy toy!" To Michael it was obscene to spend that much money on an Armani suit when his black Brooks Brothers with the new

black-and-white-striped shirt and crimson silk tie
Nina had bought would have been fine.

A tap on the parlor door signaled that the bride
and her attendant were ready to enter. As planned
and heavily rehearsed, Michael pressed the start
button on the CD player. Lohengrin's "Wedding
March" filled the room. Although the distance
from the door to the mantelpiece where Judge
Graham was waiting was more of a saunter than
a march, Nina wanted Lohengrin, so Lohengrin
it was.

The candles were lit. The lights turned off. The
door opened. Nina Slocum stood radiantly framed
against the velvet darkness behind her, her bridal
gown an apricot column of pleated silk in the
high-waisted empire style that both hid and hinted
at her impending motherhood. Her thick raven
hair was swept into a tangle of curls on the crown
of her head with a few tendrils allowed to escape.
Except for the pavé diamond earrings Michael had
slipped under her pillow that morning, she wore
no jewelry. Her bouquet was small to suit the occasion and consisted of baby's breath and baby
roses in further recognition of the child within
her.

Standing in shadow behind her, J.J. gave her
mother a gentle shove, whispering, "Go *on!*"

Mother and daughter walked slowly to the Lohengrin march step to where the rest of the small
wedding party stood in readiness. J.J. had never

seen her mother looking so exquisitely beautiful. Her own reflection had assured her she didn't look so bad, either. The plum velvet mini-dress with matching tights and shoes accentuated the shapeliness of her figure and the sexiness of her legs.

Michael had whistled and popped his eyes when he saw her, demanding to know why she'd been hiding herself in baggy jeans. Nina had pretended to scold her. What kind of an ingrate daughter was she, trying to upstage the bride? With tears in her eyes, Nina had then presented her with the pearls her grandmother had given her and which she had been saving for J.J.'s own wedding.

If only, she thought, and pushed the thought from her mind, only to have it return. If only Johnny Black were here to see how wonderful she looked. Her bouquet was a smaller version of Nina's. In secret memory of her lost love, she had added sprigs of parsley, sage, rosemary, and thyme. *He once was a good friend of mine.*

The wedding march ended. Nina joined Michael before Judge Graham. J.J. and Molly stood to one side as the two witnesses required by law.

Judge Graham began with a few remarks. "You won't be surprised to hear that I found the following quote in Bartlett's. It says better than I ever could why Michael and Nina are certain to have a successful marriage and live happily ever after.

This from an eighteenth-century sage, 'A marriage of love is pleasant; a marriage of interest easy, and a marriage where both meet, happy. Thus a happy marriage has in it all the pleasures of friendship, all the enjoyments of sense and reason; and indeed all the sweets of life.' "

He smiled broadly at the two people before him. "You asked me to keep it short, so that's what I'm going to do. Be kind enough to take hands. Michael Ludovic, do you take Nina Slocum to be your lawfully wedded wife? To have and to hold from this day forward, for better or worse, for richer or poorer, in sickness and in health, to love and to cherish until death do you part?"

"I do." Still nervous, Michael was barely audible.

Now it was Nina's turn, but J.J.'s attention was deflected by a sound coming from the lower part of the house. Was it her imagination? Could some burglar be breaking in? Or Prunella Dove? A hideous thought and one without credence. She herself had called Vera Boyle and learned that Prunella was near death at a hospice on Long Island. She listened intently, but there was no further sound.

"I *do!*" Nina called out, loud and clear.

"The rings, please."

J.J. distributed them.

"With this ring, I thee wed."

"With this ring, I thee wed."

"With the power invested in me by the state of New York, I now pronounce you husband and wife. You may kiss."

A hush greeted the sweetness and passion of the couple's first embrace as newlyweds. For a moment they seemed oblivious to their surroundings, holding each other as they whirled slowly in place, murmuring in each other's ears before finally breaking apart sheepishly.

"Champagne! My wife, my beautiful new wife, and I invite you to share our happiness!"

Their glasses filled, Nina took charge. "Now we come to the next part of this glorious occasion. Michael, J.J., and I have each prepared a special toast or recitation to celebrate our marriage. None of us knows what the others are going to do, so fasten your seat belts."

Nina cleared her throat theatrically. "This is for Michael. Elizabeth Barrett Browning said it better than I ever could:

"How do I love thee, let me count the ways.
I love thee, Michael, to the depth and breadth
and height my soul can reach, when feeling out
of sight
For the ends of Being and ideal Grace.
I love thee to the level of every day's
Most quiet need, by sun and candlelight.
I love thee freely as, as men—and women—
strive
for Right;

I love thee purely as they turn from Praise.
I love thee with the passion put to use
In my old griefs and with my childhood's faith.
I love thee with a love I seemed to lose
With my lost saints—and I love thee with the
breath,
Smiles, tears, of all my life!—and if God
choose,
I shall but love thee better after death."

Nina emptied her champagne glass and hurled it at the hearthstone. "Husband! I like that word. Husband, mine. It's your turn."

Michael licked his lips to ease their dryness and cleared his throat several times before he could speak. "As Nina and the rest of you know, I'm one of those buttoned-up types who has difficulty saying how I feel. I stand among you humbly and happily, the luckiest man in the world. And I hope that my words can express, however feebly, the depth of my feelings for the amazing woman who just became my wife."

He paused and reached for Nina's hand, raising it to his lips as if for sustenance to continue. "As we all know, couples who love each other often create their own private means of communication. Baby talk for some. Trading insults for others. Secret languages. Nonverbal winks and signs. Various ways to signal intimacy.

"For Nina and me, it's the crossword puzzle. You all know how fast her mind works. How she races through the puzzle with the speed of light. In ink, of course. Yet every so often, when it's quiet in the house and we're alone, she'll turn to me as if I were the fount of all human knowledge and wave the folded newspapers at me. 'Michael,' she'll say, ever so sweetly. 'I need you, darling. What's a four-letter word?'

"And I all bright-eyed and bushy-tailed will always reply, 'Love! Love is the best four-letter word I know.' And both of us will smile and then go on with whatever we were doing.

"Well, tonight in honor of this celebration, I would like to offer an expanded list of four-letter words appropriate to the occasion. I will begin with the newest four-letter word in our shared vocabulary: wife. Along with kiss. And care. And *hope* for the future. And the *baby* we will cherish in this our *home* where good *talk* and good *food* and good *work* are key.

"As a new husband, I take a cue from King Solomon who immortalized the erotic beauty of his beloved's *feet*. I confess to a breathless awe of my lady's *eyes* and *lips* and *arms* and *legs* and ah, yes, *toes*. All four-letter words of adoration. Yet saving best for last. The four-letter words stamped for all eternity on my heart and in the deepest recess of my mind. My *love*, my *wife*, my *Nina*!"

He raised his champagne glass to her in salute before following her earlier example of smashing it against the hearthstone.

Molly Graham lightened things up. "Remind me not to give you crystal as a wedding present."

Nina kissed her husband's cheek. "Now you know why I married you. I never know what you're going to do next."

"Is it my turn?" J.J. asked. Her selection was something she had memorized in high school. It fit the occasion admirably.

Nina made her way to the door. "Let's hold off for a minute, J.J. I have a surprise for us. A musical presentation from an international ballad singer who is especially dear to this family."

When she opened the door, John Jacob Black stood as he had earlier, his body and his guitar bathed in candlelight. He stepped across the threshold, his fingers a blur as they coaxed out the multiple chords of an old-time ballad.

Michael was as surprised as J.J. "Judge! Molly! This is the man who saved Nina's life when that woman tried to kill her! The hotel said he'd checked out. Left no forwarding address. How did you find him, Nina?"

"Now I know what you were up to, Mom!"

"Whatever do you mean?"

"Yesterday! When you left the house? And I wanted to come along and you said I should work on Julia Sands? Well, I knew you were up to something. You were wearing high heels and a skirt!"

"What's that got to do with finding Johnny?" Michael asked.

Nina laughed appreciatively. "My daughter is very astute. These days most women schlump around in pants, but when we mean business, when we want to intimidate someone, we bring out the artillery and that means skirts, high heels, and a killer attitude!"

Tired of endlessly calling the Mohawk Hotel and endlessly being told there was no way to reach John Jacob Black, that maybe he'd gone back to England or left for California, she had gone to the hotel in person with fire in her eyes and a fifty-dollar bill to jog the desk clerk's memory.

"He didn't want to double-cross Johnny. Johnny told him his ex-wife was after him for nonpayment of alimony. I convinced him I was a record producer with a record contract. Johnny's chance to be a star. So he gave me the number."

Michael, who was always so low-key, gave in to his emotions for the second time. "I owe this man my life. My happiness. If not for him there would be no wedding today. If not for him—" He could not complete the thought of Nina brutally stabbed and possibly dead, their love, their unborn child forever gone.

Judge Graham raised his glass. "Let's drink the health of Johnny Black."

"To Johnny Black."

Nina proposed another toast. "To J.J., my beautiful, brilliant daughter, friend and co-author."

"To J.J."

Almost as an afterthought, Nina had one more thing to say. She had booked a ringside table at the Spring Café for the midnight show starring Johnny Black. "He'll be introducing 'The Ghost of Julia Sands' for the first time in public. CNN is covering the Spring Café as part of its New Year's Eve round-up, so Johnny will be seen and heard all over the world!"

Michael kissed his bride's cheek and gently patted her belly. "A fine way to start a new year. But wait one minute! We're forgetting something. Nina and I did our bit. Embarrassed you all, I'm sure. In all the excitement we haven't heard from J.J. It's your turn, darling. Knowing J.J., she's found something loving and appropriate."

The younger woman's offering had been chosen with a wistful hope for the new year. Now the words of Alfred Lord Tennyson became an exultant celebration.

"Ring out, wild bells, to the wild sky,
The flying cloud, the frosty light;
The year is dying in the night;
Ring out wild bells and let him die.
Ring out the old, ring in the new,
Ring, happy bells, across the snow."

She took Johnny Black's hand. "This is for you, Johnny.

"The year is going; let him go.
Ring out the false, ring in the true."

Soon Johnny had to leave for a sound check at the Spring Café. J.J. walked him down the stairs to the front door. At last they were alone.

"Missed you," she said.

"Missed you, too."

The dormant passions of their one night together exploded once again in a convulsive embrace.

"Missed you. Missed you. Missed you," she sobbed.

"Missed you. Missed you, too."

He opened the front door. "Got to go."

"Johnny?"

He kissed her nose. "See you later. We've got the whole night, the whole new year ahead of us."

"Is it true?" She had to ask.

"What? Is what true?"

"Is there a wife?"

He considered his reply. "Curiosity killed the cat, J.J. If you must know, yes, there is a wife."

Just then Nina's voice called out from the top of the stairs. "J.J.? Are you there?"

Mother smiled down at daughter and tossed her the bridal bouquet. "The one who catches it is the one who gets married next!"

J.J. caught the bouquet. When she turned back to Johnny, he was gone.

Chapter Sixteen

It was Michael's idea. Nina totally approved. Why hadn't she thought of it first? They discussed it in whispers during the prolonged applause following Johnny's New Year's Eve performance and agreed to wait until they got back to the house to tell him and J.J. about it.

The new year's noisemakers and horns punctuated the boisterous shouts for more, more, more. One table of enraptured fans banged out a rhythmic demand for John-nee, John-nee, *John-nee*! until the emcee called for quiet. He was happy to announce Johnny Black would be back every Friday and Saturday for the next two months. "Years from now. What am I saying? Months, maybe even weeks from now when Johnny Black is a household name, you'll all remember seeing him here first at the Spring Café."

"Congratulations!" The Grahams waited until he returned to the table before heading home. Way past their bedtime, they explained. The champagne had loosened the judge's tongue. With his arm around his wife he explained that he had promised to make love to her once each year. And tonight was the night!

The Grahams had been together thirty-seven years, Nina and Michael about half as long. J.J. wondered wistfully how long she and Johnny would be together. If at all. What did he mean, there was a wife? How could she ignore his relationship with Prunella Dove? How was she going to ask him to explain himself when all she really wanted was to be with him in bed? Or on the floor or in a canoe or at the beach or in a field or any one of the secluded places flashing through her feverish thoughts.

"I hope you didn't mind my dedication." In his introduction of "The Ghost of Julia Sands," he had smiled in her direction. "The ballad you are about to hear was inspired by a young woman who is right here in the audience. Her name is J.J. Drake and as fate would have it, I met her in the Rare Book Room of the New York Public Library. Incidentally"—he grinned knowingly at several of the men—"the public library is a great place to meet smart, attractive women! But on to J.J. She was doing research into the brutal murder of a young Greenwich Village beauty nearly two hundred years ago. Right in this neighborhood. Right nearby where Spring and Greene streets meet. The murder involved two of the most famous men in American history, Alexander Hamilton and Aaron Burr, and has never been solved!"

Eager eyes strained to see the source of his inspiration. Eager heads turned to follow him to her side after the set. "Happy New Year, love," he said, pulling her to her feet in a crowd-pleasing embrace while those at nearby tables applauded and pelted them with confetti.

By three in the morning, the crowd had thinned. Those who remained tucked into the Spring Café's traditional New Year's Day breakfast of scrambled eggs, sausage, and Bloody Marys.

"Let's walk home," Nina suggested. This night was like no other in Greenwich Village. Crowds of revelers filled the pre-dawn darkness, the streets a movable feast of lovers kissing in doorways, groups singing under street lamps, and dancing to portable tapes. In one place a spirited game of catch used a man's silk hat as a ball. At another, two women in furs and bare feet played potsy with a gold bracelet on a sidewalk hopscotch.

Michael tucked Nina's arm into his and held her as close to him as he could as if to reassure himself that she was real and she was there and she was his wife. At intervals he stopped their progress and gathered her to him in a voluptuous kiss. Quite a switch for a man who abjured public displays of affection. After so many years he could still surprise and arouse her.

Following at a discreet distance, J.J. and Johnny

walked hand in hand. His mention of a wife made conversation awkward. Not knowing what to say, she had resorted to observations of the weather, how good the cold air felt after the stuffiness of the club, how wonderful the Village looked with all the holiday decorations, and of course how happy Nina and Michael looked, acting like children on their wedding day. All he could do was murmur complete agreement.

They watched the newlyweds' kisses but felt inhibited about emulating them. Johnny clutched her hand so tightly her fingers were numb. She did nothing to loosen his grip for fear of his interpreting it as a rejection. What would happen when they reached the house? Her body clamored for him. All 76,000 inches of her skin ached for all 76,000 inches of his. Throughout Nina's wedding J.J.'s thoughts had turned to him, wondering where he was and with whom. When the door flew open and there he was, she had thought she was going to faint, and when Nina said they were going to the Spring Café, she had felt queasy with desire.

As they approached the house, a group of raucous people poured out of a nearby house roaring "Auld Lang Syne" at the top of their lungs. They surrounded the newcomers, insisting they join in.

The words stuck in J.J.'s throat. Would this old acquaintance turn out to be someone she would have to forget about? And so what if she did? Get a life. Go with the flow. If nothing else, Johnny Black had shown her she was capable of sexual fulfillment. If nothing else, he had proved to her that she was ready for love. And furthermore, she reminded herself it was past time to see about birth control.

By the time they reached the front door, she had steeled herself for a chaste good night. There was no smooth way to invite Johnny upstairs to her bedroom. Even worse, there was no guarantee he would accept. Nina and Michael were most certainly grateful for his courage at Weehawken. That did not mean her mother approved of his spending the night in her little girl's bed.

"This has been the happiest New Year's of my entire life," Johnny said. He shook Michael's hand. He pecked Nina on the cheek. He traced the outline of J.J.'s mouth with his finger. "Can I call you later in the week?"

Nina opened the door and pulled him inside. "Are you crazy? You're staying here tonight. With J.J. I barged in on you once. I won't do it again. Promise."

John Jacob Black looked as if he'd been hit by a truck.

"You do want to stay with J.J., don't you?"

The strong, masterful voice that had entranced the Spring Café audience was now a hesitant growl. "If J.J. wants me." If the revelation about his wife had turned her off, there was nothing he could do but accept it.

J.J. surprised herself with the authority of her voice. "Yes, Mom. I want him to stay with me."

"That settles it, then. Why should Michael and I be the only happy ones? And oh, by the way, Michael has something to say to you, Johnny. Of course, it will interest J.J. as well."

Because Johnny had saved Nina's life, because Johnny had saved their unborn baby's life, because Nina had found him living in a third-rate hotel, Michael and Nina were inviting him to move into the guest room for as long as it took for his career to take off. Judging by tonight's audience, it wouldn't take too long.

Nina kissed her daughter. "J.J. doesn't mind, do you, darling?"

To her chagrin, J.J. did mind, although she could not explain why even to herself. Yes, she wanted him sharing her bed, but no, not her home, not her mother, not her stepfather, not the cocoon that she was counting on to protect and nourish her while she took her first faltering steps as a writer. This was hardly the time for discussion. The hour was late. Michael and Nina were beaming at her with the satisfaction of their generosity and the certainty that they were making her happy.

Time enough tomorrow to tell Nina about Johnny's wife and her own misgivings. Meanwhile, she would be in his arms for the rest of the night, and in the morning she would begin work in earnest on her theory about the murder of Julia Sands and how it might have changed the history of the United States. In her determination to separate her love life from her professional life, her game plan could be expressed in one word: compartmentalization. Johnny in one, Julia in another. No overlapping.

By morning she understood with frightening clarity the true meaning of sexual addiction to one man. Reading about it in books and magazines merely scratched the surface of her cravings. When he got up to go to the bathroom, she clung to him. When he started to dress to go uptown to get his belongings, she hid his boots, pretending to be playful but feeling a wild desperation she had never before experienced. She had read about women who had thrown all caution to the winds for a man's love. Women who had abandoned their orderly lives, deserted husband and children in the heat of obsessive passion.

Until now Anna Karenina and Emma Bovary had puzzled her. Why had they sacrificed everything for some pompous jerk who was sure to dump them? In contemporary-reality terms, there were always stories about wives getting their teenage lovers to off their husbands and about wives running away with a serial killer.

She felt helpless in her desire. Her moment to

confide in Nina came and went at the breakfast table. Michael was upstairs clearing out the guest room closet. Mother and daughter were alone.

"I like him, J.J. I think he'll be good for you."

The younger woman made a feeble attempt to disagree. "As long as he doesn't interfere with my writing."

Nina laughed delightedly. The time had come to speak woman to woman with her daughter. "*Au contraire*, teddy bear! A good lover is good for your writing. Why do you think I took on Michael in the first place? Great sex equals great writing. I was lucky. We grew together in the best possible way. That could happen with you and Johnny down the road. In the meantime you've got an exciting, demanding project that can make your career and a loving man to rub your neck and shoulders at the end of the day."

Not many girls had a mother like Nina. Perhaps if poor Julia had had someone wise and caring like Nina to guide and protect her, she wouldn't have wound up exploited and dead. A few years back J.J. had used a Diogenes quote in a high school essay. "Truth lies at the bottom of the well." She printed it large with a felt-tipped pen and taped it above WHAT HAPPENED? and HOW COME? She took a deep breath and shut her eyes briefly in order to visualize Johnny's face and feel his kiss. Keeping in mind Nina's advice that the opening sentence has to grab the reader by the throat or forget it, she began to write.

INTRODUCING JULIA SANDS

Marilyn Monroe would have been perfect casting for the role of the Girl in the Manhattan Well. To put the story of Julia Sands into modern perspective, there are distinct parallels. Both were born illegitimate, their fathers unknown. Both grew up without mothers (Julia's dead in childbirth; Marilyn's confined to a mental ward).

Both were banished to the care of strangers, Marilyn to an orphanage, Julia to a distant relative's more than a hundred miles from her birthplace. Both grew to young womanhood with the dangerous gifts of breathtaking beauty and irresistible charm, compounded by the even more dangerous gift of a childlike romantic innocence that attracted men of substance.

Neither one understood the power of her sexual impact or the rage it elicited in the men who became wildly infatuated with her and then regretted it. Having no family of their own, each sought desperately to be part of other people's families and especially the families of the men they loved.

And ultimately both were seduced and betrayed by the leading political figures of their time. Each believed she was adored and about to have her dreams come true when death came suddenly and mysteriously in the night.

Each in her own way became history's pawn, the inadvertent catalyst that triggered the events that ultimately—inexorably—destroyed her betrayers. The story of Marilyn Monroe has passed into legend. The truth about her death may never be proved. Suffice it to say that in less than a decade the two men most commonly cited as conspirators, Jack and Robert Kennedy, were murdered, occurrences that changed the course of American history.

The story of Julia Sands cries out for investigation. For its own sake in the name of justice and for what may have been the turning point in the bitter rivalry between Hamilton and Burr that precipitated the fatal duel, putting an end to the divisive policies of both men.

To put Julia's murder and the Hamilton-Burr duel into narrow perspective, here is a brief chronology of the salient events:

December 22, 1799, Julia Sands sets out from her cousin's Greenwich Village boarding house to elope with Levi Weeks, the younger brother of New York's leading builder, Ezra Weeks.

January 2, 1800, her body is found in the Manhattan Well, which is owned by Aaron Burr's Manhattan Water Company of which Alexander Hamilton's brother-in-law is a shareholder.

On March 31, 1890, Levi Weeks is put on trial for Julia's murder despite the efforts of Ezra's friends in high places to quash the indictment.

Despite their vicious political rivalry in this presidential election year, Hamilton and Burr agree to help out their friend Ezra Weeks by jointly defending his younger brother.

April 2, 1800, in a circus atmosphere, Levi is speedily acquitted and released.

Between the end of the trial and July 1804, the rivalry between Hamilton and Burr accelerates. Burr and the Jeffersonians defeat Hamilton's Federalists in the election of state legislators who in turn will cast the electoral votes for the presidency.

April 29, 1800, Jefferson and Burr are tied in the electoral vote for president. The presidential election is thrown into the House of Representatives.

February 17, 1801, outraged at the possibility of Burr becoming president, Hamilton works furiously behind the scenes to swing the vote to Jefferson on the thirty-sixth ballot.

April 25, 1804, thus thwarted, Burr runs for governor of New York State and is defeated by humiliating attacks on his integrity, sexuality, and secret dealings with New England secessionists. Hamilton's relentless accusations leave Burr with no alternative but to invite Hamilton to an "interview" at Weehawken.

If the battered body of a beautiful young Quaker girl were found today and her accused lover's connection to two of the most controversial men in American politics were revealed, the media would have a field day. Imagine how the talk shows and tabloids would treat Julia's frozen body as it lay in its coffin on public display on the street outside her house and how they would send their best reporters to her family home in Cornwall-on-Hudson and how they would pay for interviews with everyone who had ever known her, known someone who had known her, known someone who had seen her with Levi or Hamilton or Burr. Or thought they had.

All that happened after Levi's acquittal was the publication of the trial transcript by a local printer eager to satisfy the public's craving for sensation. After that, nothing! Nobody in the press or in government asked what really happened. If Levi didn't kill Julia, who did?

And most important, why did Hamilton and Burr set aside their personal animosity at the height of a presidential campaign in order to defend a young man accused of manslaughter?

Why, why, why?

In the dozens of books about Hamilton and Burr written in the nearly two hundred years since the duel, most have ignored the murder of Julia Sands and the trial of Levi Weeks entirely. Others have noted the crime and reviewed the trial using excerpts from the published transcript. Not one historian or biographer has ever asked what Nina

Slocum—my mentor as well as my mother—has trained me to ask, "How come?"

Could it be because until now most Hamilton-Burr authorities have been men? In the few books that do making passing reference to Julia Sands, I have found mention of her murder and Levi's acquittal. With hope in my heart I have turned the page in expectation of further revelations only to find—nothing! Not a grain of curiosity has prompted anyone to dig for answers or speculate on the reasons for Hamilton and Burr's questionable behavior.

What happened?

How come?

Another rule my mother taught me is this: If you want to find the end of the story, start at the beginning.

Chapter Seventeen

Being the Story of Julia Sands, "The Girl in the Manhattan Well," and How Her Brutal Murder Led to the Fatal Duel Between Alexander Hamilton and Aaron Burr and Thus Changed the History of the United States

A Speculation Based on
Established Facts and Logical Conclusions
by J.J. Drake

"Resist the Devil and he will flee from thee!" David Sands, the revered Quaker minister, quoted from his own writing as he implored the sobbing figure of his pregnant younger sister to reveal the name of the man who had seduced her. Tears streaming down her cheeks, her hair a tangle of damp curls, she lay trembling on the veranda of Rose Cottage, one arm crooked above her face as if to ward off blows.

Her scandalous and lewd behavior had brought

disgrace to the immediate Sands family and to the entire Friends community of New Cornwall. This quiet, respectable village on the western shore of the Hudson River was less than a day's ride from the Continental Army's garrison at West Point. On this hot Indian summer day in the autumn of 1776, New Cornwall was beginning to feel the immediacy of the war of independence from England. Washington troops could be seen on barges on the Hudson River below and on the roads going north to Newburgh and Albany and south to West Point and New York.

As a Quaker schooled in the pacifist principles of William Penn, David Sands was opposed to the war by conscience until Tom Paine's *Common Sense* convinced him of the colonists' right to independence. He had rallied the Friends Society in New York City to the cause and was about to leave for conferences with Quaker societies throughout Orange County when he heard about his sister's misconduct and its shameful consequences.

"No, Papa! No!" Four-year-old Catherine Sands came running from the house, her white apron covering her somber gray gown. Family and friends agreed that she must have been born singing. Never had there ever been a more warmhearted and loving child.

She threw herself at her weeping aunt's bosom, her arms tightly wrapped around the distraught woman's neck. "Please don't cry! God loves thee! God loves all of us, don't he, Papa?"

David felt mortified and betrayed by his sister's obstinate intransigence. He could not understand why she had flouted God's laws and why she would not now throw herself on God's mercy by telling the truth. Gospel love was at the core of everything he believed in. The Quaker movement had begun in England more than a century before in the aftermath of the Protestant reformation. In protest against the formality of the established church, the group called themselves Friends and described themselves as Children of Light and Friends of Jesus. In seeking spiritual reality, they brought God directly into their lives at meetings rather than churches. Because their spiritual fervor often caused them to tremble or "quake," they were called Quakers by their detractors until gradually the name lost its pejorative meaning and was used informally by the Quakers themselves.

Yes, God loved them all, he assured the little girl watching him so beseechingly. He knelt down beside his sister, hoping Catherine's presence would soften her resolve to keep her obscene secret. He had to control his exasperation. Always so quiet and demure, his sister's defiance had erupted suddenly. She had bought a length of calico from a peddler and made it into a flamboyant shawl to replace the drab gray worn by all the other women. She had worn her thick waist-length hair loose and adorned it with field flowers instead of pinning it into a tight bun under the traditional somber bonnet.

"Leave me in peace, David."

"Tell me the man's name."

Silence.

As a spinster in her brother's household, she had been a servant without pay and doomed to joyless celibacy unless she married. Not one of the local farmers asked for her hand. She had accepted her fate until fate relented by sending her a passionate love so overwhelming as to be almost religious in its wonder. Her brother would never understand. Nor would his wife or other members of their tight-knit community. It wasn't that she didn't love Jesus Christ with all her heart and soul. She did, and she also knew that He would be more forgiving and compassionate than David Sands.

"For the last time, tell me his name!"

More silence.

He rose to his feet, his manner changing abruptly. "General Washington has asked us to billet some of his troops. How can I expose these brave young patriots to a temptress and harlot without corrupting them and jeopardizing our righteous cause of freedom?"

"Oh, Catty-Cat! Thee knows I'm not . . ." She hugged her niece to her, unable to repeat her brother's words.

"What is a harlot?"

"Hush, child. See what thee has done, David? I am no temptation to innocent young soldiers. Or to any man. Ever again. There is no Devil in me. Only a child. The Devil is in man's lust. And henceforth no man shall come near me."

"And if the child is a man child? What then?"

"I'll kill it! I shall call myself Egypt and kill it as a Jew. Kill it—"

Hearing the shouts, Clementine Sands hurried from the house to her husband's side. "What is it? What has happened?"

"My sister is mad! We must suffer her sins with her."

Late that night as the poor woman lay sleepless in her attic room, little Catherine crept into bed with her. Would she really kill a baby if it was a boy?

"Oh, little Cat? Could I kill any living creature?" It was a family joke that she could not so much as wring a hen's neck or put down a sickly pup.

As months went by, Clementine's attitude softened toward her sister-in-law. She shared her husband's stern beliefs, but she was also a woman and a mother who knew full well the terrors of childbirth. By the time of Catherine's confinement, several soldiers of the Continental Army were billeted in the house and the surrounds. It was well past midnight when the contractions began. David Sands was away on one of his periodic tours of Friends societies in Connecticut and Massachusetts.

Clementine carried her midwife's bag of necessaries to the attic and stoked the fire in the grate in order to heat the water in the large iron kettle. Little Catherine watched the preparations with wide eyes. The folded bed linens and swaddling cloth still smelling sweet from the clothesline. Tin basins waiting for hot water. Knives and scissors for cutting the umbilical cord and to deal with emergency.

Clementine's attempt to slip by her sleeping daughter had failed. Catherine stubbornly clung to her mother's skirts. So be it. Little Catherine had witnessed many barnyard births. This would be her first experience with the human species. In the close confines of the attic room, her mother warned her to ask no questions and stay out of the way. She crouched on the far side of the narrow bed and stroked her aunt's hand.

So far the soldiers in the house had caused no problem. Most preferred sleeping in tents set up in the backyard and the old apple orchard. Most of the furniture had been removed from the parlor so that men who wanted a roof over their heads could kip down on the floor.

"Someone's coming," Catherine said.

David! Relieved that her husband was home safe, Clementine nonetheless wished that the baby had been born before his return. It was only a matter of minutes.

"Open the door and kiss thy father. He must be tired from his journey."

The door did not wait for Catherine. It flew open. Three disheveled soldiers staggered into the room, singing and sharing a jug of David Sands' best apple cider. "We heard women's voices! Women hiding in the attic! We're good fellows. Out for a lark. Mustn't hide from us!"

The sight that confronted them was not what they expected. Clementine Sands positioned herself between them and the woman moaning on the bed. "Leave at once! You are a disgrace to your uniform."

"Then we'll take the uniform off. Right, lads?" one of them slurred.

"Please, Clemmie, send them away!" the voice behind her gasped.

"What's this, then? A mare in foal?"

"More like a sow to me!"

"We're farmers, ain't we, lads? Let's give the ladies a hand."

Clementine stood her ground. "My husband is asleep downstairs!"

"Your husband is away. We all know that, don't we, lads? Leaving the women alone. Some husband!"

The minister's wife was not intimidated. "Get

thee and thy muddy boots and foul breath out of here."

One of the soldiers forced a kiss on her. "Foul breath, is it? An insult to Washington's brave lads!"

The remaining two planted loud, mocking kisses on each other's lips. Foul breath? Not to them. Their turn was next.

"You leave my mother alone!" The soldiers had failed to see little Catherine. From her perch beside the bed she leaped into the fray, fists flying, elbows and knees flailing, her head a battering ram seeking every target possible.

The soldiers laughed in drunken delight. One of them picked her up by the hair. "What shall we do with her, lads?"

One of his comrades thrust his face menacingly at Clementine's. "What would *thee* do to save *thy* little girl?"

A series of wild shrieks from the bed filled the room. "Help me, Clemmie. The baby! It's coming!"

Her cries sobered the intruders sufficiently to release Clementine. Not satisfied, she retrieved her daughter. "I shall need her assistance. A child is about to be born. It would be best if you leave."

Feeling cheated of their amusement, the drunkest of the trio opened the cider jug. It was empty. "Fill it first."

"Fill it yourself. With piss!" the woman on the bed screamed.

Bellowing obscenities, the man slapped Clementine nearly senseless, holding her prisoner by pulling one arm high up behind her back. Of the other two men, one clamped his hand over little Catherine's mouth to stop her cries while the third approached the writhing, sweating creature on the bed.

"More a cow than a sow!" Dawn's first light was seeping through the small attic window, revealing the filth of his hands and the caked grease and sputum on his beard as he pushed up her skirts. Blood and the mucus of childbirth covered her thighs. The baby's head could be seen. Clementine broke free of her captor and broke the empty jug over his head. Little Catherine's small, hard fists again went on the attack against his two comrades, who by now had tired of the entire episode and were ready to retreat.

Not so their leader. He hovered at Clementine's shoulder as the baby popped out, as if attracted by the ruckus. Despite the circumstances Clementine laughed in exultation at the wonders of nature and thanked God as she raised the slippery babe by its ankles for the slap of new life. "It's a girl!"

She cut the umbilical cord, knotted it, and was about to wrap the howling newborn in swaddling when it was snatched from her ministering hands and hoisted with a howl of triumph above the drunken soldier's head. His two friends cowered in disbelief.

"Not as fat as rabbit! But a tasty morsel for the stewpot!"

The newly delivered mother shrieked in terror and rose from her bed, blood streaming down her legs. Her face parchment gray and wet with perspiration, she pitched forward in a desperate attempt to retrieve her babe, a distraction that allowed Clementine to seize it.

Such was the pandemonium in the attic that no one heard the clatter of horse's hooves and the sound of heavy riding boots on the veranda.

"What wickedness is this?" The glowering figure of David Sands filled the doorway. It being against his religious principles to bear arms against another man, he drew a long-handled ax from his belt.

The three intruders pushed past him and fled down the stairs.

"Stop them!" his wife begged.

"The other men will tell us who they are! Tell me what has happened?"

She held out the baby for his blessing. "A little girl! Just a few minutes old. Those evil men prevented me from washing her. You'll see how sweet and pretty she is when I bring her downstairs. As sweet and pretty as her mother."

All eyes turned to the silent figure lying face-down on the bed with little Catherine beside her, stroking her hair. The minister pointed an accusing finger. "This woman's sins have attracted evil to this house. Those men! Those men could smell the evil. They might have robbed me of thy tender presence, dear wife. This woman is my sister, but she is accursed and so shall be her child!"

He leaned close. "Now wilst thou tell me the name of thy partner in vileness?"

Little Catherine sensed the tragedy and began to rock to and fro with a high-pitched keening sound as her father touched the silent figure. Getting no response, he turned it over. Was she dead? Her lips moved noiselessly. Her eyelids fluttered as if they were too heavy to open until with effort of will she looked up pleadingly and raised her arms for her child.

With a sob of compassion the minister's wife placed the babe at her mother's breast. "There, now. Thee has a fine, healthy girl. See to her while Catherine and I straighten things up and fetch thee a fresh gown and some nourishing broth."

Normally gentle and submissive to her husband, Clementine now turned to him and sternly ordered him to leave. "Find those louts and see that justice is done."

The new mother pressed feeble kisses to the infant's head, moaning soft, incoherent endearments. Clementine could sense the Angel of

Death hovering over the bed. She was helpless to do anything more than clear away the broken jug and other signs of the soldiers' assault and to wash and freshen the area surrounding the bed. Her experience in midwifery told her there was little point in disturbing the poor woman.

"Clemmie?" Her lips were crusted dry.

"Try not to talk." She tried to ease the doomed woman's discomfort with a damp cloth.

"Her name . . . please, I want her to have a Quaker name . . . a name David and the others will respect . . . so they won't scorn her for my sins."

"Tell me the name."

"The same as William Penn's wife—Gulielma. Gulie-el-ma!"

She half rose on one elbow with an imploring gesture. "Promise?"

"I promise."

The pallor on her skin thickened, as if coated with flour. She fell back exhausted. "Tell my brother . . . I'm sorry I . . . brought shame . . . to Rose Cottage but—"

"Hush. Don't upset thyself."

"But I'm not sorry for what happened. Catherine? Where is my sweet little Catherine?"

The child had been clinging to her mother's skirts and would have hurried to her aunt's summons if Clementine had not held her back. "Can I trust thee to hold the baby?"

Instantly mature and maternal of manner, Catherine accepted the small bundle with shining eyes. Taken away from her mother's teat, the infant's tiny mouth sucked furiously until in frustration it opened wide as a baby bird and screamed.

Catherine and Clementine could not help laughing. How could so much noise come out of this tiny creature? The little girl cradled the infant as if she were a doll and tried to soothe her. "Ah-aaah ba-bee! Ah-aaah ba-bee!"

At that moment David Sands returned.

"I've had a message from General Washington's headquarters. We are to expect a visit from Colonel Hamilton."

Hamilton? Again? Not that the family didn't relish his frequent visits to Rose Cottage. This time she'd give him a piece of her mind about the lax discipline among the troops.

"The three soldiers. Have they been arrested?"

"The sergeant said they're known trouble-makers."

"They should be severely punished."

The minister shook his head. "They've deserted. It will be up to God to punish them. Best to remember they'll not show their faces around here ever again. Now tell me. How is my sister? She seems to be sleeping peacefully enough."

To indicate that little Catherine did not know the truth, Clemmie raised a silencing finger to his lips and whispered, "She is not sleeping, David. She is dead."

His expression did not change. "And what of the child?" It was clear from his manner that if the baby, too, had perished, the shameful episode would soon fade from memory.

Little Catherine piped up. "She's sleeping, Papa. See how pretty she is? Her name is . . . Gul—Gulielma—too hard to pronounce. So I'm going to call her Julia! Sweet little Julia."

She grinned adoringly at her new cousin before once more assuming the tone of maternal chastisement she'd seen used by the younger mothers of the community.

"Jul-ia? Jul-ia! Be a good little girl or else . . ." How to cajole a newborn baby? "Or else I'll give thee to the redcoats and they will eat thee for supper!"

The baby's answering howl caused little Catherine to laugh with the gleeful sense of power and responsibility she had over this tiny, helpless creature.

"Don't cry, little Julia. I shall never let harm take thee. And one day I shall take thee to New York City, all the way to New York City by stage coach. I promise thee, little Julia."

The rat-a-tat tap on J.J.'s workroom door could be only one person.

"Johnny?"

His exasperation belied his joking tone. "Who else is taking you to the movies?"

The doorknob turned convulsively.

"What's the big idea? You locked the door!"

"Please, Johnny. Give me a minute. I'm right in the middle of a sentence. I'll be right with you."

This day, like all the previous days since J.J. had begun writing her chapter, had raced by in what seemed like minutes. Once inside her tiny basement office, locked away from the outside world, she had become a time traveler lost in that brief period around the turn of the nineteenth century. Today she felt herself transported to New Cornwall, an invisible witness to the birth of Julia and the cold indifference of David Sands as well as an invisible participant in the Rose Cottage preparations for Hamilton's impending visit.

This would be the latest of many visits to New Cornwall by the handsome young officer. As a researcher and would-be historian, dared she speculate that Hamilton was baby Julia's father? The unidentified secret lover? Factually it was possible. New Cornwall had been a popular rest stop on the journey between West Point and Albany, and there was substantial evidence in Hamilton's papers of his visits.

Emotionally drained, physically spent, she felt compelled to keep working. Into the night if necessary. She had to go on. She could not bear to leave Rose Cottage before describing Hamilton's arrival, baby Julia's life as an illegitimate child of sin and an outcast, and Catherine's unswerving devotion.

Johnny would simply have to understand. She needed a few more hours of concentration in order to cover Catherine's marriage to Elias Ring. And how the couple moved to the house David Sands had bought in Greenwich Village. And why the adolescent Julia was banished from the Quaker community and sent to live with her cousin. And how Catherine took in boarders, among them Levi Weeks!

What happened and how come? What happened and how come? How could she stop now? Nina had warned her of the syndrome. Her mother likened it to the ecstasy of the deep when ocean divers exploring shipwrecks at the bottom of the sea lingered too long, used up their oxygen, became light-headed, tore off their masks and went to a watery grave.

"You must learn to pace yourself, J.J. You can't let the people you're writing about take over. Writing can become as obsessive as drug addiction. You are alone in the world you create and soon nothing else matters! You mustn't let that happen."

The turning point for Nina had come several years earlier. She had been working through the night. Smelling smoke, she had hastily gathered her materials and fled to the street before it dawned on her that Michael was asleep upstairs. The source of the smoke had failed to materialize; perhaps it came from a coal-burning freighter on the Hudson in a sudden shift of wind.

"Remember that, J.J. Try to strike an even balance between love and work."

Johnny persisted. "It's after six o'clock!"

"Please, Johnny. I'm in the middle of a sentence!" Why couldn't he just go away and leave her in peace?

"Nina says you've been there since before breakfast and you didn't have any breakfast."

Or lunch, now that she thought of it. "Just a little while longer. I promise!"

"If you don't open the door this minute, I'm going to break it down."

Some primitive echo in the depths of her psyche responded to his threat with an erotic rush. Him Tarzan, her Jane.

"Don't you dare!" she challenged, both frightened and excited by the prospect of sexual combat. Was this how Julia Sands had felt when Levi Weeks broke into her bedroom?

"I'll count to ten and then watch out!"

J.J. watched the doorknob in breathless suspense.

"One, two, three, four, five, six, seven, eight, nine . . . J.J.? Last chance. Will you open the door?"

Her entire body throbbed with giddy anticipation. Never a dull moment with John Jacob Black.

"Okay, you asked for it!"

A thud, a kick, and the flimsy lock shattered. The door crashed open. In the split second that Johnny stood motionless before wrestling her to the floor, an odd question passed through her mind. Why was it that when she was sexually aroused, Johnny seemed taller and handsomer than at other times? She would have to ask Nina about that. Among other things. Since meeting Johnny she sometimes wondered if she was what the guys at school joked about, a nymphomaniac. Always ready, always hungry for more, more, *more!*

He had her pinned to the floor. "You asked for it, and now you're going to get it!"

Pretending to submit, she abandoned herself to his caresses until she felt him relax. "That's what you think!"

Battle cries sounded. The warriors in close combat, ambushing each other's positions, breaking down barriers, infiltrating innermost strongholds, seeking advantage by fair means or foul, giving no quarter. Wild words. Wilder acts. Power plays based on intimate knowledge of the enemy's weakness.

The jumble of bare limbs and tangled garments abruptly called a truce, a time-out while they gasped for breath and quite literally girded their loins for the next go-round. In the lull Michael's voice called discreetly from the top of the stairs.

"Hey, you two! J.J.? Johnny? Nina says to come upstairs right this minute. Or you'll miss *Jeopardy*!"

To miss *Jeopardy* was sacrilege. They dressed swiftly, scrutinizing each other for signs of their lovemaking. Not that it mattered. Anyone with half an eye could tell they were mad for each other.

"Come on, J.J. They're waiting. You've done enough for one day."

She had gone to her desk. He followed her and pulled her to him so tightly she could feel every inch of him pressed against her.

"Just let me scribble three little words."

"You mean, 'I love you, Johnny'? That's four."

She ran demanding hands down his back and between his thighs. "I mean, 'To be continued!' "

Chapter Eighteen

"Busy, Nina?"

Johnny's habit of appearing uninvited at the parlor door in the late afternoon was beginning to get on her nerves. Lying back on the chaise longue with pillows behind her neck and under her knees, she was engrossed in J.J.'s latest batch of pages, simmering in contentment. This morning the baby had kicked for the very first time, and truth to tell, the last thing she wanted was company.

But she had set a precedent of welcoming him weeks back by way of continuing to thank him for saving her life. And the baby's.

"Come on in."

"You're sure?"

What did he want, a notarized guarantee? His fawning solicitude was beginning to wear thin. Uriah Heep with a ponytail. Still, she owed him her life, and J.J. was goofy crazy about him.

"Of course I'm sure. I just have a few more

pages to read. Why don't you go down to the kitchen and fix us a cappuccino, and there's a bag of lemon cookies from Balducci's. By the time you get back, I'll be finished reading and ready to talk."

He hesitated as if to speak but changed his mind.

"What is it, Johnny? Anything wrong?"

"Well. There is something I wanted to discuss. Let me get the coffee and then we can talk."

Once he'd gone, she wanted to kick herself. Where was her generosity of spirit? Here she was, a woman with everything, a brilliant career, a loving husband, a beautiful home, a wonderful daughter, and a baby on the way. And here was John Jacob Black, alone in the world, living in a furnished room if they hadn't taken him in, pushing forty and still singing folk songs for peanuts at a Greenwich Village club!

True, he was packing them in. They had doubled his fee, which wasn't much in the first place. There was talk of agents and bookers. And most important of all there was J.J. The man might be almost old enough to be her father, but then he wasn't her father. He was her lover, her first lover, and he was making her happy. For that alone Nina Slocum could thank her lucky stars and spare an hour of her oh so valuable time for a cappuccino and a lemon cookie.

When other mothers bragged about the beauty,

style, and brilliant accomplishments of their off-spring, there was always the defensive disclaimer: "I'm not just saying this because it's my child!"

Over the past weeks Nina had joined the club, her maternal pride tinged with wonder and a touch of the jealousy the reigning monarch, though safe in her sovereignty, feels for the next in line. Never had she imagined her daughter capable of assembling her data with such clarity and of presenting her theory with such passionate conviction.

Today's manuscript picked up the narrative with the visit of Alexander Hamilton to Rose Cottage shortly after Julia's birth. He had brought gifts of knitting wool for the women of the Sands household and was visibly shaken when told about the brutality of the soldiers and the death of the minister's sister.

His tender attentions to the newborn Julia were totally in character. It was common knowledge that he had been born illegitimate in the West Indies, that his father had deserted his mother, who died when he was twelve, and that several citizens of St. Croix had sponsored his voyage to New York to further his education.

Catherine Sands was his special favorite among the Quaker children. She seemed to have been born competent. By the age of six she was bossing the other children and had taken charge of baby

Julia, showering her with kisses and shielding her from the indignation of the pious.

On subsequent visits during the remaining war years and afterward when Hamilton married into the aristocratic Schuyler family, who had originally settled the Hudson Valley, his travels as a politician and lawyer often found him journeying between New York and Albany.

As Catherine grew into young womanhood, a jesting colloquy developed between them. She confided to him her hope to marry, have children, and move with her family to New York and join the Friends Society there.

Hamilton had assured her that he believed her dream would come true, and when it did she must call on him to be of any service he could provide.

"And me, too?" little Julia asked.

"And thee, too!" Hamilton replied in the Quaker vernacular.

When Catherine's courtship with Elias Ring began, Julia was thrilled but not for long. Her mother's sin was not forgotten. She was not permitted to attend the festivities honoring the young couple or the wedding itself. There was nothing Catherine could do except assure her cousin that she loved her dearly and would take her along when the newlyweds moved into the house David Sands had bought in Greenwich Village.

But it was not to be. Julia was by then fifteen and rebellious of nature, a fair-haired creature with a complexion of polished alabaster, eyes blue as cornflowers, and a gift of song and laughter. Her wildness of spirit would have to be subdued. Her thick crown of hair must be tamed in a tight bun under a cap and her voluptuous young body concealed in drab gray.

After Catherine's departure, she felt desperately alone. The minister ignored her completely. Clementine did her best to instruct her in deportment and continued Catherine's lessons in reading and ciphering. Others in the tight-knit community viewed her with alarm, the women because of her perceived effect on the men, the men threatened in their religious beliefs by the desire she aroused.

The situation simmered silently for months with everyone on edge until one of the young farmers came upon Julia picking wild berries and tried to impose himself on her. Her screams brought help. The culprit, brought before the council, blamed his actions on the girl's lustful behavior. She had loosened her hair to feel the morning breeze and hiked up her skirts to make her berry picking easier.

Like mother, like daughter. A menace to the peaceful harmony of the community. Out of the painful humiliation of her accusers came the wish Julia most wanted to come true. To protect the orderly lives from her corruption, she was to be banished from New Cornwall and sent to live with Catherine and Elias in Greenwich Village.

New York City had been the new nation's capital until 1790, when it was moved to Philadelphia. It retained its position as the hub of commerce, banking, and culture. At the time of Julia's arrival in 1797, the population had soared to over fifty thousand, with an additional transient population of merchant seamen off the hundreds of ships that entered the vast harbor and docked along the miles of shoreline on both sides of the Hudson and East rivers, as well as immigrants from Europe and the Indies and the impecunious from other states come to the metropolis to seek their fortune.

Horse-drawn carts rattled through the streets, selling produce, dry goods, pots and pans, and fresh water. Men and women stood on corners with trays of cornbread, meat pies, and fresh oysters. Men on horseback rode hell-bent for leather through throngs of people with no regard for pedestrian safety. Children danced and sang for pennies. Men in rags earned a day's grub passing out handbills that announced everything from the arrival of Jamaican rum in barrels at South Street to *A Night of Shakespeare* at the Park Theater.

Catherine was as happy to see her younger cousin as Julia was to be there. The girl's excitement was contagious. There was much to see and do, but there were also certain responsibilities for the newcomer to the household. Running a boarding house was no easy task. There were beds to be made, chamber pots to be emptied, cupboards to be aired, linens to be washed, meals to be prepared, and dishes to be cleared. It was little more than her chores at Rose Cottage and gave her much more in return. Catherine showered her with affectionate praise for her efforts. The young men living in the house teased her in brotherly fashion, making her blush with pleasure.

One in particular seemed always to be following her with his eyes though he was otherwise polite and respectful. His name was Levi Weeks, Catherine explained. His brother was Ezra Weeks, a man of considerable influence and the builder of the famous City Hotel. Although the elder Weeks had invited Levi to live with him and his family in their downtown mansion, Levi preferred leading the bachelor life on his own with no strings.

Not too long after Julia's arrival on Greenwich Street, Levi asked Catherine's permission to invite her to a musicale evening being given by his brother at his home. He assured her that the city's most respected citizens would be there and that he would function as both escort and chaperon.

Despite her misgivings, Catherine gave in. Sweet Julia had had little enough attention in her young life. Perhaps this social event would offer new opportunities for her future. Since the poor child had no dowry or family standing, her marriage prospects were dim at best. The most Catherine could hope for would be a paid position as a child's companion in a fine house and an opportunity to read books and improve herself to the point that she might aspire to a higher calling such as schoolmistress.

Once they were out of sight of the Ring house, Levi reined in the horse and turned to the young beauty seated so stiffly beside him. "Here are some flowers for your hair. I did not think Mrs. Ring would approve."

Knowing that Catherine would be elsewhere when Levi arrived, she had brushed her hair free of restraints and covered it with a shawl to keep it neat during the journey to Ezra's.

Levi addressed her soberly. "You'll be the loveliest girl there. In fact, I think you are the loveliest girl in all New York."

There *was* one thing he wished to discuss. Ezra's musical evenings were attended by the city's most prominent men. Merchants. Property owners. Bankers. Men of power and influence in government. "Because they work so hard and have so many responsibilities, they have little time to relax and simply enjoy themselves. My brother understands that. And that's why he provides the best foods and wines set out in the most lavish surroundings and embellished by the most beautiful and accomplished young women of the city."

She panicked. "But I am not of that grand, sophisticated company."

He reassured her. "You will put the others to shame."

As if it were an afterthought, he said, "One more thing. To protect their privacy, the guests are all *incognito*—"

"What is *incognito*?"

"The gentlemen's names are never used because—in theory—they are all somewhere else."

The idea puzzled her.

"Never mind, dear Julia. Just remember, do not ask the name of any gentleman. It will offend him."

Julia shivered. "I think I should go home. I am not yet prepared for such high society."

"Calm yourself. You shall be the belle of the ball. Take this."

He gave her a vial of laudanum and helped her to take one small swallow.

The Ezra Weeks mansion glowed with the warm yellow haze of candelabras. A liveried servant opened the door where Ezra Weeks waited to greet his guests. In the background a string quartet could be heard above the hum of men in conversation and the tinkling laughter of women.

Their host bowed effusively and kissed Julia's hand. "How lovely you are. Welcome to my modest home."

"Is that your brother?" she whispered to Levi.

"Yes, but remember, no names."

She could not help being amazed at the opulence of the other women's gowns and jewels and again whispered, "Which is Mrs. Weeks?"

Such innocence. So adorable. So ripe for the plucking. Keeping a straight face, he quietly explained that Mrs. Weeks's mother had suddenly taken ill and she and the children had left for Red Bank that very afternoon.

News of the exquisite newcomer had spread. As Ezra Weeks propelled his brother's discovery through the elegantly furnished rooms, heads turned away from the punch bowls and card tables for an informed assessment. The laudanum had given Julia courage, more than courage, in fact. A sweet delirium suffused her. Like the men in New Cornwall, the eyes of the men here were all on her, stroking her breasts, kissing her shoulders, caressing her hips and thighs with hot insistence.

When one of the men stepped forward with a nod to Ezra and took her hand, she tripped lightly beside him in a haze of urgent desire. A dim passage led to a secluded room where fine wines and sweetmeats offered refreshment and a divan worthy of a seraglio welcomed them with plush pillows covered in rich fabrics.

The room began to spin and she with it into the vortex of an erotic realm beyond her most fanciful dreams of love. The laudanum had replaced her inhibitions with an insatiable greed for sensation. Surrounded by luxury, embraced by this man of prominence and sexual mastery, she gave only a passing thought to the coincidence that his blue eyes, fair skin, and russet hair were so much like her own.

Son of a gun! Nina laughed out loud at J.J.'s unmitigated gall. Alexander Hamilton inadvertently having sex with his own daughter? Why not? It happened in Greek tragedies. A speculation, J.J. said and certainly as good a theory as any. She couldn't wait for J.J.'s final pages.

"Johnny, my daughter's a genius! And so are you. Now, what's on your mind?"

Good news first: the Spring Café had booked him for the next six months at double his previous fee plus a cut of the gate.

"And the bad news?" she asked sympathetically.

The bad news was contained in the large, official-looking envelope in his hand. The National Endowment for the Arts had turned down his application for a grant to produce a film documentary on his father's life as a folk poet, singer, and victim of McCarthyism in political exile.

"I'm so sorry." She knew how much it meant to him.

"But there is another possibility, and that's why I wanted to talk to you. It's a terrible imposition and you've been so generous to me and I value our friendship and—"

"Get to the point. I won't bite."

A recently formed Folk Song Foundation had announced funding for projects designed to improve general public awareness of American folk music. He had been to see them, and they had agreed to consider his proposal.

"Where do I come in?"

"They have money. What they lack is prestige. In order to get matching funds from television and film distributors, they need prestige names on their board."

"Like mine?"

"Like yours."

As a prominent historian she was constantly asked to serve on committees and lend her name to various worthy causes. Rather than show partiality she had turned them all down, choosing instead to give direct scholarships to students of American history. This Folk Song Foundation lay well outside her field. She knew little about folk music except for some old Burl Ives and Pete Seeger records that for all she knew were still in her mother's basement.

"What would be involved?" What was wrong with her? Why couldn't she simply say no and get it over with? Why prolong the agony?

"Just putting you on the letterhead and helping to select the final proposals."

Was he nuts? "Johnny dear. I do not have the time or interest to plow through hundreds of proposals."

Of course not. What he meant was that the foundation would winnow down the submissions to two or three for her consideration.

"What are the proposals like? I've never actually seen one."

He had his NEH proposal with him. "If you don't mind reading it. The format is pretty standard."

"Do I see lemon cookies?" Michael Ludovic asked upon entering the room.

"Darling. You're home early. Just in time to catch me with this handsome man."

"I don't mind your having a lover. You're already pregnant. What I do mind is seeing you stuff yourself with cookies. You've already gained ten pounds."

"Eight."

"Nine!"

He moved the cookies beyond her reach. "Now, what's going on? It all sounded serious coming up the stairs."

He read Johnny's proposal and listened as carefully as a bird-watcher in a marsh to his description of the Folk Song Foundation. "Doesn't sound kosher to me. Who are these people? Where did you find them?"

"As a matter of fact, they found me. One night at the Spring Café. They waited around until the end of the set."

Michael pursed his lips as he always did when

pondering a thought. "Forget the foundation. I've got a better idea."

Instead of a film documentary, why didn't Johnny write a book? McCarthyism sold to a core readership who bought everything published on the subject. Folkies were an additional market. Michael poured himself a cup of tea. It was cold.

"Why don't I make some more? Johnny, why don't you come down to the kitchen with me so we can talk? I've never published a McCarthyism book. Be right back, Nina."

When she was left alone, her earlier uneasiness about John Jacob Black returned. They had taken him in, and now it looked to her as if he was taking them over. His zipper bag lay open. She could see the edge of a manila folder. Curiosity got the better of her.

Inside the folder was the résumé he had sent to Washington with his proposal and which they had returned with their regrets. Hearing the two men on the stairs, she had time only to see that he was married and the father of two.

Chapter Nineteen

The question Nina had to ask herself was three-fold. Should she reveal what she had seen to J.J. and Michael, exposing the fact that Johnny was not what he said, that he was married with children? Or should she confront him first and demand an explanation? Or should she dismiss what she had seen as none of her damned business?

In a success-oriented society, the man had the right to fudge the truth. She could credit him with some defensiveness over his marital status. What did it matter? This was J.J.'s first affair. She often said she wouldn't marry until she was thirty, at least. What's more, his being married did not diminish the fact that he had saved Nina's life and that he was clearly keeping her daughter happy and productive.

In any case, as an outspoken stickler for respecting other people's privacy, she would have a tough time explaining how she just happened to poke her nose into his belongings. Longfellow said it better than she ever could. *Tell me not in mournful numbers; life is but an empty dream.* Why make trouble? *For the soul is dead that slumbers and things are not what they seem!*

Harmony prevailed. No need to rock the boat. She felt as safe as the infant cushioned securely in her womb. Her own writing was going well. She was about to put the finishing touches on the chapter comparing the sexual fixations of her two subjects. Burr's incestuous obsession with his daughter Theodosia and predatory exploitation of women in general, including the infamous Madam Jumel, whom he married and robbed. Hamilton's intensely passionate wartime friendship with fellow officer John Lauren, a South Carolina aristocrat, with its overtones of homosexuality, and his equally passionate affair with his wife's sister, Angelica, that began during his courtship of Betsy Schuyler and continued until his death.

What fascinated her most in terms of a comparative biography was the Maria Reynolds scandal that cost Hamilton the presidency. From Nina's assessment of the known and published facts, it was clear to anyone with half an eye that Aaron Burr had set Hamilton up. In book after book about each man and in stacks of articles in prestige magazines printed on shiny paper, the details of seduction and blackmail were recounted. *But* nobody had bothered to point out Burr's widely known friendship with both Maria and her double-dealing husband.

By Hamilton's own published confession, he was home alone in his Philadelphia house when the beautiful Maria Reynolds appeared at his door late at night, a damsel in distress begging his help. The seat of the federal government was then in Philadelphia. Hamilton was Secretary of the Treasury. Everyone, including Aaron Burr, knew that Betsy Hamilton had taken the children to visit her family in Albany.

At the height of the affair, Maria's husband called on Hamilton asking for certain favors regarding the new government's plan to make long overdue payments to veterans of the Continental Army. Not only did Reynolds jeopardize Hamilton's reputation as an upright family man but also questioned his ethics as the top treasury official in charge of dispensing vast sums of money. Hamilton managed to quash the man's scheme regarding the veterans but felt compelled to explain his affair in print despite the urgings of friends to let it be.

Perhaps, Nina wondered, this act of public self-destruction was the first step toward his ultimate act of personal self-destruction at Weehawken. Or as J.J. insisted, his suicide. Nina would leave that conclusion to her daughter. It was enough for Nina to point out Aaron Burr's personal relationship with Maria Reynolds, plus the fact that as a lawyer he defended her husband in various questionable situations, and what's more when the couple ultimately divorced, guess who handled the case? None other than Aaron Burr!

Poor old Hamilton, Nina sighed. If not for Aaron Burr, he probably would have become president. And if not for Hamilton, Burr would most likely have been president, too! So much wasted talent!

J.J. slipped quietly into the room, tiptoeing to the bookcase on the pretense of looking for something. Nina had to stop herself from laughing. What J.J. really wanted was to see if Nina was reading the latest batch of pages J.J. had left on the hassock earlier in the day.

"Stop worrying, J.J. I'm just about to read it. I had to finish Maria Reynolds first. Now, give your old mom a kiss and get back to work. We don't allow lazy girls in this house."

As her daughter's satiny cheek grazed hers, she realized all the aloe verdi, ginseng oil, and bear grease could not bring back youth. The thought reinforced her sense of gratitude for all the good things in her life now and in the years to come.

Julia Sands would not be so lucky. It took only a few sentences for Nina to fall once more under J.J.'s spell

Ezra Weeks's musical evening had achieved its purpose. The contract to build General Hamilton's new house on the land he had bought in

Harlem was all but assured. There might be other builders in the burgeoning city but none with Ezra's connections in high places. His recently opened City Hotel was the quintessence of modernity with spacious private apartments, palatial public rooms, and an invention of Jefferson's called the dumbwaiter, which operated vertically from floor to floor on rope pulleys.

Ezra had taken no chances on losing Hamilton's commission to anyone else. Or to miss out on Aaron Burr's business, either. The charter for the Manhattan Water Company had been passed by the state legislature. A series of wooden pipes would soon bring fresh water to the polluted city, where it would be stored in a series of wells lined with wooden staves. As the city's foremost building contractor, he held a virtual monopoly on the sources of lumber coming into the city.

The evening at the Weeks mansion had been his clever way of solidifying his relationship with both men. They were his introduction to the highest reaches of New York society, the landed aristocracy, bankers, shipowners, and elected officials. In this new republic a man of his vision and drive might one day be mayor or sit in the Congress. If Colonel Burr could be a senator and a potential president, why not Ezra Weeks?

When his wife and family returned from Red Bank, Ezra changed the venue of his musical soirees to the City Hotel. Hamilton had been away for several weeks and eagerly accepted Ezra's invitation to another of his special entertainments.

Would that lovely young girl be there? Ezra assured him that she would. This second rendezvous of the anonymous lovers proved to be so tempestuous that Ezra dared not intrude on the idyll.

Levi was worried. It was well after midnight. "What will I tell Mrs. Ring? I promised to have Julia home at a reasonable hour. She's trusted me with her ward."

Ezra had no wish to have an angry Quaker woman accusing him of venery. "Tell me, Levi, does Catherine Ring think of you as a suitor for Julia? A potential husband for her lovely cousin?"

Levi admitted that was the case. "I have not encouraged it," he protested.

"Have you taken liberties?"

Levi bristled at the suggestion. "She has come to my bed in the night. Frightened, she says, of Catherine's husband. But I have taken no advantage. We have slept like brother and sister."

"Does Catherine know of her sleepwalking?"

"The floorboards squeak."

"Then here's what you'll do." In the morning Levi would escort Julia back to Greenwich Street with a note from Ezra explaining that the girl had taken ill and been put to bed by his wife. Levi was instructed to behave like a respectful suitor anxious to protect his beloved's good name.

Julia's condition when they reached the boarding house early the next day left no doubt as to the truth of Levi's explanation. She looked as sick as she felt, her face drawn, dark circles under her eyes, too dizzy to walk. Levi carried her upstairs and left her in Catherine's tender care.

A surly Elias Ring was waiting for him in the kitchen. That the brownish liquid in his cup was something stronger than tea was immediately proved by his belligerent attitude. "You and that brother of yours. Think you're better than us, do you? Invite our little Julia to your fancy socials, but Elias Ring ain't good enough. Is that right?"

Elias did not wait for a reply. He answered his own question. "Wrong! Does your brother know who I am? Do *you* know who I am? Have you ever heard of the Battle of Brandywine? That's in Pennsylvania, in case you're too stupid to know. Well, let me tell you this. On September 11, 1777, General Washington and his entire staff asked for shelter at my grandfather's farm at Chad's Ford. I was there. I met them all. General Knox. Lafayette. Polaski, John Laurens from the Carolinas, and Major Hamilton.

"My grandfather was Benjamin Ring. He gave up his bed to Washington. The next morning they were gone. Into battle. And days later an official scroll arrived from continental headquarters thanking us—*thanking* the Ring family for our hospitality in the face of the enemy. A good meal and good night's sleep. And we're not good enough for your brother? Does he think we'll drink our tea from the saucer? I'll tell you one thing. That little girl upstairs? That's the last time she goes to one of your fancy evenings without my wife and me as chaperones."

"I'm sorry!" was all Levi could say. Poor Julia. How he pitied her for having to live in the same house as this man and for lacking the nerve to tell Catherine how her husband pressed himself against her on the narrow staircase and touched her body as if by accident at every opportunity.

The morning was half gone. Ezra was expecting him on a building site on Mulberry Street. Before setting off, he called up the stairs to ask how Julia was. Poor little thing, she had wept on his shoulder during the entire journey home. A spark of chivalry flared within him. He experienced what was for him a strange new emotion. He felt protective toward this wretched creature and deeply ashamed that she trusted him.

Meanwhile, in a sun-filled dining room of the City Hotel, Alexander Hamilton and Ezra Weeks were enjoying an excellent breakfast of fish cakes, coddled eggs with pork sausage, and a steaming dish of fresh oysters from the Rockaways floating in cream. It was a fine day for the journey to Harlem, where they would survey Hamilton's property and decide on the exact place to build The Grange.

"I have a favor to ask you, Weeks."

"Ask away, sir."

"That girl. I know that anonymity is our protection. Even Colonel Burr and I do not acknowledge each other if we happen to glance each other's way. But forgive me, dear friend, if I ask you to tell me who she is. You have my word that I will respect your confidence and that I will on no account attempt to see her anywhere except under your sponsorship."

For Ezra this was yet another opportunity to ingratiate himself with this gentleman of such prominence. "I accept your assurances. Her name is Julia Sands. A healthy young country girl from New Cornwall. Her uncle is the famous minister among Friends, David Sands. Her mother died the day she was born without benefit of marriage. Her father is unknown and is rumored to have been one of Benedict Arnold's officers at West Point. She lives with her cousin Catherine, who keeps a boarding house in Greenwich Street. Hard to believe she's a Quaker, isn't it?"

Hamilton sagged against him, clutching his arm for support. His face had turned ashen, his breathing labored. "Forgive me, good friend. I am suddenly unwell. I'd best make my way home."

He hailed a public hack and was on his way without further discussion. Once alone he burst into wrenching sobs that slashed through his chest like a saber. Now he knew why the face that had gazed at him with such rapture had seemed so strangely familiar. It was a mirror image of himself.

Nina clutched J.J.'s pages to her breast. *Hot damn, J.J.!* Alexander Hamilton bedding his own daughter? Without realizing it? Greek tragedy mixed with a little Shakespeare. The stuff that nightmares were made of. And why not? Didn't George Washington's enemies accuse him of being Hamilton's father, for God's sake? And to give J.J. credit, her scrupulous footnotes certainly supported this possibility. Hamilton's visits to Rose Cottage, the refusal of Julia's mother to reveal her lover's name. The anonymity of Ezra Weeks's entertainments.

As for what happened next, all she could do was wait and see what her brilliant daughter would come up with.

Chapter Twenty

"We're really going to miss you, Johnny, aren't we, J.J.? And Nina, too, of course!"

From J.J. and Nina's bewildered looks, Michael Ludovic realized he'd put his foot in it. The foursome had been enjoying a rare evening out to celebrate the signing of Johnny's book contract. Michael had reserved Nina's favorite corner table at their favorite Italian restaurant, Bruno's on Thompson Street. A cushion had magically appeared for Nina's chair. Now in her third trimester, she had won the doctor's permission to have one sip of champagne.

Michael had led the first round of toasts by welcoming Johnny to Ludovic's small but illustrious publishing house. "Here's to John Jacob Black and the future success of *Wayfaring Stranger: Back Home At Last.*"

Nina picked up from there. "To Johnny! My daughter loves you. My husband loves you. Our unborn baby loves you most of all. I've heard it said that in the movie business it's not enough to succeed; others must fail. We, however, this merry foursome celebrating here tonight, we are something different. We are in the book business. It's not enough for me to succeed. Others—my brilliant J.J. and now you, Johnny—all of us must succeed."

J.J.'s turn. She raised her glass to the Rare Book room at the 42nd Street library. "That's where I first saw Johnny, and that's why I pretended to be sick so that I could get him to take me back to his hotel room and ravish me. And did he ravish me? No! Some nerve. I'll forgive you for that, but I won't forgive you if you don't write a best-seller."

And finally, the guest of honor. "When I arrived in New York six months ago, I was alone, defeated, without friends or much hope. And then the miracle of Forty-second Street happened. I found friendship. And love. And a home. And a brand-new career at the New York Public Library. Maybe one day I'll write that as a song!

"In the meantime, I want to thank J.J. for loving me. Nina for allowing me to live in her beautiful home. And Michael? Michael for believing that I can write a book. I promise you, Michael, I promise to make you proud—and rich!"

That was when, in a rush of emotional excess in good part triggered by the wine, Michael Ludovic let the proverbial cat out of the bag.

"We're going to miss you, Johnny."

"Miss him? Where's he going?" Nina asked.

Johnny looked imploringly at J.J. and reached for her hand. "I was going to tell you. Later. When we were alone."

His files were in London in the old steamer trunk that had originally traveled into exile with the family in 1952. It held his father's musical archives, diaries, letters, press clippings, old 78 RPM phonograph records, and photographs. The trunk was stored in a friend's house in Chelsea. Johnny would be flying to London tomorrow.

Would that "friend" be his wife? Nina wondered. She decided to keep her mouth shut. Why spoil her husband's pleasure in developing a new project with a new, untapped talent? And why spoil her daughter's happiness unless and until it became necessary?

Since her sneak glance inside his zipper bag, she had had growing doubts about his character and background. When you came right down to it, the family really knew nothing about him except for what he had told them. She had sometimes found his posturing pathetic but attributed it to his desire to please. And, as always, at the core of her consideration was his quick action that day in Weehawken and his unquestionable devotion to J.J. Nina would bide her time. She wouldn't mother-hen her daughter. She would keep her own counsel, keep her eyes open, and say nothing.

J.J., for reasons she could not immediately explain, felt curiously detached. She wondered what was wrong with her. Her lover was leaving town. Why wasn't she more upset? A startling revelation answered her question. If she was honest, being madly in love had begun to pall. It was hard to admit even to herself that she was beginning to feel irritated by his constant presence. He was always *there*.

Several times recently she had awakened during the night feeling clear-headed and energized and wanting to go downstairs to do some writing. Invariably, Johnny would wake up and want to know what was wrong, why was she leaving his side, he needed her to warm his feet. Emotionally intimidated, not wanting to insult him, she had stayed where she was, wondering if this kind of thing ever cropped up in Nina's relationship with Michael.

If push came to shove, Johnny could not have picked a better time to take off. She was at the point of putting together the circumstances that culminated in the murder of Julia Sands. Fitting the pieces together would require all of her concentration. If she was painfully honest, she did not want to hear about Johnny's broken guitar string or what he had for lunch or anything that required her attention.

His departure would remove a burden of responsibility that she had to admit was beginning to wear her down. She gave herself rapturously to their last night together, exchanging reassurances of abiding love and teasing demands of faithfulness during their separation. In the morning when they said their good-byes, she lowered her eyes so that there was no chance of his seeing her impatience to be alone with Julia Sands.

If there was one thing Levi Weeks feared, it was his brother's anger. Nevertheless, he had no choice but to tell Ezra that Julia was feeling poorly and would not be attending the evening's festivities.

Ezra was not sympathetic. "I want her here! No excuses! See to it! End of discussion."

Several days had passed since Julia had spent the night at the City Hotel with Alexander Hamilton. Catherine had accepted Ezra's explanation of the girl's indisposition and had caused some cynical amusement by writing him a note thanking him for his concern for the young woman's well-being.

Levi protested, "But, Ezra. She's ill—"

His brother was in no mood to argue. "Tonight's soirée is very important to me. See that she's here."

"But—" Levi stammered.

"But *what*? You're trying my patience!"

"But I thought General Hamilton was on an extended trip to Albany."

Ezra's eyes were hard and calculating. "It's Aaron Burr who requests her presence. He noticed her with Hamilton. He's always been jealous. While the cat's away, the rat wants to steal the cheese."

"You hate both of them, don't you, Ezra?"

The elder brother shrugged. "I don't care about them one way or another except that they have the power to make our fortune. And you must help me by producing Julia Sands for Burr's pleasure. And be careful about the laudanum. Don't give her more than is necessary. We want her frisky and playful. Not sluggish."

"Won't she wonder what happened to Hamilton?"

"Remember. She did not know the gentleman's identity, and for that matter she won't know Burr's either. In fact, in her state of consciousness she might not know the difference. There is a distinct resemblance between the two men. At least in a darkened room. Both are small of stature with strong physiques and small, handsome features. I'm counting on you, Levi."

On this occasion Catherine Sands Ring was adamant. Julia was indeed feeling poorly and could not be allowed to accept Levi's kind invitation. "Be good enough to convey her regrets to Mr. Weeks. Our family appreciates thy brother's patronage. A few more days' rest and perhaps she'll be well enough to attend another evening's entertainment."

Julia, however, was not to be deterred. She knew that Catherine feared that she might turn out to be a wanton like her poor mother before her. Couldn't Catherine see that she knew what she was doing? Levi's brother and all their grand friends thought highly of her. They lavished her with compliments and made much of her beauty and charm. From making beds and scrubbing floors and enduring Elias Ring's bad breath and pawing hands, she had entered a brand-new world of elegance, music, worldly conversation, and courtly men. Their sexual attentions not only made her feel valued and important but revealed a carnality she hadn't known she possessed.

Following her early experience at the Weeks mansion, she yearned for more. She longed to be lost in the skilled embrace of a knowledgeable lover, to feel the softness of satin and velvet cushions while being fed sweetmeats and sips of champagne and ultimately to match the voluptuous demands made on her person while the languor induced by laudanum oozed through her limbs like warm molasses from the Indies.

Having agreed with Catherine that she needed rest, she retired to her tiny bedroom early, locked the door, and climbed out the window to the ladder Levi had thoughtfully provided. Once again he comforted her with laudanum. Once again Ezra welcomed her with elaborate courtesy. Once again she mingled with lavishly gowned ladies and elegant, attentive gentlemen. And once again she was swept into a private room by an anonymous man who seemed familiar yet different from her previous partner.

Thus, with Levi's connivance she was able to enjoy her evening at Ezra's and be back in her room at a respectable hour and none the wiser. The next morning Catherine took Levi aside and told him she favored him as a suitor for Julia's hand and that she had saved up a small dowry as a marriage portion.

Ezra and Levi shared a good laugh at the preposterous notion of Julia Sands as Levi's wife. In Ezra's plan, Levi was made for better things, the wealthy daughter of a merchant prince perhaps.

Christmas 1799 turned out to be a season of mourning. News of George Washington's death at Mt. Vernon on December 14 had traveled slowly over wintry roads to the farthest points of the republic. In the boarding house on Greenwich Street there was another reason for gloom.

Julia lay disconsolate on her bed, her face puffy from crying. "I'm with child, Levi. What will happen to me? Catherine will send me away. Where will I go? I can never go back to New Cornwall."

Levi silently thanked his lucky stars that he had refrained from taking the ultimate liberty with her. She had always seemed like a younger sister to him. He had slept in her bed. They had frolicked like puppies. His sexual taste ran more to blowzy serving girls with big breasts who enjoyed a slap and a tickle and would raise their skirts for a flagon of sweet cider.

"Don't worry. We'll think of something."

"*Someone* has to help me. Your brother. I'll speak to Ezra. One of those fine gentlemen is the father. Ezra must speak to them. Ezra must see that I'm taken care of. A house of my own, I think. And keep for me and my little one."

"A house?" Levi gasped.

The pathetic creature looked at him with a sly expression he'd not previously seen. "And why not? Your brother's friends are responsible. I think we had best see him at once."

Levi was terrified of his brother's wrath. "We'll go first thing in the morning."

Julia Sands rose from her bed with a renewed strength nourished by resolve. "Now! We'll go now."

A servant ushered them into the library. After an unnaturally long wait, Ezra entered. "Am I mistaken or did we arrange for a meeting? I'm afraid I'm in conference."

"I must see you alone, Ezra," Levi said.

The urgency of the situation was clear. From the adjoining room Julia could hear low murmurs interspersed with Ezra's furious protestations. When the brothers returned, however, Ezra Weeks was the embodiment of soft-spoken sympathy.

"My dear Julia. We are your friends. You must

leave everything to me. You must tell no one. Levi will take you back to Greenwich Street. Behave as if nothing is amiss. I will have word for you within a day or two."

He cupped her face in his hands and gently kissed her forehead. "You are precious to me, Julia. Trust me. I will see you're taken care of."

Once they'd gone, he delayed returning to his guests just long enough to write an urgent note to be hand-delivered to General Hamilton and Colonel Burr asking them to meet with him the following morning on a matter of grave importance.

"Gentlemen, I have asked you here in the name of friendship and my deep personal respect for your good names. You have each enjoyed the considerable favors—albeit anonymously—of a lovely young woman. Hamilton here was so taken with her that I revealed her name in confidence, so I think you, Colonel Burr, should also have that information.

"She is Julia Sands, also known as Gulielma Sands. The daughter of David Sands, the minister among Friends. She lives with her cousin Catharine Sands Ring, who keeps a boarding house in Greenwich Street and—she is with child. She believes one of you gentlemen is responsible but has no wish to cause a scandal. I, of course, have not revealed your identities, not now with the elections coming up."

He did not have to remind them that they were

no longer young bucks whose randy adventures could be excused. They were established, middle-aged, married leaders whose reputations would suffer severely both politically and in their ethical integrity as lawyers.

His visitors grew impatient. What did Ezra want them to do?

"Nothing at all!" he said magnanimously. He had simply wanted to advise them of a delicate situation and to assure them he would take care of it with no possible embarrassment to either of them.

Burr expressed what was surely on Hamilton's mind as well as his own. "Why will you take on this responsibility?"

"Friendship is my motive, gentlemen. You have both demonstrated your confidence in my abilities as a builder, and I will continue to be grateful for your recommendations in the future."

Another day went by, a long and agonized day for Julia, before Levi escorted her back to the Weeks mansion. Ezra opened the door himself and greeted them with avuncular smiles. By contrast Levi had been strangely silent and withdrawn on the journey downtown, pretending to concentrate his entire attention on keeping the carriage from skidding on the icy road.

"Have you told her, Levi?" Ezra beamed benevolently.

Levi shook his head no.

Ezra grinned with unconcealed delight and put his arm around Julia's shoulder. "You must forgive Levi's shyness, my dear. He has loved you since the first moment he ever saw you at your cousin Catherine's. He never told you because he thought you regarded him only as a friend. He never told me because he was still only an apprentice and not earning enough to take a wife.

"His heart was broken when he saw you consorting with other men. But that was my fault. I never realized the depth of his feelings for you, and now that this situation has arisen, he wishes to protect your honor and make himself the happiest man alive if you, sweet Julia, will agree to marry him.

"You can see how overcome he is. Will you take him out of his misery and accept his proposal?"

Ignoring Julia's open-mouthed astonishment, Ezra added that henceforth his brother would become his partner, sharing equally in the firm's profits, and what's more, Ezra would buy them a house of their own as a wedding gift.

With the baby on the way, the important thing was to marry at once in a secret ceremony lest Catherine object. He would make the arrangements. Julia was not to tell anyone. It would be best to get the deed done quickly and without interference, he explained. "Think how happy your cousin will be when you return to Greenwich Street as a respectable married woman with a husband who loves you and a brother-in-law who has given you a fine new house!"

"Oh, Levi! Isn't it wonderful?"

Ezra slapped his brother on the back. "Look at the man! He's like all young men about to marry. He looks as if he's condemned to the gallows. I was just the same. Poor fellow. Give your bride-to-be a kiss!"

Levi's arms were stiff, his lips cold. Poor Levi, she thought. Like women immemorial, she forgave his inadequacy as an act of faith. Marriage was a big step for a footloose young man.

Ezra was saying he thought Sunday night would be ideal for the wedding. Levi would be his old self by then. They would be snug as a bug in a rug. On impulse Julia threw her arms around Ezra's neck and with tears in her eyes thanked him for everything.

It was well after midnight when J.J. stopped working and crept quietly up the stairs to bed. If she was honest, she would at this moment have liked to have found Johnny waiting to take her in his arms and kiss the kinks out of her neck. Yet she reminded herself that if he had not left for London that morning, he would not have permitted her to work so late. He would have found some silly excuse to interrupt her in the name of love when she could tell it was really because he was alone and wanted company.

Too exhausted to sleep, she lolled in a scented bath, brushed her hair, did some deep-breathing exercises, and took herself to bed with an apple and a pad. She had scribbled several pages of a miss-you love-you letter to Johnny and sealed it in an envelope when she realized he had neglected to give her his London address and telephone number.

Chapter Twenty-one

J.J. slept fitfully, images of Julia Sands, Hamilton, and Burr mingled and overlapped with John Jacob Black's.

Johnny! She reached for him from need and habit and awoke to find her arms and legs wrapped around the bolster. Toss and turn. Toss and turn. The clock said six. What time was it in London? If she'd had his number, she would have called him.

There was no point trying to sleep. She would go downstairs and get going on Julia Sands's last day on earth. This was what she wanted, wasn't it? Freedom to sleep in peace. Freedom to get up when she felt like it and work when she felt like it without worrying about Johnny Black.

She wondered if she'd ever see him again, and she also wondered if Julia Sands had wondered the same thing on that snowy Sunday in 1799 when Levi Weeks said he would come for her and they would be married.

* * *

It was Sunday, December 22, 1799, New York's official day of mourning for the death of George Washington. For Julia Sands it was a day of secret preparations for her elopement. Levi had said to expect him at eight o'clock. As the hour approached, she could no longer keep the secret. Catherine Ring was the dearest person in the world to her. Hearing her cousin on the landing outside her tiny room, she called to her and confided her plans.

Under Catherine's drab Quaker garments lived the heart and soul of a romantic. "Levi Weeks is a fine young man. He will make thee a fine husband. Fate was unkind to thee, but now thee has a chance to lead a fruitful and honorable life with God's blessing."

Having little finery of her own, Julia had borrowed a pretty little muff from a neighbor. She bit her lips and pinched her cheeks to make them rosy. "He'll be here any minute, Catherine. How do I look?"

"As pretty as thy mother. Here now, let me tie your shawl just so."

A nearby church clock struck the eight o'clock hour. "Hurry, Catherine. Stay in the parlor with Elias and keep him there until after we've gone."

No sooner did the parlor door close than Julia heard the muffled sound of hoofbeats on the icy road. *Levi.* She slipped silently down the stairs and through the front door. Levi hurried to meet her. The snow was falling in soft, enormous flakes that looked like Queen Anne's lace and glistened like stars on Julia's bonnet and muff.

The one-horse sleigh had not stopped in front of the Ring house. It waited a short distance away with a heavily muffled man holding the reins. He scarcely waited for his passengers to climb in before whipping the horse into a gallop, all the while keeping his back to them and saying nothing.

The sleigh careened from side to side on the ice, threatening to overturn, tossing Julia and Levi around like rag dolls. "Make him slow down, Levi!" she begged.

With snowflakes clinging to her lashes, she had not recognized the driver. Levi had not said a word. "Well, if you won't tell him, I will! Driver! Slow down." She tugged at his arm. He turned, his face contorted with exasperation.

"Ezra!" Panic filled her throat. She beat her fists against his back. He turned around and fought her off with his whip.

"Ezra! Please! Where are we going?"

Ezra laid his whip on the horse's rump, shrieking curses. Julia fell heavily against Levi. He turned away from her, huddling against his side of the sleigh.

"Levi? Please! Speak to me!"

She forced him to turn around and threw herself on him.

"I'm sorry, Julia. Sorry," he whimpered. There

would be no wedding. She was to be put aboard a merchant ship bound for England. Ezra's agents would provide her with money and lodgings and a midwife to care for her needs.

The terrible truth dawned on her. She had become too dangerous. She would never see England. They were going to kill her. They would wait until the ship was far out to sea and throw her overboard.

"Please, Levi! Ezra? Hear me! I'll go away. Far away! Never say a word. I promise! Levi! You said you loved me. Don't let him do this!"

The sleigh was racing down the Broad Way near the turnoff to Lispenard's meadow when Julia lunged forward in desperation and grabbed the reins. The horse reared up and bolted into the meadow, stumbling and sliding in the mud and rocks of the deserted marsh, crashing to a halt at the high stone wall Ezra Weeks had built around Aaron Burr's new Manhattan Well.

Julia jumped from the sleigh and tried to run, with Ezra close behind. The swampy terrain was like quicksand, trapping her legs and pulling her down. Ezra attacked her with all his strength.

"Ungrateful slut!" How dared she doubt his word. Or his generosity. Everything had been arranged. Money and clothes for her journey. Lodgings in London. A monthly allowance. Did she really think he'd allow Levi to marry her? A nobody? With nothing to offer but a bastard child? He had better plans for his brother than that!

With superhuman effort Julia broke free and got to her feet. "Help me, Levi!"

The younger man cowered with fear.

Ezra dragged her back to the sleigh. She struggled with him and managed to fight him off in a desperate bolt for freedom. It was hopeless. There was no escape. The stone wall of the Manhattan Well loomed above her. Panic gave her the final burst of energy to scale the wall, clawing handholds on the rough surface and kicking wildly at Ezra to fend him off.

At the top of the wall, she raised her face to the snow-filled heavens, "All I wanted was loving kindness!"

Ezra was right behind her. As he seized her ankle, she kicked him in the head hard enough to send him howling to the ground.

"Whore! There's no escape! Take hold of her, Levi!"

"No, Ezra, I can't!"

"Do as I tell you. Seize her and throw her into the well."

"Please, Ezra. Don't make me do this. It wasn't supposed to end this way. You said we were putting her on a ship for England, didn't you?"

Clinging to the wall above him, Julia's voice was strangely calm. "And you believed him, Levi?"

Her lover pulled himself up beside her. Their

faces touched. "I'm sorry, Julia. Please, please, forgive me—"

Ezra's voice rasped at Levi's heels. "Out of my way, you idiot!" He knocked the younger man off the wall and seized Julia Sands by the throat. "You have no one to blame but yourself, miss! Don't you realize that you nearly destroyed my life?"

With the little amount of breath she had left, she gasped, "You destroyed your own life."

This truth so enraged him that he lost all control.

"No more! No more!" he roared, beating her savagely with his fists until she slumped against him. With a final surge of brute strength, he hoisted her to the top of the wall and hurled her into the well.

"I loved you, Levi! Loved you! Loved you!" her voice a repeated echo until an abrupt splash silenced it.

Ten days later, on the cold, misty morning of the second day of the new century, the body of Julia Sands was taken from the well. The icy water had frozen her intact like a marble statue, Ophelia-like in her beauty, her hair in wild disarray, her bosom exposed. Only the dark purple bruises attested to her struggle.

In the aftergloom of Washington's death, the citizens were ripe for sensation. At first when Julia failed to return to the Ring house, Catherine assumed the newly wedded couple had sought privacy at an inn or at Ezra Weeks's City Hotel. Her sweet thoughts of Julia's happiness faded abruptly the following day when Levi nonchalantly reappeared, explaining that he had attended Mayor Varick's memorial service for George Washington with Ezra and his family and had remained with them overnight.

When Catherine asked where Julia was and what of their wedding, he protested ignorance of her whereabouts and vehemently denied any plans for an elopement. For ten days search parties fanned out in all directions until someone spotted the borrowed muff near the Manhattan Well and found the body.

A general hue and cry went up for the arrest of Levi Weeks. People had seen him with Julia many times. When Julia borrowed the muff, she had been unable to resist confiding in her neighbor and swearing her to secrecy. Catherine more than anyone was heartbroken at Julia's fate and held Levi and his brother responsible for her tragic end.

Ezra Weeks used all of his political clout to prevent his brother's arrest. He pooh-poohed the notion that Levi would elope in the dark of the night with a girl of such low degree. If and when his brother married, it would be a fine occasion in church attended by both family's many friends and associates. What's more, Levi was at home with him that fatal Sunday night.

To no avail. A circus atmosphere swept through the city. Julia's body was taken to the Ring house, where hundreds of excited people waited in line to view her. When the crowd threatened to riot, the open coffin was removed to the street outside the house. Women wept and warned their daughters against false-hearted lovers. Men cried out for Levi's death at the end of a rope.

Levi's arrest was not only inevitable, it was the prudent way to protect him from mob justice. Ezra accompanied him to the Bridewell. Alone with him in his cell, Ezra could see that his brother was sick with fear and guilt and on the verge of confession.

"Trust me, Levi. Everything will be fine. Just stay with our original story. You attended the church service with me and stayed the night. You were fond of this girl and are sad about her tragic fate. Nothing more."

"But what if the coroner finds out that she's with child. They'll blame it on me! They'll say I killed her."

"Don't worry. I have connections. The finest lawyers in all of the country will defend you and get you off."

The trial date was set for the end of March in the City Hall courthouse. Well before that date Ezra summoned Hamilton and Burr to meet with him once again on a matter of grave importance. Politeness prevailed. Each was aware of the Quaker girl's death; who would not be? And of Levi's arrest. Both expressed distress at the brutal murder and offered Ezra their sympathy for Levi's predicament. They considered it unlikely that he had committed so violent an act and suggested as consolation that an as yet unknown assailant was responsible. Or, as Ezra had theorized publicly to all who would listen, that Julia was mentally afflicted and had committed suicide in a fit of depression.

The courtesies having been exchanged, what was the matter of grave importance? These were hectic times. Washington's death had effectively brought the old order to an end with the end of the eighteenth century. New political alliances were being honed. A new presidential election was in the offing. The decades-old rivalry between the two men had escalated into a bitter struggle for power. The winter and spring of 1800 had turned former Revolutionary War comrades against each other, Hamilton on the side of the Federalists, Burr with the Jeffersonians. As befitted gentlemen of the legal profession, they attacked each other's principles viciously on the hustings and in handbills while behaving with civility in private situations. Would their good friend and boon companion Ezra Weeks be so kind as to explain his summons?

"My beloved brother is charged with murder.

He is innocent. The public wants to see him hang. Who better to defend him than the two most prominent and respected lawyers in the entire country? General Hamilton and Colonel Burr."

Impossible, they agreed. The demands of the coming election would have each of them traveling the countryside, making speeches and rallying their respective supporters. Burr put their objections into perspective. "Think of this, dear friend. How would it look for the two of us to put aside our enmity and skip hand in hand into court to defend a foolish young man accused of killing an equally foolish young girl? Wouldn't we likewise appear foolish?"

"Not a bit. You see, gentlemen, there are always two good reasons for a difficult decision. The private reason, in this case the desire of two prominent middle-aged men to conceal their . . . shall we say friendly acquaintanceship with the victim. And the public reason? To defend my brother's innocence and the Weeks family's good name out of compassion and loyalty to me, your always loyal and obedient servant."

On March 31, 1800, in the presence of the mayor and as many of the city's leading citizens as could be crammed into the City Hall courthouse, the trial of *The People* v. *Levi Weeks* began. Defending him were Alexander Hamilton, Aaron Burr, and a mutual friend of both, Brockholtz Livingston.

By the following day, having heard the testimony of twenty-seven witnesses challenged by the eloquence of the defense team, the jurors took less than five minutes to return the verdict of not guilty. Their goal achieved, Hamilton and Burr brushed aside the well-wishers and made their separate ways out of the courtroom. The spectators congratulated themselves for being part of a historic occasion and poured into the street to brag of their experience.

With one exception. Catherine Sands Ring rose from her seat, a distraught figure in Quaker gray, and followed Hamilton to the street, calling his name until he stopped. Pointing an accusatory finger, she cried out loud and clear for anyone to hear, "If thee die a natural death, there is no justice in Heaven!"

It was at that point that Nina called down the stairs to say Michael was home and dinner was almost ready. A perfect time to stop, J.J. decided. The day had whizzed by in a flash like so many recent days. Tonight she would gather her thoughts for the final stage of her hypothesis that Julia's murder had led inexorably to Hamilton's decision to sacrifice his own life for the sake of his country.

She knew it was presumptuous of a neophyte historian to suggest that the trial of Levi Weeks marked the beginning of Hamilton's psychological decline. What happened during the next four years was well documented. But the ever nagging question remained: How come? By presenting the facts in a logical and persuasive way, she was determined to show that Hamilton sacrificed his own life in order to safeguard the country from Aaron Burr.

"We're wai-ting, J.J. Get your butt up here or Michael and I will eat all the calamari!" Nina raised her voice in an exuberant, ear-splitting falsetto. " '*La Donna e mobile; qual piuma al ve-e-e-e-e-ennnnnnto!*' " *Rigoletto*, their favorite opera.

Michael joined in, " '*Muta d'accento; e di pensiero.*' Do you realize what you're singing, Nina? What it means in English?"

Amidst the banging of pots and the clatter of cutlery being flung on the table, she waved her ladle at him with an operatic flourish and bopped him on the head. She continued the melody with her own impromptu libretto. "What the hell do I care? What the hell do I care? I'm cooking paaaasta. For all those I love. La-laaa. La-laa . . . okay, I'll bite. What was I singing?"

"You won't like it."

"Try me."

"You asked for it. You were singing the Duke of Mantua's part and he—not I—was saying, 'All women are feather-brained. To one thing never constant.' "

She fed him an olive. "Sounds better in Italian."

This would be the first meal Nina had cooked

since the doctor had confined her to bed. The amniocentesis showed the baby had all its parts. She had refused to look. She did not want to know the child's sex until it was born.

"Angel hair primavera! Oh, Mom. My favorite."

"And a bottle of Orvietto. *My* favorite." Michael draped a dish towel over his forearm and pulled the cork with a flourish. "*Signora et signorina, per piacera.*"

They ate and drank in congenial silence.

"Nina could show that Italian chef a thing or two," her husband sighed.

It was their first home-cooked family meal in months. "Too bad Johnny isn't here," Nina said by way of consoling her daughter.

"I'm cool, Mom. I'm going to try to finish Julia Sands while he's gone."

"Good idea. No sense moping around. He'll be back before you know it," Michael said.

J.J. remembered the letter she'd written him.

"That reminds me. Did Johnny leave his London address with you?"

Nina turned to Michael, "You must have it, darling."

"I wrote him a letter, Mom. You know something? I think it's the first love letter I ever wrote."

Michael flipped through the scraps of paper on the kitchen bulletin board. "Not here."

An odd expression crossed his face. Nina instantly knew what he was thinking and prayed that they were wrong. "The fridge, Michael. He probably stuck it on with the Elvis magnet."

"Not here. He must have given it to my secretary. Tell you what, J.J. Give me the letter. I'll mail it from the office. I'm sure he wouldn't take off for London without telling us where to find him."

Chapter Twenty-two

That night before they went to bed, Nina could feel Michael's anxiety. She could tell he was only pretending to read the manuscript he had brought home.

"It's okay, Michael. Stop worrying."

He kept his eyes on the work at hand and made a few marks with his pencil. "I don't know what you're talking about."

"Johnny. We both know what's happened. Let's not kid ourselves. He's done a midnight flit."

"Don't be silly. Just because he forgot to leave his address? What's the big deal? Anyway, he probably gave it to Lisa. It's in her Rolodex, I'm sure."

"How much money did you give him."

He slammed the manuscript on the floor. "None of your damned business."

"You are my business."

"The terms of a contract is privileged information between publisher and author."

She stroked his hand and raised it to her lips for a gentle kiss. "You know something? I was reading Flexner's biography of Hamilton. He said Hamilton was the most psychologically wounded of all the founding fathers. That he seemed to be two different men. One was the paragon of charm, the other the wounded child who never got over the trauma of his early years. It made me think of Johnny. So needy. So desperate for approval and love."

"Thank you, Frau Freud. I can't wait until you analyze me. What am I, his father figure? Let's not jump to conclusions. I'll lay you odds his address and London phone number are in my office as we speak."

They both knew it wasn't so. He turned out the bed light. They held each other in the dark.

"He did save your life, Nina," he said softly, smoothing her hair.

Nina was beginning to understand what had happened. She was having a baby. Michael needed to have a baby, too, a baby of his own, an infant talent he could nurture the way he had nurtured her all those years ago.

She had drifted into a half sleep when she felt him get up.

"You okay? Not my cooking, I hope."

He was dressing in the dark. She turned on the light.

"What are you doing?"

"This thing is driving me nuts. I've got to know *now*! I'm going to the office."

In the middle of the night? Johnny might have saved her life. He didn't own it. Couldn't this wait until morning? Michael was adamant. All she could do was kiss him good-bye and call the office number again and again even before he could possibly have arrived until at last he picked up.

"Michael?"

"Who did you think it was?"

"Please, darling—"

"Or maybe you were just checking up on me. Maybe I was somewhere else. With some young thing who wants to write a book?"

She'd never seen him like this, so hurt and angry. He was always the rock of Gibraltar.

"Please, darling. Don't be so hard on yourself. Come home. I love you."

"You didn't ask me about the address. Well, it's not here. In fact, Lisa left a note on my desk asking for it so she could send him the letter I dictated this afternoon."

When he returned, Nina was waiting for him on the front steps wearing a coat over her nightgown. "Another five minutes and I'd have called out the posse."

"Have a doughnut?" He had stopped at an all-night coffee shop for the love offering, a ritual that went back to their earliest days together. It was too nice to go inside. They sat on the front steps with the bag of doughnuts. Orchestra seats for the pageant of Greenwich Village life. Dog walkers. Joggers. A pickup truck piled high with vegetables taking a shortcut to the farmers' market.

A police car slowed down. "You people okay? Locked out or something?"

"Have some doughnuts, officer." Michael tossed him the bag. He helped Nina to her feet. "As you can see, we're pregnant!"

The one discordant note had vanished. They were back in tune. "Those cops looked disappointed. They were hoping maybe we'd been mugged."

Back in bed, lights out, Michael sighed. "No question about it. I've been conned."

"You've been a decent, generous man."

"Charmed out of my socks."

"Johnny's a spoiler, Michael. There's probably some explanation. The immediate question is, what do we tell J.J.?"

"How's she doing with Julia?"

"She's working her tail off. I've got to hand it to her. Another few days is what she says."

"Then let's just say Lisa threw away his address by accident. So we'll have to wait to hear from him."

For J.J. the last part was the hardest. One of her professors had once said good writing was lean and meaningful. Don't try to say everything. Be selective to prove your points. Make every word count.

Much had happened between the Levi Weeks trial in March 1800 and the Weehawken duel in July 1804. To help her in her labors, she pinned three hand-made signs at eye level above her desk. Nina's "What happened? And how come?" Professor Canner's "Lean and meaningful!" and a new slogan of her own: "Do I need it? Do I need it? DO I NEED IT?#@+!"

The trial of Levi Weeks was soon forgotten. Hamilton and Burr returned to their adversarial positions in the battle for political clout in the elections of 1800. Less than a month after Levi's acquittal, Hamilton wrote a diatribe against his own Federalist leader, President John Adams, denouncing him as unfit to be president and urging the party to back his friend Charles Cotesworth Pinckney instead.

The pamphlet was printed and ready to be distributed when wiser heads talked him out of it. That didn't stop Burr's spies from swiping a copy from the printer and giving it to the newspapers. This further eroded Hamilton's influence in his own party while it strengthened Burr's position as a viable Jeffersonian candidate for president.

The thought of Burr as the nation's chief executive drove Hamilton into a frenzy of vicious attacks. He called Burr unprincipled and dangerous and warned that if Burr was elected president he would seize dictatorial control like Bonaparte in France.

When the electoral votes were counted, President Adams and the Federalist party were roundly defeated. But Jefferson's party couldn't celebrate because he and Burr each received the same number of votes: seventy-three. According to the Constitution a tie vote for the presidency meant that the House of Representatives would have to decide the winner.

In June 1800, the federal government moved from Philadelphia to the new capital, Washington City, on the banks of the Potomac River. The incumbent president, John Adams, and his wife, Abigail, became the first residents of the White House. Congress convened for the first time in its permanent home. But the electoral ballots for the next president would not be counted until February 11, 1801.

For six days Hamilton campaigned relentlessly against Aaron Burr and for the election of Thomas Jefferson as the "lesser evil." Although Hamilton's Federalist friends turned their backs on him and voted for Burr, Jefferson prevailed.

The outcome of the election did little to appease Hamilton's anger. Tasting the bitter ashes of his own political career, he blamed his problems and failures on one man, Aaron Burr. The lovely face of Julia Sands haunted him. He would never know if he was her father and thus guilty of an abominable act of incest. Nor could he rid his conscience of the personal shame of participating in that farce of a trial.

Considering Burr's devious connections with Ezra Weeks, he could not shake the suspicion that Burr was involved in the actual murder.

The wheel had turned. The Jeffersonians were in power. If the Federalists were ever to recapture the public's imagination, they would need a forum for expressing their theories of government. And for attacking their enemies. With the financial backing of friends, Hamilton founded the *New York Evening Post.*

His pleasure was short-lived. Once again the deadly shadow of Aaron Burr appeared like a vulture. In November 1801, Hamilton's firstborn son, Philip, and his friend Stephen Fox went to the theater. By chance they were seated beside a certain Captain George L. Eacker, a prominent Republican and friend of Aaron Burr. Before the play began, Eacker used the occasion to make snide remarks about Alexander Hamilton's military career and his financial dealings as the former Secretary of the Treasury.

The two high-spirited young men took umbrage and countered with equally snide remarks about Eacker. Eacker was embarrassed in front of his friends and tried to put the younger men in their place. "I will not be insulted by a set of damned rascals."

The situation accelerated. Stephen Fox challenged Eacker to a duel by which time both men had cooled down. The next morning they exchanged fire without injury. That should have ended the matter. Except that Philip Hamilton felt cheated. He in turn challenged Eacker to a duel.

Hamilton was proud that his son would defend his father's honor. Because Eacker fired wide in his meeting with Fox, Hamilton assumed he would do the same with Philip. Since he did not wish his son to kill or maim the older man and have that on his conscience, he told Philip to reserve his fire until after Eacker shot and then discharge his own pistol in the air.

This time Eacker's aim was true. The handsome, brilliant, cherished son of Alexander Hamilton fell mortally wounded. Bleeding horribly and in unspeakable pain, he lingered through the night. Hamilton lay beside him, holding him throughout the ordeal, heedless of the young man's mother and siblings, doctors, and friends gathered around.

Hamilton never forgave himself. He could have prevented the duel. He could have forbade it. He could have intervened. Instead, he had indulged his overweening pride. How smug he had been at the thought of his glorious golden son defending his honor! How grotesque and stupid of him to have enjoyed his son's boorish behavior in a public place no matter who the target was or how justified.

In the savagery of his grief, he placed the blame on one man. Aaron Burr had murdered his son as surely as if Burr himself had pulled the trigger. If revenge was slow in coming, he was ready when the opportunity came.

At the beginning of 1804, as Burr's term of office as vice-president was drawing to a close, Hamilton suffered yet a further betrayal from the party he had helped found. The New York state Federalists were so desperate to find a candidate for governor that they decided to back a Jeffersonian who would be grateful for their support. And who was that someone, that well-known Jeffersonian who his Federalist colleagues naively believed would be putty in their hands? Who else but Aaron Burr!

That was when Hamilton began his chaotic slide down the slippery slope to his death. Aaron Burr was fond of saying, "Great souls concern themselves little with petty morals." Therefore, when Hamilton and a group of Federalist party regulars met secretly at Lewis's City Tavern in Albany in February, two of Burr's spies were in an adjoining room, eavesdropping.

In the plainest terms, Hamilton's group wanted their party to back Burr for governor for one expedient reason. They were sure he could win. Not if Hamilton could help it. To him Burr was a danger to the country, a man motivated solely by his own ambitions who would do anything for personal power and to get himself out of debt.

From all reports, Hamilton's objections no longer mattered. Despite his humble beginnings, he was increasingly dismissed as an elitist. A newly emerging working class was giving their support to Burr. Without a public platform, Hamilton campaigned behind the scenes. And that was where Fate stepped in at a private dinner party in Albany given by a prominent judge named John Taylor.

Among the guests was the judge's son-in-law, Dr. Charles D. Cooper, who listened goggle-eyed to the vicious things Hamilton was saying about Burr. So what did the good doctor do? He wrote a letter to a friend repeating what he had heard in copious detail. And so the plot thickened.

Nobody knows how, although it's easy to know why, this private letter about a private dinner party conversation found its way into print in the *Albany Register* and was then reprinted in other newspapers and pamphlets. While the letter excited gossip, the conventional wisdom was that Hamilton's antipathy to Burr was an old story and would not influence voters. Whether it did or not remains a question. On April 25, Aaron Burr lost the governorship to Morgan Lewis by eight thousand votes. And who did he blame? Alexander Hamilton.

That would have been that except that Hamilton's father-in-law, Philip Schuyler, suddenly decided to defend the family integrity by contradicting Dr. Cooper's allegations in his own letter to the chairman of the committee. His motive was straightforward, familial, and tragic in its consequences. All he wanted to do was set the record straight and defend his beloved daughter Betsy's husband.

Cooper then retaliated by writing an angry retort to Schuyler, insisting that his original letter was true and that Hamilton considered Burr "a dangerous man and one who ought not to be trusted with the reins of government."

Furthermore, Dr. Cooper wrote, "I could detail to you a still more despicable opinion which General Hamilton has expressed of Mr. Burr." What Schuyler didn't consider until too late was the implication of the word *despicable*. In the vocabulary of the day, despicable meant aberrant sexual misconduct.

Once again somebody leaked the letter to the *Albany Register*. Once again other newspapers pounced on the scandal and gleefully reprinted the previous accusations. This time the uproar refused to die down. The New York governorship was Aaron Burr's last chance at political power. All signs had pointed to victory until the appearance of the Cooper and Schuyler letters. Burr brooded for several weeks over being called "despicable" with all its sinister implications. In mid-June he decided to act.

The timetable of destiny began its deadly acceleration on June 18 when William Van Ness, a mutual friend of both men, personally presented Hamilton with a formal letter from Burr. Enclosed with it were copies of both of Dr. Cooper's letters plus newspaper coverage of their contents. Burr's letter demanded a "prompt and unqualified acknowledgment or denial of the use of any expressions which could warrant the assertion of Dr. Cooper." In other words, if Hamilton denied calling Burr "despicable," he would be calling Cooper a liar. But if he acknowledged Cooper's report as true, Burr would have no choice but to defend his honor in the only way open to him.

To challenge Hamilton to a duel.

Hamilton mulled things over for a few days before answering with a long and rambling letter that said in essence that he could neither deny nor acknowledge Dr. Cooper's recollection of what was said at the dinner party and that he trusted Burr would see things the same way, adding, "If not, I can only regret the circumstances and must abide the consequences."

The consequences meant only one thing.

A duel.

Burr responded promptly and with growing annoyance. "I regret to find in it [Hamilton's letter] nothing of that sincerity and delicacy which you profess to value!" Once more he demanded to know whether Hamilton had expressed opinions derogatory to Burr's honor as revealed by Cooper.

By June 22, Hamilton's patience ran out. In a tense meeting with his most trusted friend, Nathaniel Pendleton, Hamilton said he considered Burr's letter rude and offensive. And that it was not possible for him to give it any other answer than that Burr must take such steps as he might think proper.

In plain English, a duel.

There was no turning back. Burr instructed William Van Ness to find out when it would be "convenient" for Hamilton to receive a "communication." For several more days Pendleton and Van Ness were kept busy rushing back and forth between the two adversaries, carrying letters that intensified the quarrel.

At the end of June, Hamilton made his will and put his affairs in order. A hint of what he planned to do was included in his papers. "I have resolved, if our interview is conducted in the usual manner, and it pleases God to give me the opportunity, to reserve and throw away my first fire and I have thoughts even of reserving my second fire—thus giving a double opportunity to Col. Burr to pause and to reflect."

On July 3, the parties agreed to meet on the morning of July 11 at Weehawken.

* * *

"J.J. Is that you?" Nina called.

The younger woman stood hesitantly on the landing outside Nina's parlor, her face wet with tears. This was one time she needed her mommy.

"What's wrong? Don't just stand there. Come in, darling."

She advanced as far as the doorway. "I feel like such a wimp. I can't stop crying. It breaks my heart. I just lived through Hamilton's death scene. Hours and hours of excruciating pain and a smile of triumph on his face at the end. He'd saved the nation from Aaron Burr. He'd paid his debt to Julia Sands and to his own murdered son."

"Well, pull yourself together. We'll talk about it later. We're about to have a guest."

"Who?"

"You'll see."

The doorbell rang.

"Right on cue. Run down and let her in."

Vera Boyle looked considerably better than the last time they'd seen her. Once settled down with a cold drink, she got straight to the point. "I saw the announcement of Johnny Black's memoir in this week's *Publishers Weekly*."

Nina clapped her hands enthusiastically. "Isn't it wonderful? Wasn't it brilliant of Michael? One minute Johnny was describing his family's life in exile after the McCarthy hearings. Next thing you know, Michael's got him doing a book. We're all very excited about it, aren't we, J.J.?"

"Very excited."

Why was her mother doing the fakey-poo routine she usually saved for book parties? Nerves. Nina had once explained that when she felt endangered, she would find herself talking in a very exaggerated manner like a road-company Katharine Hepburn. "Now, Vera, to what do we owe the pleasure of your company?"

Vera wasted no time on small talk. Following Prunella Dove's death from cancer, the network had asked Vera to clear out her office. In one of her files was a dossier on John Jacob Black.

"On Johnny? But why?"

"She may have been difficult, but she was nobody's fool. If she was getting involved with someone, she always checked them out."

"And? What did she find out? That he was arrested for spitting on the sidewalk?"

"John Jacob Black is not his name, and his father was never called before the House Un-American Activities Committee."

Chapter Twenty-three

Vera Boyle handed Nina a Bergdorf-Goodman shopping bag. "It's all here. And no, I don't want it back. Prunella Dove caused enough grief. Michael Ludovic has one of the best reputations in publishing. I would hate to see him embarrassed by a fake memoir. The media would jump on him like a pack of jackals and tear him to shreds."

She rose to go. "I hope this makes up for what Prunella tried to do to you and your baby. She knew she was dying. The pain was horrific. The drugs strung her out. She did not want to go gently into that good night. She raged against the dying of the light until the very last second. But she was truly appalled by what she'd done. Again and again she asked me, 'Is Nina okay?' I was with her when she died. The last thing she said was 'Tell Nina I'm sorry.'"

They waited until Michael got home and opened the shopping bag together. Prunella's research was prodigious. Computer printouts of the entire Mc-

Carthy hearings, newspaper coverage of all who were actually called, those who were rumored to be called, those who took the Fifth Amendment and those who announced through spokesmen that they were leaving the country.

The detective agency Prunella had hired could find no mention of a folk singer named John Jacob Black, Sr. Nothing in the Lincoln Center Library, nothing in the voluminous archives of the Library of Congress, where the most obscure record labels were catalogued.

Through a contact in Washington, copies of the family's passports were obtained. In 1952, when they fled to England, his father's passport application read John Jacob Black, Sr. "a.k.a. Jonah Schwartz"; his wife and son's papers were similarly revised.

A report from a private investigator in London further revealed the painful truth. Johnny's mother had divorced his father and remarried. She felt pity for her son and agreed to tell everything she knew. Johnny's father was a failure from the word go. He had tried desperately to have a career as a folk singer. His heroes were Woody Guthrie, Burl Ives, Pete Seeger, and the like. In his own mind he sang and played the guitar as well as they, but the world disagreed. Managers turned him down. Record companies turned him down. He went so far as to make records with his own private label.

When the McCarthy hearings were at their height, he somehow got the idea that he would be called to testify. After all, he had recorded songs about the working man. He had appeared at left-wing rallies. He could defend his rights as an American to demand equality and freedom. He could deny that he was ever a member of the communist party while passionately defending the right of the party to exist.

He deluded himself that appearing before the committee would improve his professional standing and open the doors that had been closed to him. For weeks before leaving America, he had boasted to all who would listen about how he was going to handle Joe McCarthy and Roy Cohn. When his friends began to lose interest, he spread the word that a secret informant had warned him that he would be killed if he appeared and so he was taking his family abroad under an assumed name. By that time he was regarded as a blowhard and was quickly dismissed as a nuisance.

He had heard the English were anti-Semitic. Schwartz was German for Black. John Jacob was his tribute to a ballad singer he admired, John Jacob Niles. Britain was not the best place to make a new life in those early postwar years, and as a foreigner he was unable to get a work permit. His money ran out. Johnny's mother worked as a seamstress in a tailor shop for cash.

Yet as far as their little boy knew, his father was

a famous folk singer in America who had been forced to leave for political reasons. His father played his records as if they had been distributed by Decca and blamed some top executives for conspiring against him and canceling his contract.

The youngster believed his father. He learned to play and sing like him and deeply believed that one day father and son would return to the States in triumph. Their first step was to be an audition for a folk song series on BBC Radio. Halfway through their first song, the producer curtly dismissed them. "This isn't Amateur Night at Blackpool."

The next day John Sr. cut his wrists. Johnny found the body. When his mother got home, she cleaned up the mess and said it had been bound to happen sooner or later. She said she was glad it happened sooner because if his fantasy life had continued, she would be slitting her own wrists.

A short time later, Johnny suffered a breakdown and was committed to an institution for the next five years. His future wife had been his psychiatrist. Asserting that he was no danger to himself or anyone else, she had had him released into her custody and married him.

No matter how hard she tried, she could not totally free him from his fixation on his father's tragic career, a career that never happened. Somehow he got the idea that he was like Hank Williams, Jr., and that he had to carry on his father's memory.

The London report, dated only six months before, concluded, "His ex-wife said he was determined to follow in his father's footsteps. All that saved him from the same fate was that he was taller, better-looking, and more charming than his father. Women adored him. He had read that there were women record producers in America and that the United States government was handing out grants to musicians. That's where he was going, and that's the last she'd heard from him. She'd filed for divorce, charging desertion."

Michael Ludovic sank back in his chair. "Poor bastard."

"What are you going to do?" Nina asked.

"I'm not calling Scotland Yard if that's what you mean," he snapped.

Nina reached for his hand. "You know that's not what I mean."

He raised her hand to his lips and kissed her palm. "I know that's not what you meant. Forgive me, darling. It's not the money. He's probably used it to pay debts. School fees. God knows what else. It's Johnny himself I'm worried about."

J.J. had been silent throughout the revelations of Johnny's past. "All he wanted to do was make music and make people happy. Is that a crime? Don't you see? He had no identity of his own. He had to invent one. Not like us. We've got a home.

We've got a family. We love each other and help each other and rejoice in each other. What has he got?"

Michael held both women close, the yet-to-be-born baby cossetted in their shared embrace. "He has friendship and understanding here if he wants it. I'll get the same London agency to track him down."

Over the next several weeks, Johnny might have been on their minds; he was not in their conversation. There was too much to do. The final edit of *Strange Destiny* ran parallel to the final days of Nina's pregnancy. The uncorrected proofs and the howling baby girl were delivered the very same day. Michael hefted the two pounds of book with the same tenderness as he held his six-pound daughter, feeling a parental thrill of proprietary credit for both.

A few days later, Michael and J.J. sipped coffee at the kitchen table, trying to decide how to tell Nina the good news and wondering if she would consider it good news. They had brought mother and babe home from the hospital that morning. The new nanny, Mrs. Eisel, had come downstairs from the nursery to say Nina was nursing little Michaela and would let them know when they could come upstairs.

Couldn't they wait and tell her tomorrow? J.J. suggested. "It's her first day home, Michael. She should really be resting. Why bother her now?"

"No, J.J. It's got to be now. If she hears about it from someone else, we're really cooked."

"Tell you what, why don't I wait here and let you go up alone? You know? Mother, father, and child? I'll stay here and do the dishes."

"Two coffee mugs is not dishes."

The nanny, looking crisp enough to have been dipped in starch, bustled in with the self-importance of a White House press conference. "You may go up."

Exquisite. Serene. It was hard to find words to describe the living portrait of mother and child that greeted them. The miracle of birth continued to be the most touching and mysterious gift in nature.

"Isn't she beautiful, Michael?"

"The most beautiful baby girl ever born."

Remembering her older daughter's presence, Nina quickly added, "J.J. was beautiful, too. You should have seen her, Michael."

"That's because they both take after their beautiful mother."

Nina let the compliment pass. "Okay, guys. Stop looking so worried."

"What do you mean?"

"Stop trying to look innocent. I know exactly what's going on!"

She held them in suspense for another tantalizing moment before breaking into a delighted grin. "And I think it's wonderful! I'm so proud of you,

J.J. I must be the luckiest woman in the entire world!"

The whole thing had happened so quickly. Michael's rights department had sent the first *Strange Destiny* page proofs to a number of magazines for possible reprint. The prestigious new *Young Historica Magazine* had called back within hours with an offer to excerpt J.J.'s section on Julia Sands. They wanted to run it as a cover story to coincide with publication of the book later in the year and to build a publicity campaign around J.J.

"The whole idea is to sell history to young people!" J.J. enthused. "You know. Kids who couldn't care less about either Hamilton or Burr. Give them a beautiful young Quaker girl who thinks she's getting married and winds up dead in a well, they'll stay up reading half the night to find out what happened!"

Nina nodded in agreement. "Sounds good to me. I remember what it was like studying history in high school. Deadly dull names, dates, and places. If you were good at memorizing, you got an A. I was like everyone else, yawning my way through history books written by dullards, until one day I realized how sexy and intriguing and dramatic it all was. If we can seduce young people into reading history, they should put our picture on postage stamps."

J.J. felt compelled to say what was on her mind. "I was afraid you'd be mad at me, Mom. You're the best-selling historian. *Strange Destiny* is your book. I'm just the research assistant."

"That's true, isn't it? Well, I guess I should do something about that. Michael, what do you think? Is there still time to add J.J.'s name to the cover? *Strange Destiny: The Comparative Biography of Alexander Hamilton and Aaron Burr* by Nina Slocum and J. J. Drake."

J.J. for a change was speechless.

"And you know what else? I'm thinking of taking a sabbatical from work. Devoting the next two or three years to being a full-time mother and wife. J.J. did a great job on Julia. I think it's time for her to do the next book on her own."

She turned to her husband, "Any ideas, Michael?"

He shook his head in amazement. "You're reading my mind. Funny thing is, I was talking to Johnny Black today!"

"Here? He's here in New York?"

"He's still in London. You see, my darlings, I can do research, too. The detective agency found him and faxed me his number. I told him to forget about paying back the advance for the moment. And to think about telling the real story of his life. To try to understand why his father needed to be associated with the McCarthy hearings. How humiliated he was when the folk singers he admired were called to testify and he wasn't considered enough of a threat to be subpoenaed.

"I asked him to dig into his memory, however much it may hurt, and to make notes about a childhood in exile and how he felt when his father killed himself. And what happened when he had to face the fact that his entire life was based on his father's egotistical lie."

Michael Ludovic smiled tenderly at his step-daughter. "I also told him I knew a brilliant young writer who might be interested in working with him."

J.J. groaned silently to herself. Was he kidding? Whatever made him think she wanted to see Johnny Black again? What did he think she was, some masochist? She was about to speak her mind when the loving expression on Michael's face explained everything. Clearly he was thrilled to pieces with his new role as matchmaker. Clearly he thought J.J. was carrying the torch for Johnny, and that his little scheme for her to work with Johnny on his book would bring about a reconciliation.

He was so genuinely fond of her and so evidently pleased with himself, she hadn't the heart to tell him that as far as she was concerned Johnny Black could write his own book. She had more important things to do.

Chapter Twenty-four

Six months later, J.J. Drake strolled self-consciously along Spring Street, doing her best to ignore a television crew and a crowd of the curious straining for a view. Vera Boyle was taping a segment for her new series, *Young and Hot*, for MTV. Instead of yet another predictable interview in the studio, Vera's concept was to take America's young and hot new personalities to locations that held some significance in their lives.

"Stand up straight and think sexy thoughts," Nina had advised, assuring her daughter that she looked beautiful and had no reason to fear.

"Remember to say the name of the book," Michael had added.

Vera Boyle beat her to it. "The book is *Strange Destiny*. It's about the strange destiny of Alexander Hamilton and Aaron Burr and how the murder of a beautiful young Quaker girl destroyed their lives. It all happened two hundred years ago. Right where we're standing, on the corner of

Spring Street and Greene, in the heart of SoHo. Only there weren't any streets or clubs or restaurants or art galleries two hundred years ago. Tell us what *was* here, J.J."

The words flowed more easily than J.J. expected. She opened the gate that led to the narrow alley behind the restaurant. "This entire area was open marshland. Some people called it the Lispenard meadow. Others called it the Lispenard swamp. A bleak, desolate place sort of like the moors in *Wuthering Heights*."

She pointed at the metal doors lying flat on the pavement. "This looks like a cellar door. But it's not. It covers the Manhattan Well, where the body of Julia Sands was found on a freezing cold January day in the year 1800."

The camera moved in for a close-up. It didn't frighten her. All that she knew and felt flowed easily and passionately from her lips. "The subject of battered women is nothing new. Julia Sands had thought she was going to be married the night she was killed. Some wedding night. Instead she was savagely beaten to death. Her alleged killer was acquitted, and the murder remains officially unsolved."

J.J. was enjoying herself. She smiled provocatively into the camera and added, "Until now."

Vera could sense the crowd's excitement. An unsolved murder? A well where the body of a lovely young girl was found two hundred years ago? Right here in the middle of Manhattan?

"Tell me, J.J., have you heard the stories about the ghost of Julia Sands wandering the streets late at night? I understand people have been seeing her for years. Standing in a doorway. Leaning against a lamp post. Rising up from the well? Do you believe in ghosts?"

Vera had thrown her a curve.

"I believe in energy and I believe in truth. Don't you?" Michael had warned her about trick questions. Vera's nod of respect said she had handled herself well.

Nevertheless Vera persisted in her line of questioning. "But assuming the ghost of Julia Sands can't rest ... that she does prowl the streets. What if she did appear to you one dark night? What do you think she would say?"

"I think—" Was it her imagination? Was there a figure in a hooded cloak standing at the far edge of the crowd?

"I think she would thank me for telling her story the best way I know how."

When she glanced toward the figure for a sign of some sort, it had disappeared.

Vera Boyle congratulated her. "Great interview, J.J. Want to go for a pizza?"

"No, thanks. I think I'll hang out here for a while."

"I'll let you know if there's anything more I need."

Johnny Black had returned to New York the previous day. He was a changed man, Michael told the two women after meeting with him.

"Why didn't you invite him home to dinner?" Nina asked. With so much happiness and fulfillment in her own life, she bore no grudge.

"As a matter of fact, I did. But he said he'd caused enough unhappiness. Especially for J.J. He didn't think she'd ever want to see him again. Do you, J.J.? We haven't really discussed it, but I still think you should be the one to co-author his memoir."

"I don't know. I don't think so." What's past was past. Why open old wounds? She had begun seeing people her own age, old friends from school, new friends made at parties and other social events. There were guys in her life now, young guys, as ambitious as she was, wannabe film-makers, architects, actors all struggling for success. Men, yes, but no one man. Not yet. But soon.

"At least talk to Johnny," Nina urged. His abrupt disappearance from J.J.'s life was unfinished business. It was important for her daughter to deal with it openly once and for all. Tell the man how much he hurt her. Get it off her chest. Let him know his behavior was cruel, destructive, and totally unacceptable.

Johnny had returned to the Mohawk Hotel. Full circle, he explained. He was in his old room when Michael called. "There's someone here who'd like to have a word with you."

Michael pressed the phone into J.J.'s reluctant hand and led an even more reluctant Nina out of the room. "I think J.J. would like some privacy."

"Johnny?"

The conversation was short and to the point. She did not say how nice it was to hear his voice or ask about the flight across the Atlantic or whether it was good to be back in New York. All she did say was if he wanted to get together, she would be in Greene Street at the gate leading to the Manhattan Well at two the following afternoon.

She saw him before he saw her. He looked older than she remembered, as if he had crossed the line from youth to middle age. Yet as he strode gracefully toward her, women turned to look at him when he passed. She reminded herself that he was nearly twice her age. Yet she was the more mature. He had been her first love and might, just might, be her lover again some time in the distant future, though somehow she doubted it.

For now he was the damaged child with a story to tell that might free him from the past and serve as a cautionary tale to all who replace reality with self-invention.

She waited with a certain tenderness for the

moment when he would see her and quicken his pace. Much had happened since that day in the Rare Book Room. She had honed her skills and discovered she had a peculiar talent for assembling facts and an uncanny intuition for detecting their true significance.

There. He'd seen her. He stopped in his tracks, as if trying to decide whether to turn back or continue moving toward her. She did not smile or hold out her hand to welcome him. The decision had to be his and his alone. If he joined her, it would be his commitment to telling the truth about his life.

Moving closer, his eyes sought hers, as if asking her forgiveness and her permission to keep going. She refused to allow her expression either to encourage or discourage him. He must come to her of his own volition. She held her position and her breath until finally, after what seemed forever, his pace quickened and he was standing as close to her as was possible without physically touching.

She had been up most of the night thinking about his book and whether or not she wanted to be involved. Other projects had been suggested. The history of the kiss in literature and film, for one. Biographies of famous women, famous lovers, famous murderers. Not-so-famous women who should have been famous.

Safe subjects and hardly worth her time and effort since in all honesty she didn't care passionately enough about any one of them. What was beginning to intrigue her about Johnny's life was his father's desperate need to include himself in the most sensational political event of the early 1950s.

Here was a chance to examine the McCarthy period from the unique historical perspective of over forty years through the narrow focus of one family. Johnny's father had styled himself as a glorious victim. The appeal of the victim as hero had accelerated during the intervening decades until now everyone wanted to be a victim of some one or some thing. What was truth? What was exaggeration? What were bald-face lies? Accusations and confessions abounded. Against priests, policemen, parents, teachers, bosses, neighbors, the government, the president of the United States. Abusers and exploiters were everywhere. What was fact? What was motivated by self-importance and the desire to be on TV even at the sacrifice of self-respect?

A recent talk show scandal was an example. An elderly guest had described in spellbinding detail his experiences as a young man in the Nazi death camps. He showed the number tattooed on his arm. He was a natural storyteller, moving his audience to tears. Invitations to speak, magazine articles, plans for a mini-series, followed. Michael himself had considered signing him to do a book.

It had become a classic victim-into-hero soap

opera until he got carried away by his celebrity and made his one big mistake. He told Larry King he had been with Anne Frank at Bergen-Belsen when she died. A red flag went up. Anne Frank's life was too well documented. Those who had been at Bergen-Belsen angrily exposed him as a fraud.

When confronted with the truth and asked why he did it, he said he was an entertainer, giving people what they wanted. His wife's explanation was the most touching part. Her husband always wanted to be important, to be where things were happening. But he was never in the right place at the right time.

He had read extensively about Nazi Germany and had become obsessed with the horrors of the camps. He wondered what he would have done to survive. In actual fact, he had never been out of the United States in his life. And he wasn't even Jewish. He just needed to be part of something important.

Just the way Johnny's father wanted to be part of the courageous band of idealists destroyed by Joe McCarthy. It gave his failures meaning and a spurious martyrdom that became for him reality.

Despite her initial misgivings, working with Johnny might turn out to be as rewarding as working with Nina on *Strange Destiny*. The reviews so far had been mostly positive except for some academic snarling at J.J.'s "speculation" as to Julia Sands's role in Burr's and Hamilton's lives.

Except for specific dates and places, all of history was speculation. It depended on the chronicler's point of view and personal agenda. Was each person's destiny pre-ordained? Recently she had come across an ancient Arab myth about a Baghdad merchant's servant who sees the Angel of Death in the marketplace. When Death beckons him, he flees in terror and begs his master for a horse so that he can escape to Samarra and avoid his fate. The merchant agrees. Later that day, the merchant sees the Angel of Death in a crowd and asks him why he threatened his servant.

"I was not threatening him," Death explains. "I was simply amazed to see him in Baghdad. You see I have an appointment with him tonight. In Samarra."

The concept of predestination intrigued her, but she was not completely sold on the idea. Meeting Johnny Black in the Rare Book Room of the New York Public Library could have been simply a chance meeting or could have been fate. She would need to do a lot more reading and thinking before she could decide.

Watching him approach, her thoughts turned yet again to Julia Sands. In retrospect, she could not fully explain her enduring sense of connection with this tragic young woman. Would they have been friends? She doubted it. She would have been exasperated by Julia's naivete and her willing dependence on laudanum, as opium was then called.

Emotional links were mysterious. They often defied logic. Why did she feel a link to Julia yet none whatsoever to someone like Martha Washington, say, who didn't do much more than invent a cake? Or Abigail Adams, who should have been her heroine but who didn't suffer fools and would certainly have seen how truly foolish J.J. had been about Johnny. As for other women she would like to have known, the short list would include Dolley Madison, yes! In her imagination, lunch with Mary Todd Lincoln and Jacqueline Kennedy Onassis. The subject? How it felt to be seated next to your husband when he was assassinated . . .

Johnny was the first to speak. "Would you like a cappuccino?"

The significance of where they were standing was not lost on either of them. "Don't laugh, Johnny. I thought I saw Julia today. Right here. Just like last time. Only for real."

He smiled. "Maybe it was Prunella. Still trying to get in on the act."

They fell into step and strolled slowly away from the site of the Manhattan Well, side by side but not touching. "It's not going to be easy," she said.

"I know."

"I'm going to be hard as nails. The ground rules are very simple. What I say goes. *Capisce*?"

He took her hand. "*Capisce*."

"Where are the notebooks?" Michael had told him to make notes, everything he could think of. Anecdotes. Memories. Feelings. They would be the start.

He hesitated. "Back at my hotel."

His *hotel*? No way, José. She would not be lured into a trip back in time to the good old days. Or was she being unfair, condemning him for motives that might not exist? She looked directly into his eyes as if seeking the truth from a naughty child. The eyes that returned her gaze were reassuring. Forthright. Not a glimmer of flirtatiousness.

It was agreed. She was in the driver's seat. "You can bring them down to the house tomorrow morning. Work starts at nine o'clock sharp."

Writing his life story with him was going to be in some ways far more intimate than their previous relationship. By helping him to reveal his feelings, she would learn more about her own. It would be up to her to continue to make the rules and to see that they both observed them until such time as the rules might change by mutual consent.

In the weeks and perhaps months to come, each of them would discover—if they worked hard and were very lucky—what had really happened.

And how come.

Author's Note

More than ten years ago while doing historical research for an earlier novel, I came across an obscure reference to "New York's oldest unsolved murder." It concerned a young Greenwich Village beauty, Gulielma Sands, who eloped with her lover on December 22, 1799, and was found battered to death several days later in the Manhattan Well.

When her lover, Levi Weeks, was put on trial, he was jointly defended by two of America's most notorious political enemies, Alexander Hamilton and Aaron Burr. The trial lasted three days. The jury took five minutes to return a verdict of "Not guilty!" and that was that! Or was it?

As a student of New York history I looked for answers to several nagging questions. To start with, the trial of Levi Weeks was in 1800, a much-contested presidential election year. Hamilton and Burr were power-hungry opponents, each determined to see his party in the newly completed White House.

They were viciously attacking each other's reputations in speeches and broadsides and writing nasty letters in newspapers. Why then, I wondered, did they suddenly leave the campaign trail to join hands in the defense of a rather inconsequential young man accused of killing his girlfriend?

And was the instant acquittal of Levi Weeks the result of a cover-up that led inexorably to the fatal duel between Hamilton and Burr four years later? Could there have been a personal connection between the murdered girl and her lover's defenders?

What really bothered me was the total absence of any follow-up of the trial in the press of the day or in the many subsequent biographies of both men.

Most biographers have ignored the trial of Levi Weeks completely as if a young woman's murder wasn't worth writing about. Some have mentioned the case in passing and a few have reprinted brief excerpts from the trial transcripts. But no one at the time of the trial or in the two hundred years since has questioned the curious collaboration between Hamilton and Burr.

The more research I did, the more certain I became of a sinister link between the murder of Gulielma Sands and the duel that killed Hamilton and destroyed the remaining years of Burr's life.

For over a decade, I have dug through dusty files, talked to experts, visited Cornwall-on-Hudson where

Gulielma Sands was born and the Friends Society archives in Manhattan. I have haunted the New York Genealogical Society, the rare book and periodicals collections of The New York Historical Society, the New York Public Library, the New York Academy of Medicine and more.

Ever the romantic, my feverish hope has been to stumble upon an old tin trunk crammed with letters and diaries pertaining to the case and the reasons for the cover-up. Frustrated at every turn, I have made what I consider to be logical conclusions based on existing material and have come up with what I believe to be an educated speculation as to what "really" may have happened.

I am sincerely convinced that the murder of Gulielma Sands had a ripple effect on the lives of Hamilton and Burr, resulting in the duel that changed the early history of the infant American republic. Since much of history is either speculation or interpretation depending on the writer's prejudice, I trust that my theory will intrigue as well as entertain the reader.

As a final word of explanation, Gulielma Sands was variously referred to in contemporary records as Elma, Elmore and Julianna. I have elected to take a novelist's privilege and have called her Julia.

I think she'd have liked that.

—Claudia Crawford
New York City, 1996